Leeza McAuliffe Has Something To Say

***

Nicky Bond

TAKE-AWAY-TEA BOOKS

Take-Away-Tea Books
https://nickybondramblings.blogspot.com

Cover design by Portal – Design and Illustration

Book design © 2017 BookDesignTemplates.com

Leeza McAuliffe Has Something To Say /Nicky Bond — First Edition

ISBN 978-0-9956574-1-0

Contents

For Mum, Dad, Susie, Lucy, Dom, Mon, Tim and Andi.

* * *

1.

And We Start The Bidding At...

Friday 1st January

Look, I'm not saying it was a bad idea. Just a random one. And nothing to do with me really. All because Grandma watched a documentary a few weeks ago. She went on about it to Mum. She said, 'More and more children are showing symptoms of anxiety, Molly. Schools are a hotbed of pressure. It's a wonder Leeza can function at all.' Mum did what she always does with Grandma. She looked like she was listening but carried on with what she was doing. I think she was changing Kenny's nappy at the time. Grandma wouldn't stop though. She said, 'Molly, you need to listen. Leeza is *always* in her room. How do you know she isn't stressed about being a child in today's society? You've no idea what's going on in that head of hers. She could be on the edge.' I remember listening at the door. I do that sometimes - when I need to know what's going on, but I know I won't be told the truth if I ask. Eventually Mum said, 'Stop being dramatic, Ma. Leeza's fine. She just likes her own company, that doesn't make her depressed.' And then Grandma snorted. I know. An actual snort!

For what it's worth, I'm *not* depressed. I feel annoyed at times, but then who wouldn't? I'm the only girl in a house full of brothers. I go to my room so I can hear myself think. I'm still waiting for puberty to kick in and I've got SATs this year. It's all going on.

To keep Grandma happy, I was given a diary for Christmas. If I have any negative feelings, I can shout them into the blank pages. Mum said, 'As you're getting older, you might feel no one understands what you're going through. So if you don't want to talk to us, you can talk to your diary.' Like I said, it's not a bad idea. Just a random one.

I do have things I'd like to say. Not about feeling down or unhappy. Just my news from the day - funny things that happened at school, stuff I'm looking forward to - that kind of thing. Between whingeing brothers, *Peppa Pig* and Grandma's opinions on everything, there's *more* than enough noise in my house. I don't need to add to it.

Tonight we ate yesterday's party tea leftovers. I chose cheese, potato wedges, crisps and bread. I did not choose salad. I know my own mind when it comes to eating leaves.

Saturday 2nd January

So let's do this properly. Happy New Year, everyone! I'm Leeza McAuliffe, I'm ten years old, and I'm starting a diary so I can prove I'm not depressed.

I lay in bed till dinnertime. Only because it's the school holidays, not because I felt too down to get up. The truth is, I didn't want to get up, but only in a good way. I like being lazy when I get the chance. I think that's OK isn't it? Because of 'Grandma's dramatics' I've started to doubt myself.

I got up in time for dinner. Mum and Dad have pretend arguments about dinnertime. Mum calls it 'lunchtime' and Dad calls it 'dinnertime'. They don't row for real but they *bicker*. They're usually smiling when they do it. He tells her she's being snooty like her mother. Then Mum pretends to be mad. She doesn't like being told she's the same as Grandma. Mum and Dad are both from Manchester but Dad says Mum's from the posh part. The way I see it, there are 'dinner ladies' at school, not 'lunch ladies'. So I call it dinnertime too. That's an example of alliteration by the way - *lunch ladies*. We learnt it in English in Year Four.

I got this diary eight days ago. I filled in everyone's birthday and the school holidays. Then I had to wait. That was tricky - the waiting. I like the word tricky. It's better than saying something's challenging. Mum uses that word a lot. *Challenging*. Everything I find too hard, she says is a challenge. She's wrong. Sometimes it's just too hard.

Sunday 3rd January

I can't decide if this is a secret diary or not. Here's what I think, three days in.

If I Keep it Secret...

- I can write anything I want.
- I can write about Spike when he annoys me.
- I can get rid of bad feelings that might sound mean if I say them out loud.
- I can share my worries.

Don't Bother Because...

- I've got no chance of keeping it secret.
- Spike will read it if I leave it lying around.
- Blane or Kenny won't but only because they can't read yet.
- I don't know where to hide it without it getting found.
- I don't have anything secret to write about.

I haven't decided yet but I'm keeping it under my mattress anyway. The best thing about being the only girl is that I get my own room. (Even though it's given Grandma the wrong impression about me.) This does not stop the boys from rooting but at least I have some space.

I have quite a lot to say about privacy. When you have it, you take it for granted. Meg is an only child and doesn't realise how lucky she is. It would never enter her head to change her clothes with her foot wedged against the closed bedroom door. For me, it's a daily event.

Monday 4th January

Jenna rang to see if I wanted to go round. She was bored of things being quiet after Christmas. At the time, Kenny was screaming because he'd lost his blanky and Blane had legged it in from the backyard because Spike was squirting him with the hose. It was not quiet at my house. Eventually Mum let me walk round the corner on my own. The traffic is busy now Christmas and New Year are over. I had to use the green man or it would've taken ages.

If this is a *secret* diary, no one's going to read it. I can write what I like and not worry about it being confusing. But if I ever become famous, my diary might get sold at an auction. It might sell for millions of pounds. Strangers could read this in the future. (*Hello everyone!*) They won't know what I'm talking about if I don't explain everything clearly. So let me fill in some blanks for any future auction bidders - Jenna is one of my two best friends. Meg is the other, but she's away skiing. Sometimes Jenna answers back in class, but only to make people laugh. She's been in detention the most this year. Even more than Alfie Diggs, which is a lot.

We played on her Xbox for ages today. Mum doesn't like Xboxes but she doesn't mind if I play on them at other people's houses. This is the opposite of her views on meat. She doesn't agree with us eating it and I am NOT to eat it elsewhere. Jenna's dad made sandwiches. I watched him get the butter from the fridge and spread it on the bread. My mouth was already watering. At the last minute he opened a packet of ham. It was too late then. I'd already decided what I was going to do. When he asked me if I wanted one, I didn't think twice I said a big fat YES. Mum would go mad if she knew. I felt bad but it was lovely.

I've decided. This is DEFO a secret diary.

Tuesday 5th January

It's the last day of the Christmas holidays and I've done homework ALL day. (Prepositional phrases and adverbial phrases. I'm sick of phrases.) Now my arm aches so I'm going to bed.

Goodnight any future auction bidders who are reading my words. I bet you have Xboxes in every room.

Wednesday 6th January

Back to school.

Meg was back from skiing and has a proper tan. She said she saw someone break their leg and heard it snap. I'm not sure I believe her but she liked telling the story. She told it a few times.

Ms Archer said, 'We're now on countdown to our SATs. It's a VERY IMPORTANT TERM'. I wrote that in capitals because she *said* it in capitals. She also said the same thing in September. Mum says it's only school that care about results and that I'm too young to worry about it. Maybe Ms Archer should do her speech for the parents and not for the children who've heard it all before.

The Council reopened after Christmas so Mum and Dad were back at work. They didn't look happy. They work in different offices of the same building. I have no clue what I want to do when I'm older but I don't want to come home every night wishing it were something else.

Grandma picked us up from school. She has a new coat. It looks like animal fur on the collar but she promised it wasn't real. Then she said, 'But I'm going to pretend to your mother that it is,' and then laughed a lot. It's like Grandma tries to wind Mum up on purpose.

Grandma doesn't live with us. It just feels like it because she picks us up every day. Her house is in Stockford, a couple of miles away. She walks everywhere or gets the bus, even though she has a car. Last week she decided she wasn't going to go into Manchester for shopping until the police have sorted out knife crime. It was Dad's turn to snort then. He said, 'Ursula, there have always been criminals. Your city-centre boycott won't do much to change that'. Then she replied, 'Nonsense Sebastian. The only criminal from your youth was whoever gave you that terrible teenage bowl cut.' Then Dad laughed. Even though he hates being called by his full name. It was sort of funny at the time. He did have bad hair when he was younger.

Thursday 7th January

For the future auction bidders (hello there!) let me explain what a ten year old's life is like these days. It's all about SATs. Every single minute. I liked school until Year Six but now every day is the same. Last year we used to do Music and PE and Art. (I don't really like PE but it'd be a change.) When we actually do PE, it isn't as bad as it used to be. Last year's Year Six girls did a petition. They said it wasn't fair that they had to change in the same classroom as the boys. It worked too. They were allowed to use the toilets while the boys stayed in class. I looked forward to Year Six because of that. You never want to be the girl who ends up accidentally flashing her crop top or bra. Not that I wear a bra. I want to but Mum says I don't need to yet. She also says it's the boys that should change in the smelly toilets if they can't be sensible. She's probably right but I'm not going to say that to Ms Archer. I don't want her to make us get changed in the classroom again. Anyway, we haven't done PE for ages. Or Art or Music. Or History or Geography for that matter. It's English, Maths and nothing else until the summer.

Tests are over in May and then I leave Irwell Green Primary School. I'm going to Stockford High with Meg and Jenna. It's nearly a mile away, on the same road as my house. Tyson Road is noisy, wide and busy. The houses go to over a thousand. Mine is 620. I like my road. At night when I can't sleep, I hear the double decker buses going past. I count them instead of sheep.

I don't think I've ever seen a sheep for real. Just on the television.

<u>Friday 8th January</u>

It's the first Friday Fooday since Christmas. (*Friday Fooday* - more alliteration!)

It's really called Friday *Food* Day. Mum's off on Friday afternoons and makes lovely food for the start of the weekend. When we say it fast, it sounds like Friday Fooday, so that's what we call it. Auction Bidders, you'd love it! When we get in from school there's music playing, and Mum's singing and getting covered in flour. Then Dad gets home and opens a bottle of wine for him and Mum. Sometimes they have two!

Mum and Dad's homemade bread isn't bad. They say it's better for me because they use a different type of flour. I'm sure they're right but I *really* liked the normal slices I had at Jenna's. Mum would moan about them, but they were lovely. She says when we leave home we can choose what we eat but for now she's going to decide for us. I didn't mind tonight. I never do on Friday Fooday. Tea was sweet potato and chickpea burger in a homemade bun. It was just as nice as a secret ham sandwich.

I've been vegetarian all my life. I've no idea if I'd have chosen it myself.

Saturday 9th January

Dad said the weather is going to get colder over the next few days so I lay in bed for ages.

I've started to think about the next event coming up - Mum's birthday. It's at the end of the month and she's having a party in the house. I've got a few ideas for presents but they'll take some time to organise. It's weeks off, though. I don't need to worry just yet.

Sunday 10th January

It's still freezing so I didn't go anywhere. I had homework to do - including Maths activities on a website. Homework is a pain but it was nice to have a reason to use Dad's iPad.

Mum doesn't like that Ms Archer gives us homework to do online. She thinks it discriminates against poor people. I don't think there's anyone in my class that doesn't have their own tablet. Meg has two! She uses her old one for watching YouTube in the bath. I'm the only person without. I know we don't have much money but sometimes I think that even if we won the lottery, Mum would still say no. In fact, I know she would.

I completed the online stuff in super quick time considering it was Maths (Auction Bidders – I hate Maths!) Then I FaceTimed Jenna. I told Dad I needed to check some questions with her but I didn't really. I just wanted to chat.

Jenna hadn't done her homework and said she wasn't planning to. I don't know why because she could if she tried. I told her she could copy mine but she said no. Then we talked about Ms Archer and whether or not she had a boyfriend.

Monday 11th January

Jenna was kept in at lunchtime for having no homework. I waited outside the classroom but eventually got shooed outside. I could hear Ms Archer say, 'I know you're capable,' and, 'If there's anything upsetting you, you can tell me'. I honestly think Jenna likes being mischievous. It was really cold and I was sent out but she got to stay in the warm. I might forget my homework too, next week. (Who am I kidding? Of course I won't.)

Ms Archer came into school this morning with a new hair cut. Meg thinks this is a sign she's going out with someone. She used to have long dark hair that was wavy by her shoulders. Today, when she collected our line from the playground, she had a bob! It came to the bottom of her ears and was really straight. And a fringe! It took me a year to grow out my fringe so I feel sorry for her. She doesn't realise what she's done. As we walked in, Meg told her she looked nice but then turned back and pulled a face at the rest of us. That showed she didn't mean it. I *did* think she looked nice but I didn't say anything. Meg can be quite strong-minded at times and it's easier to agree - on the outside, at least.

My old fringe is now long enough to put behind my ears. The rest of my hair stays in a bobble most of the time. I'm not that fussed about it really. That's another thing that makes me different from Meg. She thinks about her hair a lot more than most people do.

Tuesday 12th January

I went to Jenna's after school. She asked if I wanted to stay for tea. I asked her what food it was so she looked in the fridge and pulled out a box. 'Chicken casserole and mash', she said. I've never eaten chicken casserole before and it looked really nice on the picture. But even though I was hungry I told her I had to get back. How good am I! I stayed vegetarian even though I wanted to fit in.

Part of me wants to tell Mum and Dad that I did the right thing. But then they'll guess that sometimes I don't. I still think back to the ham butty from last week. I feel bad but I like ham. It's the first thing I'm going to eat when I'm eighteen and can do what I want.

Now I think about it, Jenna might have thought I didn't like the food she was offering. The complete opposite was true. It was icy cold walking home and the wind made my knees red. All I could think about was how good the casserole looked on the picture.

Tea was stuffed vine leaves, falafel and hummus. It would have been a lovely meal in August.

Wednesday 13th January

Dad had to wake me up this morning. Normally, I hear 'TEETH' being yelled at Spike and then I know it's nearly my turn in the bathroom.* I don't need an alarm clock.

This morning there were no shouts of 'TEETH' (or 'TOILET') being yelled. Dad knocked on my door and was grinning. He told me to look out of the window. I was still half asleep but I did what he said. OMG!
IT WAS SNOWING!!!!!

I woke up fast after that. The whole yard, the fences and the houses either side of us were sparkly white. Everything was covered. Blane's trike, the footballs and the last remaining patio chair were all underneath the snowy blanket. (I think I just used a metaphor!)

Then I heard Mum from the bedroom. 'They've texted, Mac,' she said. I didn't know what she meant so I went into her room. She was sitting up in bed with her phone, reading out that Irwell Green Primary School was closed for the day. Wooohoooooo! Next thing, Meg's mum was ringing, Grandma messaged and then Jenna emailed Dad's iPad (whoops – I'm not supposed to give out his work email to friends) and the whole day was planned for us to play in the snow.

Tyson Road was full of children. Normally there are cars speeding past but today there were hardly any. The ones that did drive along were very slow. Some Stockford High boys threw snowballs at them. I thought the drivers would be annoyed but they all seemed quite cheerful. Mum and Dad were inside working from home. I don't think they did any work for real. When Dad said he was 'working from home' he made speech marks with his fingers. At one point, he came out to play. He helped Jenna lift her snow woman's head onto her body. He also looked for twigs for the armpit hair. (Jenna's snow woman was very detailed.)

Today was completely brilliant.

*Let me explain for the Auction Bidders. Having the bathroom slot after Spike is **not** fair. I've raised this at Family Meetings but it falls on deaf ears. Apparently, someone has to follow him and I'm the eldest so have to get on with it. I've tried to pretend it doesn't bother me but that doesn't make him 'forget' to flush the toilet any less.

<u>Thursday 14th January</u>

School's still shut because of health and safety and the car is buried under the snow. Mum had to get a bus to a meeting. She waved as it went past the part of the road we were sliding on.

Jenna fell over and landed in the splits. She couldn't stop laughing. Meg fell over and bruised her arm so went home in a mood. I stayed out till my fingers were numb and then went in. I sat under the blanket and watched *Frozen*. It was good but for the rest of the day, every time Spike needed a wee, he sang, 'Let it Flow'. He really needs to grow up.

<u>Friday 15th January</u>

School was open but Mum let us stay off and make it a long weekend. She said I've learnt more about life in the last couple of days than I would have done at school. (She was working from home again. I think she just wanted a lie in.)

There are times when Mum can be really annoying. Her food rules for one, as well as wanting to know where I am and when I'm going to be in. (If she let me have a phone like every other parent, she could ring me.) But letting us stay off for one extra day was brilliant. I'm not sure I agree that I learnt more at home but I didn't care. I could imagine what I'd be missing. Test practices and wet playtimes. Everyone feeling cooped up and bickering. Ms Archer being shoutier than normal. No ta.

I didn't play outside today. The snow has turned slushy and grey. I've had enough of it now. Instead I lay on the carpet with my feet on the radiator and counted the drips as they ran down the glass. Mum worked on her laptop in bed before starting Friday Fooday. I was pleased when she told me there'd be mashed potato. It was defo a mashed potato kind of day.

Saturday 16th January

I'm going to start one of the books Grandma gave me for Christmas. I must be bored because when I got them, I decided I'd never read them. They looked dull. Grandma told me they were the same books that Mum read when *she* was ten. There are six in the set by someone called Enid Blyton - about twins who go to boarding school. Grandma was excited when she described them and I felt bad that they'd never get opened. Until now. So far I've taken the plastic off the box. Mum told me I should give them a go with an open mind. I'm not sure how to make my mind open but I'll start the first one now. It's 9 o'clock and I'm already in bed. That way, when I fall asleep after three pages, I won't have to move.

OMG.

It is half past midnight and I'm still awake. It turns out *The Twins at St. Clare's* is BRILLIANT! Back to it now. I want to finish it before morning.

Sunday 17th January

I'm so tired! I read until 2 o'clock then fell asleep with the book open on my bed. Boarding school sounds like so much fun. I wonder if there's a local one I can go to.

Monday 18th January

Back to school after the snow days. Mum wrote a letter explaining the value of playing outside. She included Science, (melting) Geography, (weather) Maths, (not sure - maybe from the angles of the snow balls?) and teamwork, (Jenna's snow woman was defo a group effort). To be honest, I just remember lying on the floor watching the drips on the window with *Despicable Me* playing in the background. Still, there's no need to share that with anyone.

Ms Archer wasn't impressed, I could tell. She made a sarky comment about hoping it doesn't snow on the day of the tests, which was stupid. They're in May. Obvs, it won't snow. When I sat back at my desk, Alfie Diggs leaned across and whispered, 'Your mum is cool'. I smiled but didn't say anything back. He wouldn't think she was cool if he knew her. Not when she wouldn't let him go to Jenna's seventh birthday party because it was in McDonalds.

I finished my book this evening. I'm going to start the 2nd one tomorrow.

Tuesday 19th January

Jenna was in trouble again. She has behaviour targets to work on in every lesson. Today she was sent out of English for '*distracting others around me.*' That's one of the things she's not supposed to do. She put two pencils up her nose and hid her top lip to make herself look like a sea lion. I was on another table but I could see it was pretty funny.

With Jenna in at lunchtime, it was just Meg on the playground. I told her about the book I was reading and how it would be brilliant to live at school. She thought for a minute and then said, 'There wouldn't be vegetarian options for you. You wouldn't be allowed.' I hadn't thought of that. That's *another* reason for going! Then she changed the subject to Alfie Diggs. She loves him. I don't get why. He messes around all the time and when Caitlyn Matherson wore a red hoodie last week, he called her Tomato Girl. All day. He's worse than Spike and that's bad. Meg doesn't seem to get it. She keeps lip gloss in her bag and puts it on before every playtime. I don't understand why rubbing grease on your lips is a good thing but she does it repeatedly. I was glad when lunch was over and we went inside. Jenna had been reading in the library. Once again, she dodged the cold. She's a lot smarter than the teachers think.

<u>Wednesday 20th January</u>

Something bad ALMOST happened. After school, Grandma asked me what I was getting Mum for her birthday. It's snuck up on us all! She must have noticed my panic because she offered to take me shopping on Friday after school. Obvs she won't have the same conversation with Spike, Blane or Kenny. Just me. It's always me that has to deal with this kind of thing.

Usually Dad gives me some money and I go to Tesco. (Mum doesn't like supermarkets. She prefers buying from small shops to keep them in business. But Tesco is in walking distance and it's cheap.) I can get her a book, flowers, chocolates, or a top for a few pounds. But this year is different. Mum's forty. I'm not sure *why* it's different, but it is. She says it's when her life is going to begin. This makes no sense. I don't know why the first thirty-nine years aren't part of her life anymore but that's what she says. So because it's more important to her, *I* have to make her present more important too. I'll start work on it tomorrow.

Her birthday is Saturday. I have enough time.

Thursday 21st January

I don't have enough time. The ideas I had were good, but I needed to start them weeks ago. My stomach is flipping, I keep biting my nails and I've snapped at Kenny twice today. I think I'm feeling stress. It's horrible.

I was going to write a poem like Meg's dad did for Meg's mum's birthday. It was called *40 Reasons Why I Love You*. It was soppy and a bit gross. I remember one of the reasons was, 'Because you nibble my neck like a gerbil'. (Meg did sick faces when she read me that.) I didn't want to write stupid soppy stuff for Mum so I changed it to '*40 Reasons Why You Are Nice*'.

I know the word 'nice' is a boring word. In Year Three it was crossed out on the Word Wall over a list of better choices. I could use *splendid, brilliant, wonderful, charming, attractive* or *amazing* instead. But because it's from Spike, Blane and Kenny as well as me, I thought simpler language would be easier for them. If we each think of ten reasons why Mum is nice then we'll have forty really quickly. The trouble is Spike has refused to help because Mum shouted at him for kicking the football into the window. This happened a few days ago but he's holding a grudge. Blane gave me a couple of reasons - although one was 'Mum is nice because she's nice' - and I haven't even tried to talk to Kenny about it. I know I'll be writing his ten for him, so really I have to think of twenty. So far we have twelve.

The second part of the present is taking shape a little better. I'm rewriting our own version of *My Favourite Things* from *The Sound of Music*. It's one of Mum's favourite films and is the reason why my full name is Liesl. My next challenge is to convince Spike and Blane to sing the new version with me at the party on Saturday. I'm not hopeful.

Friday 22nd January

When we got back from school, Mum had gone to the station to pick up her friend, Gina. The house was empty. We could have our first rehearsal of *My Favourite Things*.

Spike was (what Mum would describe as) challenging. Grandma was more blunt when she asked him why he was being a pain in the backside. That made me laugh a lot but I stayed sensible. I had to set an example. Blane tried his best but he kept forgetting the words. I just let Kenny toddle around as he pleased. There didn't seem much point trying to force him to stay still.

We muddled through and Grandma clapped, but she was just being kind. I don't think performing this at the party is a good idea anymore. I'll think it over.

In other news, we now have twenty-nine reasons why Mum is nice. I can't go to sleep until it's finished.

Saturday 23rd January

Mum is forty today!

I'd asked Dad to wake me up early so at 8 o'clock he knocked on the door. 8 o'clock on a Saturday - I know! I crept downstairs and made toast, a cup of green tea, and sliced up an orange. Gina was asleep on the sofa so I had to be quiet.

I put everything on a tray, and then woke up Spike and Blane. Spike told me to poo off, which I ignored. Blane was still half asleep but he got up. His hair was sticking up and his eyes were half closed.

We burst into Mum's bedroom. She was cheerful considering it was early. I know she'd been up late with Gina because I'd seen the wine bottles in the bin and the photo albums on the table. Gina has known Mum since University, and whenever she visits, Mum gets drunk which makes us all laugh. Even Dad. I missed it last night though, because I was busy in my room, thinking of reasons why she was nice.

Mum opened the cards, and then she opened the poem. I couldn't tell if she was laughing or crying, but she kept making noises to show she was pleased.

Here it is. I'd like to say it was a joint effort from the McAuliffe children but that would be a lie.

40 Reasons Why You Are Nice

1. You make us food.
2. You help us with homework.
3. You make nice bread.
4. You have long hair.
5. You gave us an extra snow day.
6. You are nice.
7. You care about the environment.
8. You get drunk with Gina and it's funny.
9. You work hard at the Council.
10. You are polite to others.
11. You do Friday Fooday.
12. You make people sign petitions about good causes.
13. You care about animals.
14. You like old films.
15. You put up with lots of children.
16. You make us eat healthy food for our future.
17. You don't want us to rot our teeth with sweets.

18. You sing loudly when you cook.
19. You like lots of different flavours of tea.
20. You make nice bean burgers.
21. You try your best.
22. You have some nice clothes.
23. You don't mind getting muddy or dirty.
24. You remind us about road safety.
25. You have hands and feet.
26. You change your hair colour sometimes.
27. You don't care about having no money.
28. You gave us names from films.
29. You stand up to people when you think they are wrong.
30. You look younger than 40 when you wear make up.
31. You make us laugh sometimes.
32. You never change your mind.
33. You have pierced ears.
34. You are younger than some other mums.
35. You giggle at Dad's jokes when no one else does.
36. Your first name is Molly.
37. Your last name is Hart-McAuliffe.
38. You are left handed.

39. You are a vegetarian.
40. You are 40.

I know the last few weren't great. But other than the ones from Blane, I did the whole thing myself. Apparently it's going to go in a frame next to her bed. We'll see. I've been waiting for a new bulb in my lamp since before Christmas. I'm not holding my breath.

The rest of the morning was busy. Gina woke up and made lunch while Mum and Dad had an extra lie in. Grandma arrived and decided to clean everywhere, because as she said, 'The place looks like a bomb's hit it'. Mum and Dad eventually came down and moved chairs around and strung up fairy lights from wall to wall.

After that I decided we should perform the song. Once again, I felt like nothing would be happening if it weren't for me. Spike sulked but he joined in. Blane tried his best, whilst Kenny sat on the floor and sucked his blanky.

We stood in a little huddle in front of the sofa as Mum, Dad and Gina faced us. They looked like they were expecting something really good and I realised this wasn't going to go as I'd planned. There was nothing I could do about that now. We just had to crack on.

We sang the first verse. I'd written down the things I thought of when I put Mum into my head. It seemed to flow as well as it could.

Movies from the 80s and veggie bean burgers
Bunting and fairy lights and Midsomer Murders
Chunky brown boots over leggings or jeans
These are a few of your favourite things...

But then it got quieter. Kenny wandered off, and Blane suddenly stopped singing. I could feel his face pressing into my legs as he hid himself.

To be honest, by the end there was only me still going. (I'm *so* glad we didn't do it at the party tonight. I don't mind singing at home but not in front of people who don't live here.) Mum had another laughing and crying reaction. Dad did lots of clapping and shouted 'encore' a lot. Grandma's smile is what I would describe in a story as *beaming.* We pulled it off. (Well, I did.)

Now I'm in my room, getting ready. I'm going to wear my Christmas jumper dress again. It'll be warm and it won't matter there's a snowman on it because the last bits of snow have only just melted outside. Grandma has gone home and will be coming back later with her friend from the dating website. I haven't met this one yet. He's called Brian or Brendan or Bruce or something. It's a *Br* name anyway. Gina and Mum are making food downstairs with Ryan from next door. Dad has taken the boys to the park for a breather.

I cannot wait for tonight. I love it when we have people over.

Sunday 24th January

Too tired to write. I'll do it tomorrow.

Monday 25th January

Mum's party was brilliant!

I didn't mind getting up for school this morning. I wanted to talk about it with Jenna and Meg. They had just as much fun as me and agreed the highlight was Grandma singing on the karaoke. I think Grandma was a bit drunk. She kept swaying and smiling. I think *all* the adults were, to be honest. Meg's mum and dad were doing a slowie at one point! Meg kept saying how ashamed she was.

Also, Grandma's new friend is now her *old* friend because she decided she didn't like the way he was chatting to Gina. Apparently he was 'lecherous'. He got sent home before the cake was brought out. I never did find out his name.

Spike and I stayed up till everyone went home. It was after 1am! By the end of the night he was watching a DVD in the corner and I was eating Quavers on the sofa. When I finally got into bed, Blane was asleep at the bottom. It was late so I got in too. This was a mistake. I woke up this morning to cold, damp legs, and the smell of wee. Blane might be five but he wets the bed regularly.

Tuesday 26th January

We've finished Mum's birthday cake. All the buffet's gone too. I was sent next door to Ryan and Tim's to return the tin that their quiche came in.

School was OK. Spike was in trouble again. I've no idea what he did today but he was standing out at lunch. Mum thinks he's allergic to artificial colours in sweets, so he isn't supposed to eat them. She thinks they make him hyper. I know for a fact he eats all sorts of things when no one can see. I still feel guilty about one ham sandwich but compared to Spike I'm the perfect child.

Tea was tofu chilli.

Wednesday 27th January

I've got my reading routine back after all the responsibility of Mum's birthday. It's such a relief to get back to normality. After school I finished the 2nd of my St Clare's books. I still think a boarding school would be brilliant. I asked Mum, but apparently all the boarding schools are in London. I didn't point out that it wouldn't matter how far away it was, as I'd be staying there all the time. I just let her say her fib. Sometimes it's easier to let her think she's right.

Thursday 28th January

After school, Grandma wanted me to pass the remote but instead of saying 'Leeza' she said, 'Spike... Blane... Kenny... Molly... *Leeza*.' She came out with three boys names and my mum's before getting it right. Then she fell about laughing. Apparently this was a *senior moment*. Grandma says she's happy she can tell she's having senior moments because the real worry is when you don't realise. The other day Dad made a joke about her being an Old Aged Pensioner. She went mad. She said, 'Sebastian, I will never be old, or aged, or a pensioner.' We all just smiled at her.

Dad hates being called Sebastian. He used to be called Seb, but when he met Mum she called him Mac and now everyone does. Grandma doesn't, but then she doesn't call him anything usually.

Maybe I'll change my name. I'll give it some thought overnight.

Friday 29th January

I slept on it but renaming yourself is harder than it sounds. Mum calls me Liesl if I'm ignoring her or if she's trying to tease me. And Spike calls me Loozer - which he finds hysterical and which I find childish. To be honest, I quite like Leeza. Having a Z makes me stand out from the crowd. I won't make any hasty decisions.

Friday Fooday was gorge. It was cauliflower crust pizza - which always tastes better than it sounds - and sweet potato fries. Grandma stayed because she didn't have a date planned. Since the lecherous man with the *Br* name was sent packing she said she's been 'footloose and fancy free'. Dad wound her up by saying no man could handle her. She laughed and in her posh voice said, 'I have no intention of being handled'. And then Mum laughed too. I think it was a bit of a rude joke. I smiled but made sure I looked grown up as I did.

Nearly done with book three. I have no idea what I'll do when I finish the set.

Saturday 30th January

Mum has started a new behaviour chart with Spike, and Dad went to the park with Blane. He's trying to teach him to ride a bike without stabilisers. Spike and I managed this no problem but it's been a long-term project with Blane. I don't think he really cares about riding a bike but Dad won't give up. At one point I heard him say, 'This will not beat me, Moll.' I don't think Blane realises how much stress it's causing.

Sunday 31st January

Mum used her new milkshake maker and made the best smoothie ever. Frozen banana, milk and homemade Nutella. (It's the same as real Nutella but not as sweet, not as chocolatey and not as nutty.) It tasted GORGEOUS. I wanted another but Mum said it'd make me go to the toilet if I had too much. I have to wait for tomorrow. I can't stop thinking about it.

I started book four, did my homework and thought about all the food I love.

When I'm eighteen, I will eat ham sandwiches, and banana and fake Nutella smoothies. Actually, I will buy r*eal* Nutella. I will do what I like.

* * *

2.

#nappygate

<u>Monday 1st February</u>

Mum wrote down the smoothie recipe so I made it myself after school. Even Grandma agreed it tasted good. What she actually said was, ‘Not bad, considering’. I said, ‘Considering what?’ She said, ‘Not bad, considering it’s trendy vegan nonsense’. This confused me. I know we’re vegetarians but I didn’t think we were vegans. I hope Grandma’s mistaken. (Anyway, I used normal milk, not one of Mum’s special ones.) I really hope Mum isn’t trying to make us vegan without anyone realising. It’s hard enough to avoid meat in the real world but this would be too much.

I let Blane have a taste of my smoothie. He deserved it. It was his class assembly today. When I walked into the hall I spotted him. He had his head buried in Mrs Miles' lap. She managed to get him to sit on the stage just before it began. I tried to smile encouragingly but the Year Sixes are at the back so he wouldn't have seen me. When it came to his part, I'll admit I was worried. But he stood up and held his painting in front of his face. In a tiny voice he said, 'The lollipop lady helps us'. Then he sat down. I could see his relief the second it was over. He managed a small smile when everyone clapped at the end but it was mainly fear. There's no way I can see him getting rid of his stabilisers.

Tuesday 2nd February

I think Mum's a vegan. She uses almond milk in cereal and she has special cheese for herself. It all adds up. I don't want to be a vegan. I don't want her to try and make me.

It's hard enough being the only vegetarian in the class. I don't tell anyone unless I have to. It gets tricky when I refuse food from people who don't know. And then there are times when I don't. Jenna doesn't care - she'd never tell *anyone* - but if Meg saw me eat meat, she'd be shocked. Her mum and dad give me special food when I go for tea. It's really kind of them, but I'd rather have the beans and chips *without* the chicken, instead of them cooking me a mushroom omelette from scratch. They're being nice, but sometimes I feel like a kind of... *freak*.

It was such a good feeling when Jenna's dad asked if I wanted a ham butty. He thought I was the same as everyone else.

Wednesday 3rd February

Something funny happened. Blane came into my room. He said, 'Spike told me to ask you about pyramids'. I was really pleased with Spike. He must have remembered the Egypt project I did last year and realised I was the household expert. I rooted under the bed and found my Year Five history book. There were pictures of the Pyramids, as well as Tutankhamun and the Sphinx. I explained it all as best as I could remember. He looked a little blank but I assumed that's what all teachers have to put up with. It was a few minutes after I'd sent him back to his room that Spike shouted across the landing. 'Not pyramids, Loozer. *Periods!*' And then he spent the next ten minutes laughing hysterically at me.

I ignored Spike and thought about explaining it to Blane, but his attention span had gone. He'd listened to a lot of Egypt talk already. I decided this was a job for a parent so sent him down to Mum.

I'm surprised Blane doesn't know what periods are. Mum talks about them *a lot*. Like every month. When we learnt about them in school, I already knew everything and it was as if they were treating us like babies. But then Jenna went bright red and looked in shock the whole time. She hadn't known. Only having a dad must be a nightmare at times. I don't know what happened to Jenna's mum. She was there when she was little and then she left. Jenna doesn't talk about it.

Blane has just come upstairs and seems fine. I don't think this new information has changed his life in any way. I guess periods will never affect him. I'm hoping they won't change my life much either. I want them to start but only when I'm at home and not wearing white. If I could pick the perfect time, I'd be in the bath so there'd be no mess. It's just a waiting game.

Thursday 4th February

It was wet play all day. Ms Archer said we had cabin fever.

The funniest thing happened after school. Blane asked Grandma if she knew about periods! She actually spluttered. I could tell she didn't know what to say. Eventually she mumbled, 'I don't think that's something with which you need concern yourself.' Then she tried to change the subject by pointing out a police car that had just driven past. She's very different from Mum. Mum answers every single question we ask. In the past she's told Grandma off for not doing that. Sometimes it's hard to believe that Grandma is Mum's mum. They are so opposite.

Mum's dad is dead, but according to Grandma, 'was very little use when he was alive'. They were divorced when Mum was small and she doesn't remember him. He left a lot of money in his will, and Mum and Grandma had a big house and lots of holidays. Mum's been all over the world but when she met Dad, they started from scratch and so we're poor. Sometimes I think we aren't as poor as Mum and Dad say, but they simply prefer that we don't have expensive things. Grandma's always trying to give them money but they never take it. I wish they would. It'd be nice to have a holiday on a plane, instead of Wales all the time. I really like Wales, but when Meg spends every half-term in a different European country, it's hard to make the Welsh Coastal Pathway sound as cool. I do like Wales, though. I can take big breaths of air and not cough. And we get an ice cream every day.

I forgot about ice creams! I defo can't be a vegan.

Friday 5th February

For the first time in ages, we had PE. Mr Eskbrook's wife went into labour during third lesson, so his class had to double up with ours. We did rounders on the field.

Because there were twice as many girls, we couldn't use the toilets to get changed. Rubbish! It was a hard fought battle to get that rule changed. I thought of last year's petition as I struggled to pull my arms out of my sweatshirt whilst my PE top was pulled down over the top of it. Meg didn't have as much of a problem. She seemed to be doing all she could to show the straps of her crop top to anyone nearby. They were like bra straps that could be made shorter or longer. She kept adjusting them as she got changed. I'm sure she was hoping Alfie Diggs would notice. He didn't.

As much as I dislike PE, it was a nice change. I said I'd field on the side where the left-handers aim. There's only Ellie Rogers and me that hit that way so I knew it would be an easy afternoon. Then, when Ellie came to bat, she missed! I got an easy ride.

When we got home, Mum was cooking and listening to the soundtrack from *Pretty in Pink*. It's another of her favourite films and the reason why Blane is called Blane. There are two boy characters in the film and when she was a teenager she loved them both. When she was pregnant, it was a toss up between Blane or *Duckie*. I know Blane's a weird name, but it could have been a whole lot worse. Imagine having a brother called Duckie McAuliffe! I'd be well embarrassed.

It was a quieter Friday Fooday because of Kenny's birthday tomorrow. We had baked sweet potatoes and veggie chilli. It was lovely but defo vegan-friendly. It bothered me for the whole meal. When Dad was doing the dishes I just came out with it. I said, 'Dad, is Mum a vegan?' He chuckled to himself, kept scrubbing the chilli pan and eventually said, 'She bobs in and out, Leez.'

She can bob in all she likes. As long as she doesn't expect me to bob in with her.

Saturday 6th February

My youngest brother is three today. Happy birthday Kenny! We celebrated by watching back-to-back *Peppa Pig* in Mum and Dad's bed. After an hour, I stopped watching and got my book. I got back into the bed though. It was cosy.

Grandma came for tea and made a joke about not bringing the lecherous man that she brought to the last party. She didn't call him the lecherous man. That's what I call him. When I asked Mum what *lecherous* meant, she said, 'It means he was talking to Gina like he fancied her but she didn't fancy him back.' I'm worried that one day *I* might be lecherous and not realise. Meg is defo lecherous to Alfie Diggs. He hasn't noticed, but she's used a whole tube of lip-gloss since Christmas. When the wind blew the other day, her hair flew into her face and stuck to her mouth. Me and Jenna found it hilarious. Meg fake-laughed and then went off in a mood.

Sunday 7th February

Today we had the first Family Meeting of the year. I can't remember what the last one was about. Sometimes they're regular and sometimes they don't happen for months. Mum called today's meeting. This isn't unusual. We all have the power to call one as long as it's a Sunday. It's only ever Mum or Dad, though. Mostly Mum. Still, I could if I wanted.

There was one item on today's agenda. *Operation Potty*. Now that Kenny's three, Mum and Dad want to start potty training him. Apparently this'll be a team effort. We have to ask if he needs a wee, as often as possible. If we can suggest he goes before he wets himself, it's a good thing.

I understand why they want to tackle this sooner rather than later. They must've realised they never got it right with Blane. Even though he uses the toilet now, he still shouts for Mum to wipe his bottom every time he does a poo. She used to tell him to have a go himself but it's just quicker for her to do it. It's well embarrassing when people are here. Let's hope it's different with Kenny. I'll do my bit and be encouraging. He's still going to wear a nappy at night but be in little undies during the day. It starts tomorrow, so really it's Grandma's problem most of the time.

Monday 8th February

I'm in a dilemma! When we got back from school, I asked Kenny if he needed a wee and he said no. But under his shorts I spotted a nappy! Grandma must have put it on after Mum and Dad went to work. I don't know whether I should tell anyone. I can't blame Grandma. She doesn't want to be cleaning up mess all day, but I know Mum won't be happy. What do I do?

I asked her about the *Br* man from Mum's party. Just to distract myself from the nappy stress. I'm still unsure why it's bad to look like you fancy someone, but I left that alone. Instead I asked if she'd seen him recently. 'To be brutally honest, Leeza,' she said, 'I've decided to let him go his merry way.' When I asked why, she didn't even mention the Gina thing. Instead she straightened her back, stood tall and said, 'Leeza, I am sixty-eight years old. There are many places I want to visit, many experiences I want to have, and many people I want to meet. I DO NOT want to spend my days with a man who rolled his eyes at the thought of climbing Machu Picchu.' I didn't really understand what that meant but it seems Brian was boring. (The *Br* man's name is Brian.) Grandma is very adventurous for an old lady. In a couple of weeks she's going on a plane that takes six hours.

All the talk about Brian meant that I forgot about the nappy situation until I'd gone to bed. I'll investigate after school tomorrow and see if it was a one-off blip. Maybe I won't need to get involved.

Tuesday 9th February

I think I need to get involved. First thing this morning I heard Mum tell Kenny he was a big boy and would use the potty all day. Then straight after school, I checked and he had a nappy on.

I wonder if this is why it took so long with Blane. Did Grandma go against our efforts then? Kenny is defo getting mixed messages. The right thing to do would be to tell Mum, but I don't want to get Grandma into trouble. Mum has to tell her off a lot and sometimes it's not that important. Maybe this isn't that important too?

Tea was veggie burgers. They weren't as nice as proper veggie burgers that get made on Friday Fooday. They were just bits of left over carrot, potato and broccoli mashed together. I think calling them veggie burgers was a bit of a stretch. I couldn't have asked Meg round tonight.

Wednesday 10th February

I finished my last book of the St. Clare's box set this evening. I'm gutted. I let the last one stretch out for ages because I didn't want it to end. I don't know what I'm going to do now. All my other books seem a bit flat. I liked how I could follow the same characters over lots of stories. Who'd have thought the Christmas present I said was my least favourite, is now my best present ever!

There was another nappy on Kenny today. Grandma might have got me a good Christmas present but she's causing me problems in other areas.

Thursday 11th February

Jenna had an idea. She told me I should tell Grandma about Kenny's potty training as if I thought she didn't know. I should pretend to notice the nappy for the first time, and then say, *Oh no, didn't you know? We're trying to potty train Kenny. I can't believe Mum didn't say anything*. That way, I don't get her into trouble but l let her know what we're supposed to be doing.

I did my best. After school, I made a big show of asking Kenny if he needed a wee, in front of Grandma. She was flicking through a magazine so I don't think she heard me. Then, with my best ever acting, I pretended to notice the nappy. I was all, 'Oh NO, Kenny. What's happened here? How come you're in a nappy? Did Mum put that on this morning because she forgot you're a big boy now?' Kenny looked at me like I was stupid. When I looked across at Grandma, she was still reading her magazine and hadn't looked up. I think I blew it.

Grandma must sneak the nappy off before Mum and Dad get home. I'm tired of it today but maybe I'll catch her in the act another time.

<u>Friday 12th February</u>

I woke up to find my toothbrush in the toilet. I thought Kenny had grown out of that but he must be playing up. It's all the wee-related issues he's experiencing. When I saw it floating in the bowl, it was like old times. I did exactly what I used to do. I gave it a good rinse under the tap, put it back until tomorrow when I'll have forgotten, and chose someone else's brush to use. At first I picked up Spike's because it looked the newest but I couldn't bring myself to put it in my mouth. I ended up with Blane's. No one will know. No one will care. (Sorry Blane.)

Friday Fooday was GORGEOUS. After the rubbish burgers in the week, tonight we had spicy chickpea and leek burgers. They were delish! You can't mush any old thing together and call it a burger. I asked Mum where she got the idea from, and she said from a recipe book. Then I asked where she got the idea for the rubbish ones in the week (I didn't say they were rubbish to her face). She said she made it up with leftovers. I said, 'Oh'. She smiled and could see I was telling her that she shouldn't make up her own recipes.

Saturday 13th February

For homework we had to complete a book review of something we've recently read. I loved it. It was like re-living the best bits of the St. Clare's stories all over again. I could only choose one book so I picked the first, but I made it clear they were all brilliant. When I got to the part that said '*Would you recommend it to others?*' I wrote '*I would, because you can lose yourself in the stories.* Then I added, '*But also I wouldn't recommend them because when they end, it feels like a secret boarding school world is over. It's like the characters have died and nothing you read can ever make you happy again.*' I felt like crying when I wrote that. It made me feel sad. I don't cry as a rule. There's no point. When you're a baby, it's the only way to communicate. But I have words. Besides, parents are too busy dealing with the crying babies to worry about the nearly teenage crying kids.

On a different topic, it occurred to me that as it's Valentine's Day tomorrow, Grandma might be lonely now she's binned off her lecherous boyfriend. I made her a card and asked Mum if she would drop it off tomorrow. She agreed and said I was a lovely granddaughter. Then she said I was a lovely daughter and tried to give me a hug. I let her but had to tell her to stop being weird. What with the wrong burgers and now this, Mum is losing the plot.

Sunday 14th February

Because I did my homework yesterday, I had lots of free time today. Dad let me borrow his iPad, so I messaged Jenna and Meg. Apparently Meg got three Valentine's cards. I'm sure her parents send her a couple so it's not that big a deal. I know she gave one to Alfie Diggs because I watched her put it in his bag on Friday. I don't think he'll find it. Alfie Diggs is the sort of boy who drops his bag on the floor as soon as he walks in and then picks it up on Monday morning when it's been emptied, cleaned and refilled by his mum. His mum is always coming to see Ms Archer when she thinks he shouldn't have been in trouble. If Alfie Diggs' mum could see him in school, she'd realise she's made a mistake. He's a nightmare. I have no idea why Meg likes him.

Jenna didn't get any Valentine's cards either. I'm glad about that. It's not that I *wanted* to get one - I find it a bit embarrassing - but I didn't want to be the only one without. Sometimes Meg thinks she's older than she is. It's not just the lip-gloss. It's the way she talks about people. She once said she was 'desperate' to be Alfie Diggs' girlfriend. I asked her what that would mean. She just shrugged and said, 'It would mean I'd be his girlfriend'. I didn't get it. I still don't. Why would anyone want that? He never talks to her or treats her in a friendly way. He's quite rude actually. But this seems to make Meg like him even more.

What makes me laugh is what Meg's mum and dad would say if she ended up marrying Alfie Diggs. They would hate it! They call her their little princess and would *not* be happy if Alfie Diggs was in their family. I don't see how being called a princess is a compliment either. Princesses don't do anything. They have to look pretty and do what the Queen says. When it was Prince Harry's wedding, Mum spent the day shouting at the telly, saying, 'Run for the hills, Meghan! Be your own woman!'

<u>Monday 15th February</u>

OMG! There are more Enid Blyton books!

Ms Archer saw my book review on her desk. As the lesson was about to start, she glanced at it and said,

'Oh, Leeza, good choice. I read those when I was your age.' (Just like Mum. But I cannot believe Ms Archer is anywhere near forty). Then she said, 'Have you read any of the other school books?' I must have looked blank because she came over, perched on the edge of the table and said, 'There are the *Malory Towers* books and *The Naughtiest Girl in the School* books. Then there are *The Famous Five*. They were my favourite. Not really about school but a group of children having adventures. You should look them up'. And then she moved away. My head was full of questions, but I had to be quiet and get on with the comprehension. The next chance I get, I am going to the library. Auction Bidders, do you still have Enid Blyton books in the future? I hope so. They're great.

Tea was veg and bean chilli with rice.

<u>Tuesday 16th February</u>

Mum KNEW there were more books! Everyone's kept this from me! She said that Enid wrote hundreds and the school books are just the start. I'm going to work my way through every single one.

In all the book excitement yesterday I forgot about the nappy situation. I only remembered today after Grandma had gone home. Kenny wees in the potty some of the time. Then other times, he wees on the floor. This evening, when he was saying night-night, he weed on Spike's leg. I thought it was funny but Spike didn't see the joke. He was annoyed he had to have a bath before he got into bed.

Tea was the same as last night. The pan of chilli sat on the hob all night. I'm not sure if that's the healthiest way to store food but as far as I know, no one's been sick. I'm the only one in the family that worries about these things.

<u>Wednesday 17th February</u>

My plan to read every single Enid Blyton book has failed before it started. The library had six of her books, and three of those were for babies. I had no idea she wrote *Noddy*! As much as I'm impressed with her range of stories, I'm far too old for *Noddy*. I borrowed one of *The Famous Five* stories that Ms Archer told me about. I'll give it a go and use my open mind again. I'm still not sure how I do that but it doesn't stop Mum from saying it.

Thursday 18th February

Well, Auction Bidders, it all kicked off today. I walked home with Jenna, ahead of Grandma as normal, so we got to the house first. We were sitting on the step when the front door opened and we fell back into the hall. Mum was home early! A meeting had finished sooner than she thought and there was no point going back to the office. As Jenna lay giggling on the floor, Grandma turned into the path with the buggy and saw Mum in the doorway. She looked *astonished*.*

Mum got Kenny out of the buggy and took him into the house. I could see Grandma lingering in the background, pretending to fuss with Blane's coat. I didn't understand because Grandma is so bossy, but she looked...*scared*.

A minute or so later I heard Mum say, 'Ma?' in a careful voice. The type of voice when she's about to shout at Spike but wants to make sure she has all the facts. And that was it. Kenny's secret nappy had been discovered. We stayed in the lounge pretending to watch *Fireman Sam*, while they shouted in the kitchen. It was loud. We heard Mum say, 'You have never taken my parental decisions seriously', and Grandma replying, 'Yes I have, even when I think you're doing it wrong.' Then Mum said, 'How dare you comment on my abilities as a mother. It's not like I had anyone to set me a great example.' Then Grandma said, 'I did my best! You wanted for nothing.' Then Mum said, 'I wanted for stability and a mother who'd put me before her social life.' Then Grandma said, 'I look forward to the day when Leeza throws all your efforts back in your face.' Then Mum screamed, 'At least I'll train her child to use the potty when she asks me to.' I turned the TV volume up at that point. It didn't seem to be about a nappy anymore. Besides, Mum might not potty train my children when she sees I eat ham sandwiches for breakfast.

In the end Grandma slammed the door and went home and Mum sat on her yoga ball, deep breathing. When Dad got in, they sat and talked in the kitchen whilst Spike and me listened at the door. I don't know who'll be picking us up tomorrow.

**Astonished* is on the Word Wall. I've used it every day this week.

Friday 19th February

This morning Mum acted liked everything was normal. She knows we heard it all but she's pretending we didn't. She put on a fake smile and said that Kenny was spending the morning at Teeny Tots and she'd be picking us up from school 'for a nice change'. Even Blane looked at her like she was mad. Fair play to Dad, though. He saw I was confused and gave me a smile that I took to mean, *Yeah, I know you know what's happened, but let's just pretend this is normal for Mum's sake.*

Saturday 20th February

In the weirdness of yesterday, I forgot that I am now on half-term. A whole week off school! It seems such a long time since the Christmas holiday.

Apart from the mountain of homework I've got, I'm looking forward to starting my *Famous Five* book. It also means the Grandma situation isn't a problem for a week. She is going to America tomorrow and Mum and Dad had already booked time off so they can look after us.

Grandma is visiting a place called Maine, which is on the top right part of America. She is going because the weather is similar to our weather (she doesn't like hot places) and because it's where *Murder She Wrote* is set. I really hope her row with Mum doesn't stop her buying presents. I love getting presents from Grandma's holidays.

I wonder if we'll ever see her again.

Sunday 21st February

Today I asked Dad if we'll ever see Grandma again. He was doing the dishes. He stopped, looked at me, and said, 'Why do you ask that?' I said, 'Because of the row with Mum.' Then he smiled to himself and said, 'That wasn't really a row. It was two people who love each other, letting off steam.' I am not convinced at all. He must have seen my doubting face because he added that if it hadn't been for half-term and her holiday, she'd be picking us up tomorrow as normal. I didn't tell him I'd known about the nappy situation all along. I'm still torn about whether I did the right thing by keeping quiet but I'll stop thinking about it. Kenny's toilet training is back on track and that's all that matters. He only had four changes of undies today so he's getting better.

I'm having an early night tonight. I think worrying about Nappy Gate (Dad calls it that) has taken it out of me. I've also started my book. I'm one chapter in but still not sure. There's a character called Georgina who tells everyone to call her George. I really like that. I'd do the same if that were my name.

Monday 22nd February

First day of the holidays. Dad's off work for the start of the week and then Mum's off towards the end.

Dad was happy he didn't have to wear a suit. He came downstairs wearing his holiday shorts. I asked him if he was cold and he said, 'Freedom from the tyranny of the neck tie is what's keeping me warm today'. I didn't really understand that but I did notice him put on a jumper after *Homes Under the Hammer*.

With Dad being there full time, Kenny only wet himself once. This is a massive improvement. He was really pleased with himself - Kenny not Dad - and kept saying, 'Kenny wees,' like it was a new game.

Tuesday 23rd February

Today was the same as yesterday. Kenny weed in the potty, Spike played with sticky tape and loo roll, Blane did colouring, Dad enjoyed being in shorts, and I read my library book.

I read back my whole diary from January 1st. It took ages - I've written loads! I'm glad I decided to keep it private. It's been a useful place to share my worries - Nappy Gate, not wanting to be a vegan, and my lapses with meat. I hope all you Auction Bidders are enjoying it in the future. Did you spend lots of money on my writing? Have I taught you about life as a ten year old from hundreds of years ago?

I don't plan to be famous but I hope I do good things so people will want to read my words. I don't want reporters in my face, but it'd be nice to have people stop me in the street to tell me they liked me. I just need to find a job that makes that happen. When I was little I wanted to drive ambulances. But then Mum told me that was a paramedic and I'd have to help people who were injured or smashed up. So I stopped wanting to do that. Then I wanted to be a YouTuber but that was so I could have a phone. Then I wanted to be a chef. Except I wouldn't want to work in a restaurant and be shouted at when the peas were late. I'd want to cook for a nice family and make all my favourite foods. I don't want to cook for MY family - Spike would tell me it tasted like sick even if he liked it - but a LOVELY family would be great.

Wednesday 24th February

It's taken some time but I think I like the Famous Five book. It's called *Five go to Smuggler's Top* and it's scary in places. It's exciting too - I'm not sure what's going to happen. The only weird thing is that the boys (Julian and Dick) treat the girls like they're not as good as them. George is a girl and won't take it but

Anne does. Anne needs to tell them to grow up. The mystery part is good though. I'll keep reading to find out what happens.

It was Dad's last day off today. He took us to the park. It was cold but we wrapped up in scarves and hats. (Dad had to put on actual trousers.) He wanted to get Blane cycling without stabilisers but Blane was having none of it. Instead we took the football and kicked it about. Kenny fell in some mud and I sat on a bench after a while and read. Spike decided to build a bonfire with broken twigs and branches. By the time we left, all the wood was piled up like a pyramid. Dad said it was a shame we couldn't light it as he'd worked so hard, but that we *definitely* couldn't light it. He looked a bit worried that Spike might come back later with matches. Spike wasn't bothered. He always stays out of trouble when he's building something. It was never about the fire.

Thursday 25th February

It was Mum's turn to be off. She didn't wear shorts, but put on clean pyjamas as soon as she'd had her shower. She said we were going to have a lazy day together. I didn't like to tell her that the whole week had been pretty lazy so far.

I finished my book. I was happy with how it turned out. I liked how the children solved the mystery when the adults couldn't. It reminded me of Roald Dahl stories where the grown-ups are useless.

I'm not saying the grown-ups in my life are useless. But I defo don't get credit for being as sensible as I am. I always set a good example to the younger ones, and I've been the only person giving consistent wee messages to Kenny. Dad forgot to ask about the potty a couple of times, which meant he had to clean up a wet puddle on the floor. Apart from that, we're all trying. Since Grandma went on holiday, we've been good at making sure he gets to the potty in time. I think he'll have a completely dry day soon. Then Mum will get the credit because she's off now, when really it's been a McAuliffe family effort.

Friday 26th February

We went food shopping on the bus. Normally, whoever has the car does it on their way home from work. I am never involved. But today Mum wanted to get some special ingredients for Friday Fooday, and for Dad's birthday tomorrow. She also gave me £5 to get him a present. The responsibility of being the eldest can be very full-on at times. We didn't go to the supermarket because of Mum's feelings about them. 'Only as a last resort,' she says. (Or when time is tight, or when she forgets she doesn't like them.) Instead she took us to the Farmers' Market on the other side of Stockford.

Even though I moaned about having to go, it turned out better than I thought. There were lots of stalls selling food. Some of it was being cooked outside in big pans and on BBQs. The air smelt gorgeous. Mum said that Spike and me could wander on our own as long as we stayed together. (Neither of us wanted that but it was better than having to walk in a big huddle with the pushchair.) The very best bit about the market was that some stalls were giving away free samples. Free samples! We walked to the cheese stall, and a really friendly woman with an accent told us to help ourselves. Help ourselves! We tried them all. There was a really soft, creamy one that was squishy to pick up. Then there was a spicy one with red bits all the way through it, and there was a strong smelly one. I wasn't sure, but Spike had two pieces because he said it smelt like feet. He thought that was a good thing.

Another stall that we stopped at was more of a problem. A man from Spain was selling different types of ham and sausage. We must have looked like meat-eaters because he gave us a big smile and told us to have a taste and tell our parents how good they were. Now, I'm very good in this situation. I've been doing this for a long time. I can smile politely and say, 'Thank you but I'm afraid I'm a vegetarian'. And then sometimes I even make a joke and say, 'Blame my parents,' as I roll my eyes. Just as I was about to launch into my reply, Spike leaned forward and helped himself to a big piece of sausage.

I didn't really know what to do. Should I tell him off? That's what Mum would do. But then I'd be a big hypocrite because I've done things like that too. Spike looked at me like it was no big deal. And then he tried some other stuff - ham I think. He ate it right in front of me. Next thing you know, the man is waving as we're walking away, telling us to tell our parents it was good. For the rest of the day, we never spoke of it.

Friday Fooday was a bits and pieces tea, where we could help ourselves from the middle of the table. Cheeses, olives, marinated peppers, special bread. It was brilliant. I watched Spike but he was just the same as he normally would be. I wonder if he's done this before. I did my best to put it out of my mind as we ate and chatted. I have far too many worries. Grandma is back from America tomorrow so that's another thing to stress about. I have no idea if Nappy Gate is really over.

Maybe Grandma was right. Maybe I do need this diary so I can share my problems. I still don't think I'm depressed though. Just really annoyed by other people. A lot.

Saturday 27th February

Happy birthday Dad! Forty-two today. Because his age isn't a special one, I didn't have the stress of writing a song and a poem. The hand-made chocolates and real ale were enough. Mum had to buy the beer but I found the chocolates on a stall yesterday.

Dad seemed very happy. He opened the chocolates in bed and tried one before he was up. He said he'd save the beer for later. While we were sitting on the bed, Mum's phone pinged. She picked it up, read it and then tossed it on the bed. 'She's back. She says happy birthday.' Mum sighed but didn't say anything else.

Even though it isn't strictly true, Grandma is my only grandparent for real. Apart from her 'dead, useless husband' (her words) I also have my dad's parents. But, the thing with them is, they're not very nice. I don't mean that in the way that Grandma talks about Mum's dad. She says mean things about him to be funny. Dad's mum and dad are not very nice for real. When Dad wanted to marry Mum, they didn't like her and didn't want him to go out with her. In the end, he told them to like it or lump it, and they decided to lump it. I met them once when I was a baby but I don't remember.

I think that's why Mum puts up with Grandma when she does things like Nappy Gate. We aren't speaking to any other relatives so we have to keep things going with the ones we have.

Sunday 28th February

I wonder if I'll ever go on a plane. I think it would be the most exciting thing in the world but I just can't see it. I'd fly to a deserted island that had peace and quiet and no little brothers barging into my room. I could handle that very easily. I'd need a couple of books of course. And it might make Mum realise I could do with a phone.

This was one of the thoughts I had today as I tried to get through all the homework I'd left to the last minute. (It was adding fractions with common denominators. I will never need to do this in my life, ever.)

Monday 29th February

Back to school.

It's a leap year so today is extra. It should be used for something spectacular. Instead I'll be in school having a normal Monday. What a waste.

We had *another* SATs lecture. Some people hadn't done their homework, which is NOT GOOD ENOUGH. I felt very smug even though I only finished it at 9.30 last night. Jenna hadn't done hers. I don't think any of us thought she would.

Grandma was back. She picked us up and teased us all the way home, saying she hadn't had time to get us presents. Then when we got through the door, there were bags waiting for us. I knew she'd been joking but it was still a nice surprise. I got a sign for my door saying L's Room. It had been written on a chunk of wood that is the shape of the map of Maine. I didn't know that before Grandma told me. The boys were given similar Maine shaped pieces of wood, but as they all share a room, they had different things painted on them. Spike's had a skull on it. I'm not sure why but he thought it was great. Grandma kept saying things like she needed to go to the 'restroom', when she meant toilet. And later she described her hotel, saying she had to get the 'elevator' to the fourth floor instead of the lift. Mum laughed in her face when she said Blane had been careful to stay on the 'sidewalk' and not the pavement.

Things seem back to normal. Grandma even asked Kenny if he needed the potty. He did, and he weed, and everyone clapped. He'll feel very disappointed when we all stop doing that. I think Nappy Gate is finally in the past. It's such a relief.

* * *

3.

OMG!

<u>Tuesday 1st March</u>

St David's Day. (We had an assembly about daffodils.) While we were at school, Grandma and Kenny made Dad a birthday cake. Because of Grandma being away, it was three days late. No one cared! It was a chocolate sponge but with a can of Guinness mixed in. That sounds like it should be horrible but it wasn't. It was gorgeous. Grandma made a big deal of telling Mum that the alcohol had baked out of it in the oven. I've no idea why. Mum likes beer. Maybe she thought we wouldn't be allowed to have a piece. Although I ate trifle at Christmas and that had a LOT of sherry in it. We were full of cake so we had toast for tea. Sometimes

Mum's healthy eating rules get forgotten when work has tired her out.

Wednesday 2nd March

Kenny had his first dry day! He had three wees on the potty with Grandma, and a couple more in the evening with us. We gave him a standing ovation as Dad carried him upstairs. I'm not sure if he understood what was going on, but he clapped himself as he went.

Thursday 3rd March

Mum and Dad came home from work in moods. I couldn't tell if they were angry, sad or both. I heard them tell Grandma that some changes are coming at the Council. I don't know what they are but they forgot to sign my form for the Stockford High taster day. They're defo not themselves.

This evening Kenny pooed in the potty. Yuck. It feels wrong to celebrate something so smelly as you're watching TV but we had to cheer him on so he knows he's doing well. Before bed, Spike was actually funny (first time ever) when he went to the toilet. He came back saying he couldn't go until we all clapped. That made Mum and Dad smile even though they were still thinking about the changes that are coming. I went to bed early because apart from Spike's joke, the atmosphere was weird.

Friday 4th March

The atmosphere was still eerie this morning. (*Eerie* is on the Word Wall and means 'strange' or 'odd'. I used it in English to describe a haunted house.)

Jenna asked me over for tea but it was Friday Fooday so I said I couldn't. When I got home though, it wasn't like a normal Friday. Everything was quiet. Mum was sitting at the table with a cup of green tea, staring into space. It was very strange. In the end, Grandma said, 'Crack on and set to, Molly. This is getting you nowhere.' Mum started chatting then.

Apart from that, Kenny had an accident (only wee, not a real accident.) Spike repeated his joke from last night but it wasn't as funny the second time. And Blane seemed a bit quiet. He didn't manage to get rid of his stabilisers before everyone's attention turned to Kenny. At least being the eldest has given me practice at being left to get on with it. I'm used to achieving things in silence.

Tea was cous cous, sweet potato and cheese tart. It sounds eerie but it tasted fine.

Saturday 5th March

Mum and Dad are still being mysteriously moody. (Alliteration!) I kept out of their way and did my homework. It was another dry day for Kenny though. I think he's cracked it.

Sunday 6th March

Mum called a Family Meeting. I knew something was wrong as we sat down. The last few days have been weird and my stomach was churning.

This meeting was about the Council changes that are coming. Apparently there might be some redundancies. No one knew what that meant so Dad explained. He said, 'It's when you get sacked from your job even though you didn't do anything wrong.' I must have looked confused so he added, 'It's usually when companies don't have enough money.' It sounded bad. I asked Mum if her and Dad were going to lose their jobs and she said, 'I'm sure we'll be fine, Leeza'. But then Dad put his hand on top of hers and squeezed it, so it looked like we were defo NOT going to be fine. They must think I'm thick. I notice everything.

After that, the meeting turned into the type of meeting we often have. It was the 'We Don't Have Any Money Right Now, So Don't Ask Us For Anything' speech. I've heard this before. I think it's directed at Spike because he's always wanting sweets. I'm sensible about money. I *know* we don't have any to spare. Compared to Meg, I'm really poor. She acts like having lots of money makes her a better person, which I know isn't true. But compared to Jenna, I'm loads better off. She doesn't care and I prefer her attitude. She couldn't stop laughing last month when the snow soaked through the hole in her shoes.

Monday 7th March

I'm not sure if it's the worry of the Council changes or if there's a bug going round but I woke to hear

Mum throwing up. I thought it was part of my dream at first. It was only when I woke up that I realised it was coming from the bathroom. (Having a wash after Mum has thrown up is still better than using the bathroom immediately after Spike. This says a lot about Spike's hygiene habits.)

I thought Mum would stay off work but she didn't. She said she'd be fine by mid-morning. I don't know how she can be so sure. When I got a bug last year, I was off for a week. I couldn't stop being sick AND going to the toilet. It was horrible. Sitting at a desk would have been beyond me.

Tuesday 8th March

Mum and Dad keep whispering to each other when they think we're watching TV. No one else seems to realise but I do. The Council changes have changed them. When Mum smiles it's like she's forcing herself.

Jenna was off school so I walked home with Grandma and the boys. I used the opportunity to ask Grandma if Mum was OK. She didn't really answer my question. Instead she said, 'Leeza, your mother is as stubborn as a mule and will always do what she thinks is best. Good luck to her. That's what I say.' Like I said, she didn't really answer my question.

Tea was veggie bolognese with whole wheat pasta shells.

Wednesday 9th March

I had tea at Jenna's. Having a break from home was good. We watched YouTube videos and talked about Alfie Diggs. Jenna thinks he's funny, but that's all. She doesn't fancy him. She did an impression of Meg and her lip-gloss that made me laugh a lot. Then I felt bad for laughing but it *was* funny. Meg should laugh at herself too. She takes everything so seriously.

The *real* best bit was the food. I'd been trying to work out what to do if I were offered meat. I think I'd decided it would be rude to turn it away. But then Jenna's dad said we were having a chippy tea, so I got to have my absolute favourite. Chips and curry sauce!

I *think* the reason we hardly go to the chippy is because of the cost. Or maybe Mum's trying to keep us all healthy. Either way, I didn't feel I was doing anything wrong at Jenna's. It felt good.

Thursday 10th March

Things were more normal today. Mum and Dad are still quiet but we're getting used to it.

Grandma took Kenny shopping while the rest of us were at school. She wanted an outfit for a date tomorrow. Dad said, 'You must be nervous if you have to tart yourself up, Ursula.' Then Grandma snorted and said, 'Who are you calling a tart, Sebastian'. Then Dad laughed and said, 'I think I've touched a nerve'. Then Grandma said, 'I haven't been nervous since 1963.' That was it. As Dad and Grandma's funny conversations go, it wasn't their best. Usually there are funny insults and *grown-up* comments at each other. This one was fairly tame.

Grandma's date is with a man called Willard. I've never heard that name before. It sounds like a type of tree.

Friday 11th March

I asked Grandma about Willard. She met him on her website. She always gets her 'menfriends' from there. (Mum says they're too old to be called boyfriends.) Grandma said she'd asked him about his name. He said his Dad was an American soldier in the war and it came from there. I still think it sounds like he should be planted in the ground.

After school, me and Jenna were sitting on the step waiting for Grandma and the boys to catch up when Ryan came out from next door. He said, 'How's your mum feeling?' I said, 'She's fine thank you'. Then he said, 'Tell her I was asking after her. It can't be easy'. I said, 'Will do'. And that was it. I've no idea what isn't easy. Spewing up every morning, I suppose.

Tea was jacket potato, cheese, beans and salad.

Saturday 12th March

Mum has called another Family Meeting for tomorrow. I know *I* haven't asked for money so it must be to remind Spike. Or maybe it's to congratulate us all for getting Kenny off nappies so smoothly. Family Meetings are happening more and more these days. They're losing their power.

I spent all day doing homework (relative pronouns). My hand hurts.

Sunday 13th March

OMG.

In shock.

Monday 14th March

Still in shock.

Tuesday 15th March

The last two days have been a blur. My mind is bewildered. (Word Wall!) Everything is a confusing mess. I feel so discombobulated. (My head might be all over the place, but I'm using excellent describing words. Ms Archer taught us *discombobulated* the other day.)

The Family Meeting seemed normal at first. We sat round the kitchen table as usual. Kenny was asleep in his chair but the rest of us were awake. Then Mum said, 'I've called this Family Meeting to discuss some of the changes that are coming.' Spike rolled his eyes. He said, 'I know we don't have money, I haven't asked for anything'. I nodded because neither had I. But Mum explained this was about something else.

She paused for a moment. I saw Dad do his hand squeeze again so I was suspicious. Then she said, 'Last week we talked to you about money being tight, and we said there'd be redundancies at the Council. But this week we have some news to cheer us up.'

For a second I was excited. I wanted her to say we were going on holiday. It's been ages since we've been away. Now that Kenny's toilet trained, staying in a caravan would be loads easier. I was picturing myself paddling in the water with an ice cream in each hand, when she carried on. She said, 'So we wanted to ask you what you'd think if...we had another baby?

Just then, Kenny woke up and started crying. He'd weed in his chair. When Dad picked him up, his top got covered in wet. He took him upstairs while we sat in silence. Eventually Mum said, 'So what do you think?' I looked at Blane who was picking his nose. I looked at Spike who was open-mouthed. I knew I'd have to be the mature one. Again.

The Family Meeting rules are to listen when someone is speaking, and to be polite. I had listened to Mum and now she had to listen to me. I *politely* explained that we'd been told money was tight so maybe a new baby should wait a bit. We'd know whether the Council changes would be bad, and we'd know if we could afford another mouth to feed. I also explained that now Mum was forty, she should concentrate on the children she already had, rather than bother having a new one.

When I finished, Mum smiled. She said, 'Those are really good points Leeza, thank you.' (I agreed with her.) Then she said, 'It's a bit late to consider them though. I'm already pregnant. We have to make the best of it and look forward to the new baby. It's due in September.'

I sank back into the chair unable to find words. Spike got up and said, 'It better not be a girl', then went over to the TV. Mum wiped Blane's nose and asked him if he'd like a baby brother or sister. He just shook his head.

Wednesday 16th March

I haven't told anyone yet. Mum said she'd prefer we kept it to ourselves for now. Even if she hadn't said that, I'm not ready to share the news.

I don't hate babies but I know they're a lot of work. We've just got to the stage where Kenny can do more things. Apart from the odd accident, he doesn't need changing every few hours. Walking to the shops is easier without loading the pushchair with baby stuff. He doesn't cry in the night anymore. He's easier in every way. When September comes, it'll be like stepping back in time.

Thursday 17th March

This morning we did a test practice and even though I answered the questions, I couldn't concentrate. This 'baby situation' is taking up my thoughts.

I think I'm putting on a *good* brave face. I'm smiling even when I don't feel like it. That's what Mum's doing too. She was sick again this morning but acting like she wasn't ill at all.

Ohhhh. I just worked it out. *That's* why she was throwing up. If I were in a film, I'd be smacking my hand against my forehead now. I can't believe I didn't realise what was going on. I wonder if Grandma knows. I might drop some hints tomorrow and see if she gets what I'm talking about.

Friday 18th March

Grandma *so* knows. I tried to bring it up on the way home. I said, 'It's good you're back from America now because Mum was throwing up this morning.' I waited to see if she'd try to change the subject, or just ask if she was OK. Almost immediately she replied, 'Leeza, are you dense? She's three months pregnant. Of course she's throwing up in the morning. That's what comes of carrying the miracle of new life inside you.'

This annoyed me. I am *not* dense. I was thinking of her feelings in case they hadn't told her. I decided not to ask how her date went with Willard the Tree.

I think Grandma might have known about the 'baby situation' before me. This isn't right. She won't be the one having to live with it. I also think she was being sarcastic when she said 'miracle of new life'. It's like she was teasing Mum, even though Mum wasn't there. Everything feels very complicated right now.

I had an early night and carried on re-reading St. Clare's. It wasn't really a distraction, as I know what's going to happen. I need to go to the library. I also need to stop stressing about the 'baby situation'.

Saturday 19th March

When the baby is my age, I'll be twenty. That's ridic.

I've just remembered it's the taster day at Stockford High on Monday. My mind is all over the place. I was nervous about it last week but now it'll be something to focus on. I'm meeting Meg and Jenna at 8.30am and walking down together. We will be like *proper* teenagers.

Sunday 20th March

I spent the day doing homework. I can't pretend I'm excited about the baby when I'm not. It didn't affect me when Kenny was born. I was younger and didn't have much responsibility. Now I'm nearly in high school. It'll be down to me to do everything when Mum and Dad are tired. I'll be the one bringing this child up. I don't think I can handle another Spike.

Monday 21st March

Stockford High taster day. I feel so grown up!

It went well from the start - walking with no adults and no pushchair was brilliant. Even though Stockford High is on Tyson Road, it took us twenty minutes to get there. When we arrived, we were divided into groups. Meg and Jenna were together, but I was on my own. I didn't mind. I ended up in Alfie Diggs' group so I don't think Meg was very happy.

We did Science, Art and German. In Science we were shown what a Bunsen burner was and we watched the teacher light it. In Art we mixed paint and used watercolours on special paper. In German we learnt to say *Ich heiße Leeza. Ich bin zehn jahre alt.* I can speak German now! And I learnt a new letter. I can't remember what it's called but it made a ssss sound.

Some of the older children are massive. They aren't really children at all. They're as tall as Dad. I saw one boy with a beard! I thought they might pick on us, but they were OK. A group of older girls walked past and said, 'Ahhhhhh', like we were babies. I suppose I have to ignore it. Soon I'll be here every day.

By home time, I was shattered. Mum kept asking me how it went but I was too tired to go into details. I'm only writing this now because I want to remember how much I enjoyed my first time at high school.

<u>Tuesday 22nd March</u>

Meg spent break time asking about Alfie Diggs. She wanted to know everything he'd done yesterday. I couldn't remember. Apart from when he was told off in Art for putting paint on Caitlyn Matherson's neck. He needs to grow up. He's nearly in high school.

Mum was also full of questions about yesterday. The new baby is making her act weird. What I enjoyed yesterday was forgetting about it for a while. She even patted my head as I went to bed. I had to roll my eyes to show her she was being strange.

<u>Wednesday 23rd March</u>

It's been a busy week for Year Six. First it was the Stockford taster day, then today it was Sex Education! (That's the last thing I want to hear about right now.)

At least it was a change from the SATs. Ms Archer said we should treat Sex Education exactly the same as Maths or History. Except we never have to agree ground rules in those subjects. And Alfie Diggs never laughs so hysterically that he turns purple in those subjects either. He's such a child.

I enjoyed today. We learnt how babies are made in Year Five so this year's topic was about adverts and why they often have half-naked ladies on them. Ms Archer said that advertisers think that pretty people sell products better. But half-naked people could never make me buy sweetcorn no matter how pretty they were. I can't stand sweetcorn.

When Dad got in he said, 'Tell your grandma what you've been learning today, Leeza'. I knew he was winding her up but it was quite funny. I said, 'We did about sex in adverts.' Grandma looked startled for a second, then said, 'I'm very happy for you, Leeza.' She was quiet for a minute and then said, 'See, Sebastian, not such a fuddy-duddy am I?' She was quiet for another minute and then she left. I don't think she knew what to say. She *is* a bit of a fuddy-duddy sometimes and I still don't know what's happening with Willard the Tree.

Tea was veggie sausages and mashed potato. Mmmm.

<u>Thursday 24th March</u>

It's nearly Easter. The bank holiday weekend starts tomorrow, then there's four more school days till we break for the two-week spring holidays. I can't wait.

Tea was baked sweet potato and home made coleslaw.

Friday 25th March

Good Friday.

Today has been a very *good* Friday. Did you spot my joke? Ha ha.

Mum and Dad were off work too, so it was Film Day. Dad bought the double duvet from the bed and we all squashed onto the sofa.

The first choice wasn't a choice. It was a no-brainer. *The Sound of Music* was on BBC1 at 10.30am so we started off with that. I ate my cereal under the duvet and it felt *so* much better than being at school. Liesl is my favourite character. Not just because it's my name, but because she's the eldest like me, and sneaks out and disobeys the rules. I disobey the rules sometimes (like with meat!) so I know how she feels. It's a long film though. By the end, everyone else had got bored. Although I heard Spike whisper *cool* when the nuns messed with the car engine.

After that we watched kids stuff. *Peppa Pig* and *Fireman Sam,* mostly. I didn't really care. I was very snug under the covers and every so often Dad would get us drinks or popcorn. It was a very *good* Friday. (I've said it again! Ha.)

Saturday 26th March

Easter Saturday.

Grandma is coming for lunch tomorrow so we had to go food shopping. It was crazy! People were snatching things from under each other's noses. The shelves were almost empty. Dad drove us to Tesco to save time but Mum kept making sarky comments like, 'You don't get this at the Farmers' Market, Mac'. Dad wasn't impressed but he ignored her. I think everyone's stress levels were up.

We don't celebrate Easter. I suppose Grandma coming for lunch makes it a celebration but we don't do anything else. When Mum was little, Grandma made her go to church every week. Mum once said to me, 'I hope you appreciate the fact I would never force religion on you.' I don't care about that but the odd Easter egg would be nice.

I do get Easter eggs in a way. At school, everyone was given a cream egg on Thursday. And Grandma buys us something too. I just find it hard when Meg's eggs run to double figures and she's still eating them in the Summer.

I think Meg is a bit spoilt.

Sunday 27th March

Easter Sunday.

Grandma is officially dating Willard the Tree. It came up over lunch. Dad asked how her love life was. This made Mum laugh, and Grandma roll her eyes. She said, 'Sebastian, I assure you, it's merely a social life, not a love life. It isn't love when there's been a smattering of dates and I'm not sure about his jumpers.' Mum found this really funny. 'What's wrong with his jumpers?' she said. Grandma sighed. Then she said, 'I suppose it comes down to the fact that they're very *busy*. The patterns play havoc with my eyes when I'm wearing the wrong glasses.' At this point Dad snorted and left the table. He pretended he was taking the plates away, but he was laughing a lot. Grandma takes things very seriously. I don't get why jumpers are such a problem. Surely the issue is that the man is called *Willard*.

The good news is that I got a full sized Easter egg! (Thank you, Grandma!) I've eaten the buttons but am saving the egg for tomorrow. I'll try and make it last for ages like Meg. Maybe till the Summer?

<u>Monday 28th March</u>

I ate the egg for breakfast. Oh well.

<u>Tuesday 29th March</u>

It's been over a week since Stockford High. I'm glad it was good. I'm not thinking about leaving Irwell Green yet because it's still ages off, but now I've had a bit of insight into the future, I'm getting excited. I can't wait to be one of the high school students that walk past my house. I've decided I'm going to carry files - a pile of files in front of my chest like I'm grown up and intelligent. That's my plan.

Mum asked me about high school *again* over tea. She said, 'It's OK if you didn't enjoy it as much as you thought you would.' I stopped her right there and said, 'Actually I enjoyed it far more.' Then she said, 'Oh,' and that was that. I don't get her anymore. It must all be pregnancy related. At least I've stopped waking up to the sounds of her vomit.

Tea was quiche and salad.

Wednesday 30th March

I was worried I'd spoken too soon with writing that last night. No puking today though - so far so good. Although it won't be long before there will be *baby* puke everywhere.

Once, when Kenny was a baby, I went to school with his sick on my shoulder. Mrs Johnson noticed it in the cloakroom and got a wet paper towel to wipe it off. I think she felt sorry for me. It wasn't so bad then. I was in Year Three. I could get away with things like that. If it happens in high school I'll be mortified.

I'm still not keen on this baby idea. It's on my mind all the time.

Thursday 31st March

I've decided to make a list of all the reasons why I think the 'baby situation' is a bad idea. At the moment it feels confusing. I need to work out what the problem is. Here goes.

- The house is full - no spare rooms.
- It's already a squeeze around the table when Grandma eats with us.
- Babies cost money.
- We have no money.
- Mum threw out all Kenny's baby stuff when he was done with it.
- I don't want to share my room. If it's a girl that will happen.
- If it's a boy, there'll be four boys in one bedroom. Too many!
- I'll have homework every night and a crying baby will make that harder.
- Mum and Dad are too old.
- It's bad enough when Mum and Dad hold hands in public, so telling people they are having another baby will be embarrassing.
- Meg will be disgusted.

- I don't want things to change.
- I don't like change.

I know it's not about Meg. And if I were excited then I wouldn't be bothered what she thought. I think, looking back over my list, it's the money and the space issues I'm most worried about. I'd love there to be more space at home. I should be having more privacy as I get older, not less. Sometimes I go to bed early, just so I can get away from everyone. I never realised how lucky I was to have my own room until the thought of sharing it came up. I don't think I can handle any more brothers, but on the other hand, a sister would mean life as I know it is over. It's a no-win situation. For me, at least.

Tea was courgetti spaghetti.

4.

Grown-ups Are Confusing

Friday 1st April

After the register, Ms Archer stood up with a very serious face. She said, 'I'm sorry to do this but I've just been told there's a change. One of the SATs tests is in French.' There was a shocked silence. It didn't make any sense. Then Jenna shouted out, 'That's stupid!' really loudly. Ms Archer said, 'It *is* stupid but we only have a month to start learning'. As soon as she said that she launched into lots of fast French words as she walked around the classroom. At one point she was standing over Alfie Diggs, asking him something over and over again in foreign, but he hadn't a clue what she was saying. Meg looked upset and Jenna kept saying, 'This is mental,' repeatedly. I couldn't say anything. I felt sick. There's no way I can learn French in a month. I haven't learnt all the English words yet.

After a few minutes, when we were all speechless, Ms Archer stopped talking fast and walked to the Smart board. Without saying anything else, she wrote big, tall letters. Only when she moved away, could we see what it said - APRIL FOOL. It took five seconds before everyone burst out laughing. Caitlyn Matherson kept wagging her finger, saying, 'You really had us, Miss'. Alfie Diggs shouted, 'Miss! I thought you'd gone mad!' and Jenna laughed till she was bright red. To be fair, it was pretty funny. It's nice to see Ms Archer relax again. The SATs can't be fun for her either. Only Meg stayed annoyed. I don't think she likes jokes.

In the playground afterwards, everyone was talking about it. I said it was the funniest thing that has ever happened in Year Six. Jenna said it was between that, and when Olivia Tyler ran into Mr Eskbrook when she was fielding in rounders. It was a close call.

The rest of the day felt light-hearted. Breaking up for two weeks helped too. When we got home, Grandma didn't stay for long because she was meeting Willard. Mum said, 'Have you got over his busy jumpers yet?' and Grandma replied, 'Patience Molly. It takes time to convince a man that the changes he must make are his own idea.' I have no idea what she means but his jumpers don't stand a chance. Not if Grandma is against them.

Friday Fooday was Moroccan cous cous and veggie burgers. It was gorge.

Saturday 2nd April

I had a massive lie in today. Till 11 o'clock. Eventually Dad said I had to watch Kenny while he was sorting out the yard. Mum and Dad have started binning things they don't need. They must have realised there's not enough space for a baby and now one is coming whether they like it or not.

I made a list of aims for the next two weeks.

- Go to the library and get more Enid Blyton books
- Read the books
- Rearrange my room
- See Jenna
- Maybe see Meg
- Do my homework
- Have fun

I've called them *aims* because I don't want to feel bad if I don't achieve them all. It's OK if I miss. The only one I *have* to do is homework. I ran out of ideas by the end. I wasn't sure what else to put other than 'Have fun'. I don't know what that fun will be but I would like to have some. I'm also looking forward to re-arranging my room. I'd like my bed under the window, I think.

Sunday 3rd April

My room looks so different now. I've worked all day - my arms ache and everything.

One good thing about Mum and Dad is they don't mind me changing my bedroom around. I have a bed, a bookcase, a wardrobe made out of canvas and a little desk and chair. They're too small for me now so end up being covered in clothes. Nothing's hard to move. The bed has wheels so I can pull it across the floor easily.

Not only have I rejigged everything, but I've also tidied. I never tidy! I got the hoover out, dusted the window ledge and put my clothes away. I take after Mum and Dad when it comes to cleaning. They're quite relaxed. Grandma is the opposite, though. She changes the sheets on all three beds every weekend. And she lives alone! It doesn't make sense. She says she has to keep her standards up, but I think she must get bored. Why would she do more chores than were needed? I did need to do *my* tidying though. The last time I vacuumed my room was the last time I rearranged it. That was last Summer. It was time.

As well as having a new bedroom, I also found three socks, several felt tips (all dried up) and Kenny's blanky. I had no idea he'd lost it. I gave it back to Mum who looked a bit surprised, before she put it in the bin. 'Let's not mention we did that', she said.

Monday 4th April

Dad's off work for two days to give Grandma a break. I told him I needed to go to the library as soon as possible. He said, 'What's the rush, Leez? You're off school, you can chillax.' I said, 'I need my holiday reading before the holiday goes too far.' He didn't argue with that. He knows reading's a good thing. He needs to stop saying things like *chillax* though.

The trouble with the library is taking Spike, Blane and Kenny. Controlling the three of them in a place they're supposed to be sensible is impossible. I *needed* Dad to let me go on my own. It's only a fifteen-minute walk and in September I'll take longer than that going to school. I decided to do what Grandma is trying with Willard and his jumpers. I had to make Dad think he'd come up with the solution, even though it was my own idea.

I sat on the sofa as he was watching *Loose Women.* First I said, 'It's a shame I have to rely on Stockford Library when I'll be at high school soon and will get books from there'. (That was me reminding him I was old enough to be leaving primary school.) Then I said, 'The library's closer than Stockford High when you think about it. (That was me showing him it isn't a big deal to walk to the library alone.) Finally I said, 'It's a lot of hassle to take the boys, just so I can get books to help develop my reading. It'd be easier to go on my own.' (That was me giving him the idea to let me go on my own.)

I'm not sure which bit did it, but it worked! I think he knew I'd been trying to suggest it, but I didn't care. The second he said yes, I got my shoes and my library books, and set off. Dad insisted on watching me cross the main road from the front window but then I was free! Straight past the park, right at the next road, left at the next. It felt amazing to be treated like a grown-up. I practically am one, really.

One thing I do know. There's no *way* that tactic would have worked on Mum.

Tuesday 5th April

In all the excitement of yesterday's freedom, I forgot to say what books I got.

The high hopes I'd had when I walked through the door were dashed as soon as I saw the shelves. I searched through loads of books I didn't want before I found a few I'll read. I got *Second Term at Malory Towers* (which is written by Enid Blyton, just like the St. Clare's books) and *Matilda* by Roald Dahl. I've read *Matilda* quite a few times so it's like an old friend. I like how she reads books and sorts out problems. If I could use my mind to control things, I'd be sorted. I'd never have to move Spike's undies from the bathroom floor, ever again.

Wednesday 6th April

I'm forty-nine pages into *Malory Towers* and I've worked out there's another book that comes first. I thought it was confusing. I'll keep going but I'm not as glued to it as the St. Clare's books.

It was Mum's turn to be off today. I'm glad I had a book to read because every time Spike moaned that he was bored, she gave him cleaning jobs to do. He wasn't happy. She also said we should go through our things and see if there's anything we've outgrown or don't want anymore. I'm not being funny but we don't have much. The few possessions I own are precious! I looked in my room but the only thing that doesn't have much sentimental value is the sign that says L's room. I've only had it since February. I think it'd be rude to get rid of it so soon. Grandma might be offended. I'll tell Mum I haven't got anything. I've no idea why she's so obsessed with cleaning and sorting right now.

Thursday 7th April

Mum's still at it. I kept reading my book so I'd be left alone. Spike hasn't worked out he needs to pretend to be busy if he doesn't want to be nagged. I looked out of my window this morning and he was picking all the weeds from between the flags in the yard. It didn't look like he was enjoying it.

Mum needs to calm down.

Friday 8th April

I didn't have to fake-read to avoid anything today. Mum took us all to the Farmers' Market which I actually enjoy. Like last time, I was allowed to wander off on my own as long as I was with Spike.

But unlike last time, I wasn't shocked when I saw Spike stuff his face at the Spanish Meats stall.

On the bus home Mum reminded us to sort the things we don't want anymore. I asked her why and she said, 'We have too many things.' This is the complete opposite of the truth. She wants to see the inside of Meg's bedroom. Then she'd know what too many things look like.

Saturday 9th April

There's a Family Meeting tomorrow. Mum called it. No one else ever wants one except Mum. One day I might call a Family Meeting and discuss that we should stop having Family Meetings.

Sunday 10th April

Family Meetings have started to become stressful. They're never called for good reasons. Today's Family Meeting was all about being poor. (This is not news.)

Mum started by saying that we have to make changes now a new baby is coming. She repeated the line about not asking her or Dad for money because they have none. I think I rolled my eyes. I NEVER ask for money. I'm not even going on the Year Six holiday because it cost £160 and there was no point showing them the letter. Mum needs to talk to the people that keep asking. It *must* be Spike.

Then she said she'd been asking if we'd got unwanted belongings because she plans to sell them on eBay. She hasn't thought this through. Even if I *did* contribute my bedroom door sign, it wouldn't raise a pound. (I think she's lost the plot.) Dad told us he was selling some of his records and Mum said she was going to sell her exercise bike. (It's in her bedroom under loads of washing.) She said that any old toys or clothes we've finished with, should be left on the landing to be photographed.

When Mum finished, she asked us if we had anything to add. I couldn't sit in silence. I felt I HAD to say the stuff that's been in my head. It needed to come out. First of all I said that we have no room in the house for another baby and selling a door sign wouldn't make a difference. (This caused confusion because I hadn't told them I'd been thinking of contributing the door sign in the first place.) Anyway, I carried on and explained I didn't know where the baby was going to sleep. I said I had no idea how we'd fit round the table when Grandma stayed for tea. I finished by pointing out that the Farmers' Market was more expensive than Tesco so maybe we should change what we eat instead of selling our belongings. (That was stupid, to be honest. I really like the food from the market. I was just trying to show it wasn't all my responsibility to save money.) Mum was quiet after I finished. Then she said, 'Leeza, thank you for your comments. We're working on all these issues.' Then she got up and said, 'Meeting over'. I couldn't work out if she was cross or not. That's the problem with Family Meetings. You have to listen to everyone's opinions even when you don't want to. It wouldn't surprise me if we stop having them from now on.

<u>Monday 11th April</u>

Grandma was back today. She said she'd been conserving her strength for the past week because she has us for the rest of the holiday. I certainly don't take any energy to supervise. It must be the strain of reminding Kenny to have a wee fifteen times a day.

Saying that, I think we all agree that Kenny is now completely potty trained. He also uses the toilet when the special seat is attached. It's funny to remember how stressed I was a couple of months ago. Hopefully the 'new baby/selling things' worries will ease soon, too. Mum said she was working on all the issues although I don't think there's much she can do to fix things.

Tuesday 12th April

I was woken up at the crack of dawn by Grandma banging on my door and saying, 'The sun is shining, the sky is blue. We are going to the park to blow away the cobwebs.'

I groaned but I didn't say anything. There's no point with Grandma. I wanted to point out that blowing away the cobwebs isn't a real thing. I have no cobwebs and there is nothing to blow away. I'm sure it would've made no difference if I'd explained that.

Grandma was right though. It *was* a nice day. She put a football and tennis ball in her bag and the five of us walked together. It was different from walking home from school. This felt more like a daytrip than the school-run. As we walked, we chatted a bit too. I asked her about Willard the Tree (although I was careful to just call him Willard to her face.) She smiled and said, 'He seems a very decent man, Leeza, and there are precious little of those in this world.' I asked if she thought Dad was a decent man. She laughed out loud before saying, 'He'll do'. I must have looked a bit surprised because she quickly followed up with, 'Of course your father is a decent man. He makes your Mum happy so that's what counts. Of course he isn't *my* type for a second.'

I'm glad that Dad isn't Grandma's type. (That would be disgusting!) But even if Dad were really old and not her son-in-law, I can see what Grandma means. They are totally different. He laughs at her when she's being serious and winds her up a lot. Grandma wouldn't stand for that. I'm now really curious about what Willard is like. Perhaps he's scared of her. Or perhaps he's serious and boring too. I wonder if we'll ever meet him.

Wednesday 13th April

I think yesterday's park visit must have taken it out of Grandma. Today she was happy for us to watch TV and have a lie in. I got up just before eleven.

I felt tired too. It's not like I did much at the park. For a few minutes I kicked the football with Blane but he fell over and cried on Grandma's knee. Spike was busy building a den out of grass and sticks. Kenny stayed in the pushchair. It wasn't *that* tiring but we still lazed around today.

Thursday 14th April

I finished *Second Term at Malory Towers*. I'd spent so long fake-reading to get out of jobs that I had to go back to the beginning to find out what actually happened. I enjoyed it but I prefer the *St. Clare's* books. At least I'm using my open mind, as Mum would say. After that I started to reread *Matilda*. It made me think of Ms Archer. Sometimes she's like Miss Honey because she does April Fools' jokes with us and she liked my book review that time. But other times she's like Miss Trunchball because she goes on and on about the tests in May.

When Mum got in she told me Jenna's dad had rung to see if we could look after Jenna tomorrow. Mum said it was fine. This made me laugh. It won't be Mum that has to look after her. It will be Grandma. Because we're helping Jenna's dad, it feels perfectly acceptable that Meg isn't invited. I feel bad but she can be hard work. Jenna on her own is much more fun.

Friday 15th April

Today was brilliant. Jenna's dad dropped her off at 11 o'clock and we went to my room. (She said she liked the new layout.) We talked about Ms Archer and Mr Eskbrook and whether or not they fancy each other. Jenna thinks they do but I've never noticed.

Jenna spotted the junk on the landing that's been left out to sell. She was asking about it so I told her. (Not about the baby, just about being poor.) She understands. She's another person not going on the

Year Six holiday. Jenna said she didn't want to go anyway but she might just be saying that. I think it would've been fun but I also think I'd find Meg hard to handle for a whole weekend. It's probably best I'm not going.

Mum came home after lunch and asked Jenna if she wanted to stay for tea. I had a little panic in case it was going to be weird food, but then I remembered it's Friday Fooday. The holiday has got me confused about the days. Jenna said, 'Yes please,' straight away and so that was it. She stayed.

A really funny thing happened when Grandma was getting ready to leave. She told Mum she was heading into town because she needed a new handbag. Straight away Jenna said, 'You should sell that bag to raise money. You'd get at least £5 on eBay.' Grandma looked horror-struck (Word Wall!) and said, 'Jenna, this bag cost over £300.' Jenna looked a little shocked and then - and I KNOW she didn't mean to be cheeky - said, 'OK, maybe £8.' I fell about laughing and so did Mum. Grandma looked even more horror-struck and then left. I don't think she knows how to handle Jenna. I don't think she gets her.

Tea was lovely. I was proud of Friday Fooday and glad I had a friend round for a change. We had tomato and halloumi bake. I LOVE halloumi. Jenna had never had it before but said it was gorgeous *and* she had seconds. I think Mum's bobbing back into veganism right now as she'd made herself a chickpea thing. It didn't matter. All the more *crispy-on-the-outside, gooey-on-the-inside* halloumi for us. Even though I get annoyed with being a veggie, I'm glad I get to eat things like halloumi. I might never have discovered how much I love it if I were busy being distracted by mince.

Jenna went home at 9 o'clock. I had a really good day. Having another girl in the house made a brill change. (This does not mean I want a sister.)

Saturday 16th April

I started my holiday homework but gave up after half an hour. I'll do it tomorrow.

Sunday 17th April

I spent all day doing Maths homework. Rubbish! I shouldn't have left it till the last day of the holidays. I don't want to see a mixed operation for the rest of my life.

Monday 18th April

Back to school.

Ms Archer only used to speak in capital letters every so often. Now it's the only way she talks. 'WE HAVE STARTED THE FINAL COUNTDOWN'. That's what she said. This time next month, the tests will be over and I can get excited about high school. I'm looking forward to a time when I can learn things again.

Meg's mum and dad have booked a holiday. Meg was full of it today. She's going to Portugal for two weeks as soon as we break up. I smiled and said it sounded great. I wasn't lying. It really did.

One day I might go to Portugal. It won't be till I'm an adult though. Mum and Dad don't like carbon footprints. So instead of going on a plane for three hours, we drive in a car for five. Apparently it's better but not sure why. I don't even know what a carbon footprint is, except that it's bad.

Tuesday 19th April

Spike's got nits again. His class came home with the head lice letter. This happens every time one is spotted. The class get a letter but the teacher tells the parent of the nitty child, face to face. All the parents saw the letters as the children came out. There was a loud groan. Then Mr Peacock walked towards Grandma to have a 'quiet word'. I didn't hear what he said - I think he was trying to be subtle. All I saw was Grandma take a step back, and in a really loud voice, say, 'Young man, I think you'll find that Spike's *buzz cut* is an utterly inhospitable environment for habitation!' Then she marched us off the playground and out of the gates.

It's nice that she was defending Spike but I can easily believe he has nits. When the letter gets sent home, the teachers go on about nits only liking clean hair, but I'm sure that's a lie. Spike is full of germs. It's easy to imagine a wide range of bugs choosing his body to make a nest. I go after him in the bathroom, remember.

Grandma texted Mum so she picked up special shampoo on her way home. We all had to wash our hair over the sink with the stuff. It stank! Spike thought this was hilarious but I was annoyed. Mum handed the bottle to Grandma before she went, but she refused to take it. 'I think you'll find no creature would dare take on my mousse, spritz and spray medley', she said.

Sometimes Grandma talks utter nonsense.

Wednesday 20th April

I made a mistake today. I'm sure of it. There's always *some* kind of worry in my head. I've only just stopped thinking about the whole baby thing, and now this.

At home time, Grandma was making conversation about Year Six and Ms Archer and whether I was looking forward to high school - blah blah blah, that kind of thing. (I like the phrase *blah blah blah*. I should use it more often. It's perfect for when grown-ups go on and on about the same thing.) Anyway, we were chatting when she suddenly said, 'Leeza, what's your Mum planning to do with all that jumble on the landing.' I didn't see anything wrong with telling the truth (which should *always* be the way - I'm sick of having to keep quiet about things like Nappy Gate, the baby, and my meat eating activities) so I said, 'It's all going to be sold on eBay because there's not much money at the moment.'

I suppose I'd been distracted by the *blah blah blah* conversation. But as soon as I said it, I knew Mum was going to go mad. She's very careful about the stuff she shares with Grandma. I walked in silence, hoping it wasn't a problem, but deep down knowing it was. Grandma was quiet for a moment and then said, '*I* see', in a firm voice. She put lots of expression on the *I*. It was as if she were making it clear that SHE was very important and now that SHE sees, everything was going to be different. I'm not sure what she *did* see, but I knew I shouldn't have said anything.

I went to my room early tonight. I needed to be out of everyone's way. Sometimes it'd be nice not to worry about the adults all of the time.

In other news, the nits seem to have left the building.

Thursday 21st April

It never takes Grandma long to meddle. It all kicked off after school. I missed how it started because I was on the toilet. Too much information, I know, but that's why I didn't get all the details. By the time I came downstairs, Grandma was speaking loudly. She was using her firm voice again. She said, 'Molly, I think you'll find as your mother it's my duty to help if you're going through financial difficulties.' At this point I was outside the door. It didn't look like I was listening. Not like in films where people have their ear to the wall or are holding a glass. I was sitting on the bottom of the stairs pretending to tie my laces. Except I was only wearing socks. It still looked less suspicious than in the films, though.

Mum kept answering Grandma but I couldn't hear all of it. Sometimes she shouted but mostly she had a very low voice. I know this voice. When she's angry, she goes lower, quieter, and much more scary. The one thing I did hear her say was, 'One of these days you'll realise money doesn't fix everything. It never did when I was a child, and it won't now.

Mum is funny about money. Funny-*strange* not funny-*ha-ha*. She thinks having too much of it means you miss out on the important things. She said when she was a kid, she never experienced the joy of watching the sun set or walking barefoot on the grass, because Grandma was too busy taking her to expensive hotels and exotic places that all merged together in her head. They didn't speak for a few years. But then they did. Around the time she met Dad. I think, compared to his parents, Grandma is still the best option.

Mum might reckon that having too much money and too many things, spoils people. Well that's fine for Mum, but what about me? I still haven't been to Portugal and the only thing I own that I could sell is a door sign from Maine. I wouldn't say no to too much money. Too much money would be a lovely problem to have.

Eventually I went back upstairs. Dad was standing in the doorway of his bedroom, pacing about. It was as if he couldn't decide whether to go downstairs and help or not. When he saw me, he smiled. His expression said, *What are they like, Leeza?* Then he laughed. I suppose if Dad isn't too bothered, I shouldn't be. Except I am, of course. I'm the only person that sees all the consequences. If Mum annoys Grandma too much, she won't pick us up tomorrow. And I am *too* young to be responsible for Spike's road safety on the way home.

Friday 22nd April

There were ripped up pieces of paper in the wastepaper basket this morning. It was defo a cheque. Grandma still writes cheques. She gets cross when Dad tells her to get Internet banking. She says, 'If I want to lose my life savings because NatWest's Wi-Fi has a virus, you'll be the first to know, Sebastian.' Dad just laughs at her.

The good news was that at home time, Grandma was there to pick us up. Back at the house, Mum and Grandma were polite to each other but not relaxed. I would say the atmosphere was 'strained'.

The other thing on my mind is that I want to tell people about the baby. I know sharing worries helps. It made things easier when I talked to Jenna about being poor. I reckon it'll be easier when I can share the baby worries too. I just need Mum and Dad to say it's OK.

Saturday 23rd April

It rained all day so I finished my homework by 2 o'clock. That shows how bored I was. Mum has started to sort out the eBay stuff. I saw her taking photos of everything from lots of different angles. I asked her why she was opening all the curtains and she said, 'I need as much light as possible so they look as bright and colourful as they are in real life'. I smiled and said, 'OK Mum'. I don't think it will help. No amount of light can make Dad's grey joggers look appealing. I think they should just focus on the exercise bike, to be honest.

At teatime Mum told us about the row with Grandma. She began when we'd started to eat our sandwiches, so we couldn't respond straight away. She said, 'I know you all heard me and Grandma exchanging words the other day...' I think I raised my eyebrows at that. Exchanging words? Yeah right. Having a full on slanging match, more like. Still, she continued. '...and I don't want you to worry. We both got things off our chests that needed to be said, and now we're back to normal.' I listened to all that but carried on with my butty. She wasn't finished. Just as I took a big bite, she said, 'So none of you need to tell Grandma about us being poor again. I know we said things are tight, which they are. But we don't need any help. We're working on all the issues.'

'*Working on all the issues*' has become the new '*Don't ask us for anything*' line. It gets said a lot. I wonder what she actually means when she says, '*Working on all the issues*'. What is she actually doing?

I decided I should ask a question. As the eldest, I have the responsibility to speak for Spike, Blane and Kenny. I waited for her to finish and then said,

'How're the Council changes going? Has anyone been made redundant yet?' There was a definite silence. Mum and Dad looked at each other really seriously before Mum spoke again. 'There *have* been some redundancies, yes. So far, your dad and I are fine. There're more to come though, so we don't know for sure.'

And with that, tea was over. I went up to my room to relax whilst everyone else seemed to make more noise than it's possible for human beings to make.

Sunday 24th April
Still raining. I slept in till after 11 o'clock. Tea was root veg casserole and mash.

Monday 25th April
There was a message from the office, first thing. Ellie Rogers has chicken pox. Ms Archer went pale. She said no one else was allowed to get chicken pox and we had to be in school for SATs week. Mum says she's obsessed. I agree.

After school, when I was learning my spellings, I could hear Blane and Kenny banging around on the landing. At one point they came to my door and shouted, 'Jumble? Any jumble? Give us your jumble!' I shooed them away so I could get on, but they carried on going in and out of the bedrooms. I didn't pay much attention because I was learning words with the suffix '-ology'. Then at teatime it became clear. Blane stood up and with his tiny voice said, 'Please come to Blane and Kenny's jumble sale. It's after tea.' Then he sat down. Mum looked like she was going to cry at how sweet it was. She kept touching her heart with her hand and saying, 'What lovely boys', to herself. So after we'd eaten, we went upstairs to buy their jumble.

They had loads of things for sale. Scraps of paper were propped up against each item with a price. I couldn't see anything dearer than 30p. I think that's as high as Blane can count. I was suspicious before I walked in but I knew for sure as soon as I saw the things for sale. There was *my* red plastic desk tidy, priced at 12p. *My* Year Five English and Maths books from under my bed (25p each.) And of course, *my* L's

Room door sign. That was a bargain at 9p. I smiled because they had tried but I looked at Mum and Dad's faces to check they weren't going to let my belongings be sold to Spike without my permission. Dad laughed and did lots of hair ruffling on Blane who was within reach. Then, just as Spike spotted his first Lego box (30p) and was about to start shouting, Dad put a hand on his shoulder. He said, 'This is such a good jumble sale, I want to buy everything you have in stock.' Blane looked really proud of himself. Kenny clapped his hands and laughed. Dad went to his copper jar in his bedroom and came back with a handful of change. He whispered, 'Buy your stuff back', to me and Spike, and gave us some coins. *I* got that we were humouring the younger members of the family but I think Spike thought we'd all gone mad. He kept shaking his head saying, 'This is messed up,' over and over again.

Later on, after Blane and Kenny had sold everything back to their original owners, Dad helped them count it all up. They had made £2.46. Then they handed it over to Mum for the new baby. It's not the first time

I've seen Mum cry but it's the first time it's happened over the theft of my red desk tidy.

Tuesday 26th April

The bad thing about being in Year Six is that the rest of the school are carrying on with normal things whilst we're practising test questions. This week is officially Medieval Week. Apart from the assembly yesterday morning, you wouldn't know it in our class. When I went to the toilet this afternoon, I saw Year Five jousting on the quad. I knew it was jousting straight away because I've seen *A Knight's Tale* and that's got jousting in it.

I asked Ms Archer if we'd be doing anything for Medieval Week. She said, 'It depends on how much we get done before Friday.' That means no. I'm not stupid. I can always tell what adults are secretly saying.

Wednesday 27th April

We've had our first eBay sale! It was when Dad was cooking tea. Mum had been staring at her phone for ages when she suddenly yelled out, 'Yesssssss!' We all laughed because she sounded funny. Kenny couldn't stop giggling but that's because he was copying us. Mum told us that a bundle of Kenny's old baby clothes had gone for £8. She rushed upstairs to wrap them so she can post them out tomorrow. I was pleased for her. I didn't want to point out that baby clothes were one of the things we *would* be needing soon.

While Mum was in a good mood, I decided to take advantage of the situation. I followed her upstairs and as she was wrapping the clothes, I asked her if I could tell my friends about the baby. After a minute, she took the tape from between her teeth and said, 'Which friends?' That was a good question. I know who I trust (Jenna) but I know who I feel I *should* tell (Meg). I said, 'Jenna and Meg'. Mum was quiet for a bit longer then she said, 'Yes. Of course you can. It's your news too.' Then - and this is the most interesting thing I've ever heard her say – she said, 'I've been putting off telling Chris (Meg's mum). I suppose I need to bite the bullet myself.'

When I think about it, Chris is exactly like Meg. She's always getting a new car.

Thursday 28th April

Knowing I'm allowed to talk about the baby doesn't make it any easier to choose a good moment. There were a couple of times on the playground when I thought I might pop it into conversation, but just as I was building up courage, something would happen. At morning break the bell went, and then this afternoon a bee flew at Meg and her screaming stopped all conversation for a while.

There's no rush. It will come up when the time is right.

Friday 29th April

After hearing every other year group have medieval fun this week, it was finally our turn!

The morning was normal. We did a comprehension and then went through the answers as a class. So far so boring. But just before the lunch bell, Ms Archer announced that this afternoon we were going to have... a medieval banquet!!!

We all cheered and clapped and got very excited. Caitlyn Matherson shouted out, 'At last we're delivered from this SATs hell!' At that point Ms Archer told us to calm down and go to lunch. (And not to use the word hell, or to exaggerate.) Literally none of us knew what a medieval banquet was. We were just happy to be doing something new.

When we came back, the desks had been moved into one long table covered in a red paper cloth. We sat in two rows facing each other, giggling a bit. No one knew what was going to happen. Then Ms Archer showed us a picture on the board of a real life medieval banquet from years ago. She said there were no knives and forks and that people ripped bread from big loaves in the middle. She said herbs were scattered all over the table to make everything smell nice. She explained that people ate big chunks of meat with their hands, and finally she said everyone drank beer. It looked like LOTS of fun.

And then it all kicked off. Packets of herbs from Tesco were passed around and we were told to scatter them all over the table. I opened some basil and threw it about a bit. Then Miss put a big loaf of unsliced bread in the middle. We had to rip it with our hands! It was hilarious. Next came chicken legs (also from Tesco in a plastic container) that we had to pass along. That's when Ms Archer came over to me with a Quorn fillet in an individual tub. She whispered that she'd cooked it at home the night before and so it was cold but not uncooked. I found that really lovely. My mum's strict food rules had caused Ms Archer to cook me a veggie option in her own time. I said, 'Thank you', as meaningfully as I could. It was at that point that Alfie Diggs shouted, 'Miss, what about the beer?' Everyone laughed but Ms Archer didn't say anything. She just went back into her bag and brought out a stack of cups and two massive bottles of *ginger* beer. There was even more laughter. I honestly can't remember having this much fun in school before. Glasses were passed along and Miss walked along the table, filling everyone's up. When she was done, she walked back to the front of the room and picked up a glass of her own. She waited for quiet and then raised it in the air. 'Year Six', she said, 'Let's congratulate ourselves on what we've achieved this year and look forward to the future. Cheers everyone.' We all yelled, 'Cheers', and drank our pretend beer. It was the best feeling I've had in ages.

On the way home, I didn't stop to think about it anymore. I turned to Jenna and said, 'Oh yeah, my mum's pregnant again'. She looked at me, smiled and said, 'That's gross.' I smiled back and agreed. She wasn't wrong. Then we carried on walking home. It's a big relief that it's out. And I'll get around to telling Meg another time.

<u>Saturday 30th April</u>

Slept in.

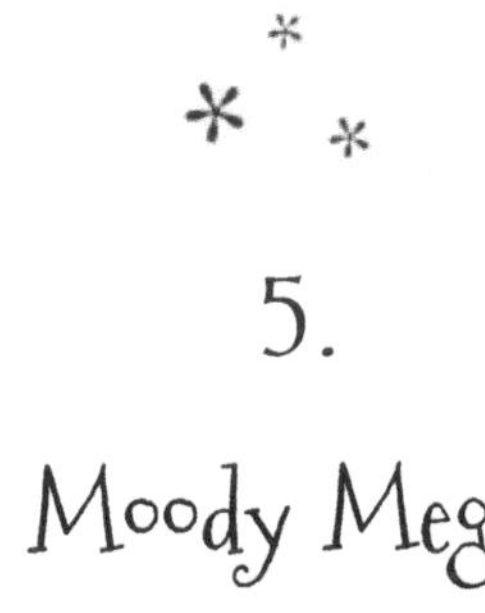

5.

Moody Meg

<u>Sunday 1st May</u>

It's Sunday so I was half-expecting another Family Meeting. I still hope that one day we'll have something good to discuss.

Tea was pasta and sauce.

<u>Monday 2nd May</u>

Bank holiday. The day went nowhere.

<u>Tuesday 3rd May</u>

I was on the playground when Meg walked over. I said, 'Morning', but she didn't listen. Then in a sarky voice, she said, 'I heard your good news, by the way.'

I was confused. I haven't had any good news for ages. She glared at me and said, 'I cannot *believe* you didn't tell me about the baby.'

The penny dropped. I smiled and said, 'I'm glad you know now.' Meg looked furious. I'd been worrying about telling her, but the way she acted made me feel calmer. She was being silly about nothing. I carried on. 'I'd been told to keep it to myself for the last few weeks but I only told Jenna on Friday. Now it's all in the open.' At this point Meg's face turned bright red. 'Jenna! Jenna knew before me?' she spluttered. 'I'm your best friend, not Jenna. I should have known first!'

Meg is ridic. First of all, her and Jenna are my *two* best friends. But also, if I had to choose, it'd be Jenna. Anyway, it seems Mum had got round to biting the bullet after all. She'd told Meg's mum, who'd told Meg, who'd kicked off at me. Meg was moody all day. The one positive thing to come out of it was that it stopped me worrying about what she thought. It made a nice change to *not* care about Meg and her moods. (Alliteration!)

Wednesday 4th May

I still feel relaxed today. It's like I've gone back in time before everything started changing. Before Kenny's toilet training, before the SATs, before Council changes and before new babies. The feeling of a relaxed tummy is far better than the feeling of being worried. I know people call it 'butterflies' but that isn't enough. Butterflies are fluttery and light. They tickle but they don't hurt. To me, worries feel like insects burrowing inside my skin. Rubbish.

I'm going to enjoy this feeling of relaxation for as long as it lasts. Was it about Meg all this time?

Thursday 5th May

Meg seemed normal with me in school, but I think she's still annoyed. She doesn't chat as much as she did. I've stopped teasing her. It used to be for fun but if I did it now it'd sound mean. I didn't mention it once when she flicked her hair over her shoulder when Alfie Diggs ran past. Even though it made me laugh inside.

At lunchtime, Jenna said, 'Is it just me or is Meg acting weird?' I told her she'd been annoyed about finding out about the baby, second. Jenna's reply was, 'Oh for God's sake.' That summed it up for me too.

Friday 6th May

It was the last SATs practice before they start for real on Monday. This time next week they'll be over and I won't have to think about them ever again.

Meg defo kept her distance. She thinks she's making a point by staying away. She doesn't realise playtime is more fun when she's not there. Me and Jenna talked about Stockford High. Jenna doesn't think it'll be any better than Irwell Green - or as she put it, 'a school's a school, innit' - but I'm convinced it will be *so* much better than primary school.

Friday Fooday was veggie hotdogs, caramelised onions, mustard and gherkins. I pretended I was in New York eating a hotdog in the street! I closed my eyes to imagine this. I also shut out the image of Spike shovelling food into his mouth with the bits falling out.

Saturday 7th May

Yesterday, school sent home a letter from the Year Six teachers. It was to tell us to relax this weekend and remember that we've worked hard all year so not to worry. I'd have liked the chance to relax. Instead Mum told us we had to spring clean our bedrooms!

I think Mum's gone mad. She's never been bothered about cleaning before. I don't mean everything's dirty, but her and Dad do a 'quick hoover', or a 'quick dust' just before we have visitors. That's it. But recently, Mum's become obsessed.

I was lucky. It wasn't that long since I'd rearranged my room. It was more or less OK. The boys' room, however, was defo a health hazard. Spike moaned and groaned so in the end Dad helped. Between them, they found eight pairs of dirty undies shoved down the side of the mattress. Spike is disgusting.

Sunday 8th May

I did have a little relax today. I lay in bed until 11 o'clock and finished *Matilda* - I've been taking my time. At some point I need to go back to the library, but now I've tasted the freedom of going alone, I can't go back to being supervised. I'll wait till Dad is on his own so I can ask him again. Between my parents, he's defo the weakest link.

Tea was sandwiches.

Monday 9th May

It's SATs week! After all the months of TALKING IN CAPITAL LETTERS, today wasn't anything special at all. I had a few creepy crawlies in my stomach when we lined up at 9 o'clock but I didn't show them. Meg was talking to Ellie Rogers about how she'd been awake all night (which I didn't believe) while Ellie looked like she was going to cry. Maybe because Meg was talking to her? (Ha ha. I'm funny!) Or probably because she's not long had chicken pox.

By the time we got inside, all the tables had been separated and we had to sit on our own. It was very serious! Ms Archer reminded us not to talk to each other and to answer every question, and then we began. Today was the SPaG paper. There's nothing to say because I just got on with it. It's English but it's the boring side of English. It has to be done and I can do it, but I don't get anything out of it.

When it was over, we got an early playtime. The rest of the day was normal. It seems mad that every day since September has been working towards this week.

Tuesday 10th May

Mum was funny before she left for work. She said, 'Good luck, Leeza. Even though they mean absolutely nothing, you should still try your best.' Mum really hates the SATs. She thinks it's bad that there's so much pressure on us. I don't feel too much pressure with schoolwork. Well, I do a bit, but mostly I know I'm good at some things and not good at others. And the things I'm not good at are boring so I don't care.

Today was the Reading test. I liked this one. I read the booklet quite quickly, and then started to answer the questions. I checked back for each answer, even when I didn't need to. I don't remember much about the actual stuff I had to read – there was a bit about space and something about snails – but I finished it before the time was up. Ms Archer saw me put my pen down and mouthed 'check it' at me. So I did. But I hadn't missed any pages, I'd answered everything and I was happy. I'm not cocky. I just like reading. I'll feel the opposite when it's Maths tomorrow.

At teatime I told Mum the test had been OK. She smiled and said, 'That's great to hear. Good for you. Me and your dad are proud of you.' Then she paused and added, 'As long as you remember it is a complete waste of time and doesn't teach you anything you need in the real world.' Then she ate her salad and the conversation was over.

I'm starting to think that EVERYTHING I learn at school doesn't teach me anything I need in the real world. But it's just what you have to do, isn't it.

Wednesday 11th May

It couldn't last. The relaxed feeling went. The sense of achievement from the past two days disappeared. Today was rubbish.

It was Arithmetic and Paper 2 Reasoning. Two Maths tests to make us all feel bad! I took ages. I had to read each question about ten times just to work out what it wanted me to do. I felt the clock ticking. I didn't enjoy it one bit. This must be what it's like for Alfie Diggs. Maybe I should've been having extra help all year too?

I managed to finish but I did *not* feel happy as I walked outside. If I were in charge of schools, I'd ban Maths. No one needs it.

To make matters worse, Meg kept going on about how easy it was. She still isn't officially speaking to me or Jenna, so I know she was doing it on purpose. Jenna told me not to worry. She hadn't finished the paper and hadn't answered any question where you had to show your method. When I asked her why not, she just shrugged and said, 'I couldn't be faffed.'

Thursday 12th May

Paper 3 Reasoning is done and the SATs are over! Wooohooo.

In terms of the test, today felt a bit like yesterday. I was fed up while I was doing it, but once it was over it felt amazing. Ms Archer told us to put our pens down. We had to stay in silence as she collected the papers. As soon as they were on her desk, she turned to the class and said, 'Congratulations Year Six. The SATs are over!' We cheered and banged our desks and made lots of noise. Then we had our last early playtime.

Meg was talking to Ellie Rogers the whole time. I like Ellie but I don't think she's very comfortable with Meg. Every time she's with her, she looks terrified. Meg can be a lot of work. I'm used to it so I know how to deal with her.

Me and Jenna wandered about on our own. We agreed we didn't want to talk about any of the questions. There was no point now it was over. Then Jenna said, 'Let's choose names for your new baby'. I was surprised. I hadn't thought about it needing a name, but of course it will. We spent the rest of the day making a list.

On the way home we shared it with Grandma. If it's a girl, we came up with Sofia, Ariana, Casey, Lacie and Jenna. (She insisted!) If it's a boy, we came up with Justin, Harry, Bieber and Styles. Jenna's choices were quite specific. I can't imagine having a little brother called Bieber McAuliffe. But then I suppose I never thought I'd have brothers called Spike, Blane and Kenny either.

Grandma added her own name - Ursula - to the girls' list. I didn't say it to her face, but there's no way Mum will call the new baby after Grandma. No way, José.

Friday 13th May

It's a good job it was sunny because Year Six were outside all day. We joined with Mr Eskbrook's class and did PE straight after the register. (Girls in the toilets, thank you very much.) We had a rounders tournament in the morning and sports day practice in the afternoon. It was certainly better than silent tests. I did my usual trick of choosing to be a fielder for the left-handers. I got to sit on the grass most of the time. Ms Archer and Mr Eskbrook didn't seem to care. I think everyone was happy to chill out.

At teatime Mum was weird. She started asking how Meg was. I told her she'd been in a mood all week because she hadn't been first to know about the baby. Mum said, 'Ah that makes sense,' and left it at that. I know I should be more bothered that Meg isn't talking to me. But the truth is, I'm enjoying the space from her.

Friday Fooday was mushroom and halloumi burgers with salad. Just like Nandos!

Saturday 14th May

For the first time in forever (yeah, I know it's a song) there was no homework. This meant I slept in till after 12 o'clock! To be honest, I wasn't asleep all that time. I was thinking how I could go to the library on my own again. With Mum downstairs, it wasn't as simple as just asking. I'm pretty sure Dad hadn't told her that he'd let me go last time. I had to tread carefully.

As it turned out, it was less hassle than I imagined. Mum was going though a box of paperwork in the bedroom. She had a plastic bag for the stuff she was binning and a box for things she was keeping. She seemed harassed. (Word Wall!) I crept in and said, 'Mum?' in a quiet voice. She didn't look up and just said, 'Yeah?' absentmindedly. I told a little, but necessary fib. I said, 'My books are due back at the library today. (Lie!) Can I take them back if I'm quick?' She didn't look up. She was reading a document from the box and trying to decide if she needed to keep it. She just said, 'Yeah,' quietly under her breath. I was amazed. It was too easy. I said, 'Thanks' and went to get my books. Just as I was heading out of the front door, I told Dad that Mum said I could go to the library and did he want to watch me cross the road like last time? (I think that was the clever bit. I was reminding him I'd done this before.) He was also a bit preoccupied. Kenny's bare bottom was sticking out from under his arm so I'm guessing there was a puddle of wee somewhere. He nodded and walked towards the window as I left the house.

Of course when I got back, it all kicked off. Mum swore she'd never heard me ask permission. Dad was mad because he thought I'd lied about Mum saying

OK. I knew it had been too easy. I had to explain *very clearly* to Mum that she'd said I could go. Then I had to explain *very clearly* to Dad that he'd let me go before and this was the second time. (Dad has defo not told Mum because her face was mad!) Then I had to remind them *very clearly* that in four months time I'll be walking further than that, every day. That was always going to be the winning argument. They can't keep me locked up from the library when high school is further to walk. Mum had calmed down by then. (She must have remembered giving me accidental permission). Also, I'm good at being *very clear* in situations like this. Mum still looked annoyed but knew she couldn't do anything. This is what happens when you get obsessed with cleaning. Your kids get on with life around you.

Sunday 15th May

Dad took the boys to the park this afternoon so I read my book in the backyard. We don't have garden furniture as such, but there's an old yoga ball of Mum's. I sat on that. Normally Spike nabs it before any of us get a look in. Then all that's left is the stepladder. I've had many an outdoor tea on that.

It's been sunny for the past few days. I lay back against the ball and read my book. This time I went with *The Story of Tracy Beaker* by Jacqueline Wilson. We read extracts of it in Year Five for English and I always wondered what happened. So far, so good.

Other than that, it was a normal Sunday. Except I didn't have to waste most of it with homework. Woohoo!

<u>Monday 16th May</u>

We did Art all day! The change in Year Six is unbelievable. Everyone is smiling. It isn't like school at all. Also, Meg spoke to me. I asked her to pass the red paint and she did without being stroppy. She said, 'There you are,' and it sounded like she meant it.

After dinner, Ms Archer talked to us about the rest of the year. She said that as well as doing more Art and PE we had to start on transition activities for high school. Then she reminded us of the end of year performance, the Year Six holiday (which I'm not going on) and the final assembly for the parents. I have no idea how it'll all fit into the next two months.

Tuesday 17th May

Mum asked weird questions about Meg again. I repeated what I told her the other day - that Meg was being moody because I hadn't told her about the baby. Apparently Meg's mum had rung to see if I'd said anything about her behaviour in school. I explained she was being funny with me and Jenna, but we were leaving her to get over it.

Then Mum filled me in. Apparently Meg has been terrible at home. She keeps answering back and being rude to her mum and dad. Also, she called her mum a bad word yesterday. (The name for a lady dog! I laughed out loud.) Mum told me to stop laughing but she was smiling too, I could see. Then she said, 'I think Meg is finding puberty difficult. Try to be nice to her, yeah?' and then she went downstairs.

I don't think Meg has started having puberty yet. She's been wearing a bra top with adjustable straps since Year Four but she doesn't need it. It's all for show. And I know she hasn't started her periods because she would have told everyone. She was really annoyed when Caitlyn Matherson did last year. It was like she thought Caitlyn had done it on purpose to annoy her.

Meg's mum will not be happy that her little princess has gone bad.

Wednesday 18th May

I've been thinking a lot about puberty. I know what it is of course. I've known since I was four when I asked Mum why she bought herself nappies. Yeah, I know they aren't nappies but that's what I thought back then. Anyway, I know all about it, I just don't want it to happen to me. At least, not without me being in control. Periods sound messy, and as for boobs - they make no sense. I don't want to topple over because I have a massive chest. But also, I want to wear a bra some day. Just not a big one.

There's no point talking to Mum about this. She says that change is part of growing up and not to worry. The fact it's part of growing up is exactly what makes me worry. I like being in control of myself. I don't want to start my periods anywhere except the bath. That's the only place I will accept them arriving.

Thursday 19th May

I decided to ask Grandma about puberty. At first I thought it might make her embarrassed, but then I decided this wasn't true. Grandma is a grown-up and had to deal with Mum having puberty (even if it was like a hundred years ago). She could be the person I need to be honest but reassuring. I waited till we were walking home from school and I went for it. I said, 'Meg's mum says Meg is badly behaved at home because of puberty.' Grandma looked at me. Then I said, 'I don't get how it makes her cheeky, just because her body's changing.' Grandma kept looking at me. Then I said, 'Mum says change is part of growing up and I shouldn't worry about it.' As I said that, Grandma looked up at the sky, sighed, and then answered me. She said, 'Leeza, your mother was an absolute cow between the ages of ten and eighteen. Even after that she wasn't much better. Living with a hormonal daughter is utter hell and I hope you cause her as much trouble as she caused me.' I laughed a bit, because I thought she might be joking, but she kept looking grim-faced as we walked along.

I wonder if Mum will ever describe me as an absolute cow.

Friday 20th May

Finally. Someone has bought the exercise bike. It went for £49. I think it was over £300 when Mum bought it and it's been used about twice. The buyer got a real bargain. It's getting picked up tomorrow. I'm not sure how this affects the day, but tomorrow is my 11th birthday. I know! I'm eleven years old as of tomorrow. In all the Meg/puberty/SATs drama I haven't thought about it. Actually, the only time I did think about it was when we had the 'We Are Poor' Family Meeting last month. I thought it was just my luck the family austerity measures were kicking in before my special day.

Eleven isn't very exciting. I'm already in double figures and I'm still not an official teenager. Nothing has changed. Tomorrow won't be that extraordinary.

Saturday 21st May

OMG! Today was brilliant! I will write about it tomorrow. Too tired now.

Sunday 22nd May

I had the loveliest birthday. I didn't think I would feel any different but I really do.

When I woke up there were presents at the end of my bed. I could hear Mum and Dad (who were in bed across the landing) shouting, 'Finally, she wakes!' Considering the fact money is tight, I did very well. I'm really lucky to be honest. I got a new school bag - it's meant to be for Year Seven, but Mum said I can use it now if I want. I got a posh pen that I'm using to write this. The ink is really smooth and it feels heavy and grown up to hold. I also got a bra top with adjustable straps! I will only wear it on special occasions, not like Meg for PE days.

Because it was my birthday I got to choose everything. I sat on my favourite chair (the arm chair that Dad usually uses) I chose cheese and baked bean toasties for lunch. And then I asked Mum if I could have a fake Nutella and banana smoothie in her blender. I think she'd forgotten that she had it as it was in the back of the cupboard. It was just as gorge as I remember.

Grandma came round in the afternoon. I am very excited about using her present. It's a book token. It means I get to go to an actual bookshop and choose a book to buy. I've only been in a bookshop 'just to look'. I like the library but being able to buy any book I want will be amazing.

Teatime was my favourite. It was a cheese board with crackers. Mum had bought all the interesting cheeses from the Farmers' Market - no boring mild cheddar on my birthday! I ate a lot of my favourite, which was the Camembert. Spike's favourite is the soft garlicky one so he had most of that. I'm not sure what Blane and Kenny went for, but between the whole family, we managed to demolish five blocks of cheese and a whole packet of crackers.

I think I even saw Mum eat some Gouda. She must be bobbing out of veganism this week.

Monday 23rd May

Jenna made me a card and got me a packet of Maltesers. I opened them at break and we shared them. If Meg had come over we would have offered her some, but she didn't.

At lunchtime Ms Archer asked me if everything was OK between us all. She must have noticed that Meg has been different. I told her everything was fine for me, but that Meg is getting into trouble at home and not being herself. Ms Archer said, 'So you haven't fallen out with her?' I shook my head and said, 'No, but I think she's fallen out with us.' I was really honest. Jenna agreed with me. Her words were, 'She's gone well weird, Miss.' After Miss had gone, we carried on talking about Mr Eskbrook's baby. His wife came into school with it and walked into class to show Ms Archer. Everyone said, 'Ahhhh', really loudly so it woke up and cried. Mrs Eskbrook left then.

I'd forgotten how harsh a baby's cry could be. It really hurts your brain.

Tuesday 24th May

We've been given our first piece of homework since the SATs finished! I knew it wouldn't last. It could be worse, though. It's a class novel to read. In a few weeks, we'll be working on a booklet about it. It isn't anything I would choose in the library but I'll give it a go.

Wednesday 25th May

On the way back from school, Grandma got a text. She said, 'Oh good, your Mum and Dad are back from the hospital.' This completely threw me. I had no idea there was anything wrong. Grandma must've realised I knew nothing because she went all reassuring and calm. She said, 'Don't worry, nothing's wrong. It's just the next scan.'

I hadn't even realised there was a *first* scan. When I asked Mum later, she said it was back around the time when she told us about the baby. She said neither her nor Dad had any coins with them so they hadn't got a photo. This time, however, they had.

We passed the picture round while we had tea. As photos go, it's not the best. Just lots of grey, black and white. You can see a circle that's the head. I asked if they knew whether it was a boy or girl, but Mum said they hadn't wanted to find out. (I *hate* the uncertainty of not knowing whether I'll be turfed out of half my room!) Mum did say that the nurse had known, though. She said, 'If you're an expert you can tell, but me and your dad have no idea'. Spike stared at it for ages. Then he decided it was a boy. He kept pointing at the bit he thought was the penis. (I can write that because I'm being biological.) Anyway, he reckons he can see it. Dad said he thought that was an arm. Basically, no one has a clue.

I *don't* like not knowing the future.

Thursday 26th May

I told Jenna about the scan photo. She said, 'Did it have a willy?' I said I didn't know but that Spike thought so. Then she said, 'Well that's sorted then,' and we both laughed. I've appreciated Jenna's relaxed nature about this baby. I'm glad she isn't a drama queen about these things.

Friday 27th May

Meg has officially gone off the rails. Today, she was sent out of class!! It was all so silly too. Ellie Rogers was walking back from sharpening her pencil and tripped on someone's chair leg. She stumbled into the back of Meg and accidentally shoved her arm as she was writing. Meg's pen slipped across the page and made a big line over her story. Just as Ellie was straightening up and saying sorry, Meg flipped! She stood up really fast, turned around and shoved Ellie in the shoulders. It was unbelievable. Ellie started to cry.

I was watching from my seat because I'd seen Ellie trip in the first place. It really was an accident. Ms Archer shouted at Meg to calm down, and then - and this is the most shocking bit - Meg turned around and shouted, 'Get lost', at Miss! I know! This was the naughtiest thing I've ever seen with my own eyes.* Even Alfie Diggs looked shocked. He's always in trouble but he doesn't lose his temper. He gets told off for messing around and being silly but not like this. Ms Archer told Meg to stand outside and cool off, and that she'd be speaking to her at lunchtime.

It was the most exciting thing to ever happen in class. It was all we could talk about on the way home. It's a shame we've broken up for half-term. I won't see Meg for another week now. Who knows what kind of monster she'll have become.

*Actually it's not. Jonathan Paignton that left last year, once had a fight lining up for dinner. Actual punches.

Saturday 28th May

After all the excitement of yesterday, today was very dull. Last night I told Mum about Meg. She checked I wasn't being horrible to her, but I'm really not. I think she's worried that Meg's mum might blame it on me. I promised her it was Meg being weird. I said it should be me and Jenna that are cross with her. The fact that me and Jenna don't care, isn't the point. If we *did* care, we would be cross with her.

Even though Meg's weird right now, my tummy is still relaxed. It feels like all the changes that are happening will be OK.

Sunday 29th May

I learnt something new today. I was reading the class novel from school. Dad saw me on the sofa and said,

'I didn't know you liked sci-fi, Leeza'. I had never heard that phrase before. Apparently sci-fi is short for Science Fiction and is when books are to do with space and other worlds and things. I also learnt something else. I do not like sci-fi.

Monday 30th May

I've finished the sci-fi book. I wanted it out of the way so it wouldn't ruin my holiday. Grandma looked after us all day. She said that today could be lazy because it was our first day off, but tomorrow will be different. I defo eye-rolled. I wonder whether it was things like this that turned Mum into a cow when she lived with her.

Tuesday 31st May

Grandma wasn't lying. She turned up this morning with sponges, spray bottles and buckets. We had to clean! I couldn't even pretend I had to read that book because she saw me finish it yesterday. I opened my mouth to speak but she threw a pair of rubber gloves at me and said, 'Look lively, Leeza. There's mouldy grouting in the shower that needs your attention.' She gave me an old toothbrush and a pot of cleaning stuff that makes things white again. It was a tip from Kim and Aggie, whoever they are.

For three hours I was on my knees in the shower. The worst bit was Spike kept coming in for wees. I scrubbed and scrubbed and eventually got rid of most of the black gunk from between the tiles. My arms ached from working so hard.

I am not suited to physical labour. It is not my friend. I could never have lived in Victorian times.

* * *

6.

Life Isn't Fair

Wednesday 1st June

Everything aches! When Grandma arrived, I told her I couldn't move my arms. She replied, 'Nonsense, young lady. You experienced healthy, hard work, that's all.' I think deep down she could see she'd broken us. Spike had woken up with inflamed hands from the soapy detergent. He'd had to clean the outside window ledges with a sponge. That's why he kept needing to wee - because of all the water. To be fair to Grandma, she'd been busy too. I'd half expected her to be sitting eating chocolates with her feet up when I came down, but she wasn't. She'd washed all the duvet covers and made all the beds. Every single one. I don't get why people do this. They're only to sleep in. If you haven't wet the bed -

which let's face it, most of us manage *not* to do every night - they're good for months.

After our hard work yesterday, the house has a weird lemony smell. It's not a bad smell, but it doesn't feel like home. I'm sure the Auction Bidders reading this in the future, will be amazed at how hard life was for me. They'll have robots and gadgets to do all their chores. No one will suffer with achy arms in the future. It's just my luck to have been born too early.

<u>Thursday 2nd June</u>

Grandma was on another cleaning mission, but it wasn't as bad as yesterday. Just tidying. Before the mouldy grouting, I'd have thought tidying was as bad, but it defo isn't. Straightening books and plumping cushions is well easier. As I was doing that, Grandma was dusting around me. I said to her, 'Grandma, why're you obsessed with making everything clean?' She replied, 'In life, or in here?' I said, 'Both.' She said, 'In life, fewer germs and less mess make everything run smoother. Here, however, I think your Mum and Dad need all the help they can get with their latest hare-brained scheme.' I let that lie for a second before realising I didn't have a clue what she was talking about. 'You mean the new baby?' I asked. 'Something like that,' she replied. And that was it.

It's not just Mum that has lost the plot.

Friday 3rd June

Today was odd. Mum and Dad had the day off work to go to a meeting. That's what they said. They had to 'go to a meeting'. They only left the house at 10 o'clock. I asked what it was and they said, 'Council stuff.' They must think I'm stupid. They don't work in the same department so they never have the same meetings. I wonder what they're hiding?

I've thought about it all day. It could be another hospital appointment. Maybe there's something wrong with the baby? Or perhaps they both lost their jobs and are pretending they still go to work? It's very mysterious and proves two things. Firstly, they've no problem fibbing to their children. And two. They're terrible liars.

They got back this evening. I didn't bother pointing out that it was the longest Council meeting ever. It wasn't all bad though. My anxious tummy calmed right down when they bought in a chippy tea. Mmmmmm chips and curry sauce. It fixes everything.

Saturday 4th June

This half-term holiday has been strange. Grandma with her mad cleaning, and Mum and Dad with their poor attempts at lying. I'll say it again, but I'm the only one that picks up on these things. I tried to talk to Spike yesterday. I waited till he was on his own in the lounge, and I said, 'Where do you think Mum and Dad have *really* gone?' He looked up from the telly and grunted, 'Meeting'. I tried again. I said, 'Yeah, that's what they said. But you don't believe it, do you?' He looked up again. I think I'd got his attention. If it looked like I was interested in his opinion he might open up to me. He's nearly eight so he might have noticed their lying too. He thought for a moment and then said, 'Maybe they're spies. They've been summoned by their handler for a top secret mission, assassinating baddies and freeing the world of all evil forces.' I looked at him for a second, and then he turned back to the TV. I don't think I'll bother chatting again.

Things had calmed down by the evening. Just as I was getting into bed, Mum put her head round the door. All casual and smiley, she said, 'Family Meeting tomorrow, Leez. Yeah?' And then she had gone.

What on earth is happening?

<u>Sunday 5th June</u>

<u>Monday 6th June</u>

<u>Tuesday 7th June</u>

I haven't slept well since Sunday. I'm shattered. Mum and Dad are horrible.

<u>Wednesday 8th June</u>
I thought about talking to Grandma on the way home. Then I realised she's known all along. That's what the cleaning was about.

Thursday 9th June

I've still not told anyone. I need to get my head round it. Everything is rubbish. I've no control over anything. Mum and Dad need to realise I'm nearly a grown-up. I have rights.

Friday 10th June

It's Friday Fooday but I wasn't in the mood. Mum and Dad haven't said much to me since Sunday. I think they're cross I had an outburst, but they know they're ruining my life so they can't say anything. I wish there was something I could do.

I still can't sleep. I'm writing this at 1am!

Saturday 11th June

I'm fed up. I can feel tears coming into my eyes when I think about it. And I NEVER cry.

As I was tossing and turning, I thought of one thing I *can* do. I will call a Family Meeting. They ignored me about the baby, but that was after it was already on the way. This time they can change their minds before it is too late.

Just being able to do something made me feel a little better. I'm going to work out all the things I need to say and write them down.

Sunday 12th June

I told everyone about the Family Meeting this morning. I could see Mum was a bit shocked but she knew she had to come. That's the rule.

When it was 3 o'clock we sat around the table and I stood up and read my speech. I'd worked really hard on it and used the persuasive writing technique of repetition. Maybe all that SATs practice was useful after all. I'll write it out below so there is a record forever. I was very proud of it.

'It has been a week since this family were informed we were selling our house and moving miles away. It has been a week since Spike and Blane learnt they would not be returning to Irwell Green in September, and that I learnt I would not be starting Stockford High with my friends. It has been a week since we were told why you have been cleaning, sorting and binning our things. It has been a week since you told us you had lied about a

Council meeting and had in fact been looking at a new house to live in-– a house the rest of us have never seen. It has been a week since...'

At this point, Mum interrupted. 'Leeza, I think we get the gist.' I was really cross she butted in but I was mature. I said, 'You need to listen. It's the rule.' I saw Dad smile. This annoyed me but also showed he knew I was right. He said, 'You *will* insist on democracy, Molly,' and then smiled properly at me. 'Go on Leeza, we're listening.' I carried on.

'It has been a week since we all had to rethink the future we thought we knew, and a week since we realised we were going to be moving away from the only home we have ever known. It has been a week since we heard the name Applemere Bridge and a week since we learnt we were moving to a completely different place. It has been a week since everything has turned upside down. I am asking you to change your minds about this decision. A decision you made without asking any of us. Change your minds and let us get on with things as normal.'

Now I don't know about you, but I thought that was an absolute belter of a persuasive argument. I made really good points and included all of us in it, so it wasn't just about me. *And* I used the same phrase over and over again. Ms Archer would have put a big smiley face next to that in my book. I looked round the table to see the reaction. Spike was fidgeting because he wanted to watch TV and Blane was trying to stop his nose running with his tongue. Mum looked sad. I felt a bit sorry for her because she'd been excited last week when she told us. She thought we were going to be happy. She thought she was telling us good news, when in fact it was the complete opposite.

This week it was Dad that did the talking. He let me sit down and then said, 'Leeza, thank you for such a well-prepared introduction to a Family Meeting. I think we have learnt a lot about how to share our news.' I knew he was sucking up, but I listened anyway. 'You've made some great points but more importantly you have told us how you feel. So thank you. Last week, we didn't expect you to react the way you did. It was a surprise. You know you shouldn't swear at home.' Immediately Mum jumped in with, 'Or anywhere!' Dad looked at her and she was quiet again. He carried on. 'Yes, yes, or anywhere. So we weren't happy with that. But we do appreciate it was a shock. We just thought you'd be as excited as we were. It was silly of us not to realise how big a change this is for you all.'

I was sort of listening to him, but also trying to work out where he was going with this. Was he going to say it had all been a misunderstanding and they had decided to stay in Stockford after all? He carried on. 'So let us share a few more details that we know now. That way you might feel a bit more comfortable with what's happening.' Dad went over to the kitchen unit where all the post is piled up. He pulled out a bunch of papers and brought them back to the table. He gave me the top sheet. 'That is the house we went to see. We heard yesterday that they've accepted our offer.' Spike decided to pipe up then. 'What offer? What have they accepted?' Mum sighed. 'We offered them some money. They agreed to take the money and give us the house.' Now it was Blane's turn. (If I've done nothing else I've opened these meetings up to involve all the family). Blane said, 'But we have no money. You always say that.' Dad said, 'You're right. We *do* have no money now. But if we sell this house and buy the house in Applemere Bridge, we'll have some spare money. Because that house is cheaper than this house. And it's bigger. So we win all round.'

I was feeling less wound up than when I'd started this meeting. But I had lots more questions now. The past week had been filled with outrage and anger. (And tiredness!) Now I was able to hear what was being said, there were loads of things that didn't make sense. I went for it. 'OK, I have a question. How come the house we're moving to is bigger but costs less? Tyson Road is busy and scruffy but the countryside is where people go on holiday. It should be loads more expensive than here. How will we have spare money?' Mum and Dad did a 'look' at each other. I have no idea what they were trying to secretly say but in the end Dad spoke. 'You are mostly right. The Lake District is beautiful and people pay lots of money to stay there. I think the part we're moving to is a little bit away from the expensive places. The good thing about where we'll be is that there'll be no tourists. It'll be quiet. Lots of fresh air and space. We'll have a proper garden.' I must have looked up at that, because Dad jumped on it like it was a really positive thing. 'Yes, exactly Leeza, a garden! We'll be able to get proper outdoor chairs and there'll be space for footy and running around and stuff.' I'm not sure those were winning arguments for me as I've never shown a big interest in footy or running around, but still. He kept talking about all the marvellous things we'll be able to do and I started to tune him out.

I'd done my best. I'd called the meeting and shared my thoughts. There was nothing else I could do.

Monday 13th June

Yesterday's meeting carried on all evening really. Even when we were sitting in front of the TV, there was lots of discussion. The pictures of the house are black and white and small. Mum showed me which room could be mine but it was hard to see. Apparently the house has been empty for a while so there was nothing in there to show what the room might look like. Just a window with fields outside.

I haven't talked to Jenna about it yet. I feel terrible that she'll be left on her own. Meg is still being odd. She walked around with us on the playground for a bit but ran off when Alfie Diggs came out. She is what Grandma would describe as 'flighty'. Lots of people are flighty according to Grandma.

I've just thought. This means I won't have to share a room if the baby is a girl. Interesting.

Tuesday 14th June

I did some detective work today. We'd been in the computer suite all morning so we could type up stories for our Leavers' Files. I'd finished early so Ms Archer said I could use the Internet. She knows I don't have much computer access at home. Anyway, I went on Google Maps. I often do this. I like seeing Tyson Road from the sky, or searching for people's houses that I know. When you type in Grandma's address, you can see her on a stepladder outside the front door, scrubbing the window frames. She was fuming when we showed her. She said she'd write to the Internet to complain.

I took the chance to look at Applemere Bridge for myself. All I know is that it's in The Lake District, which is the countryside, and that the Lake District is a couple of hours north in a car. We went for a day trip when I was seven. Other than that I've no idea. I typed it in the box and saw the map zoom out, move up and then zoom back in. That's when it became obvious it's a very different place from Stockford.

Right now, if you look at the map of where I live, it looks like a really detailed grid. The roads are white, so you see lots of white criss-crosses everywhere. I thought there was something wrong with Applemere Bridge at first. There was no white. All I could see was green. There's no green in Stockford. It doesn't appear until you zoom in far enough to see the park down the road. And it's only a little speck amidst all the white roads.

I typed in 'Applemere Bridge' again but it took me to the same place. I zoomed in as far as I could. That's when I saw it. One white line. Just one. And it was a thin one, not a main road. More like a lane. One lane that runs through the new place I am going to be living. I don't understand. How does anyone get anywhere if there's only one teeny tiny road?

I dragged the little yellow person over to the map to see what was actually there but all it showed were fields and tall grass.

I think the map must be broken.

Wednesday 15th June

My nervous feeling is back. It arrived about a week ago.

I tried to break down what I'm nervous about. Moving house? Yes, obvs. That's the biggie. But there're other things too. I need to tell Jenna. She should know before anyone else. Meg will find out at some point but I've stopped thinking of her feelings these days. (It sounds bad to say that but it's true.) But Jenna will be going to Stockford High without me. She'll be with Meg on her own and I can't do anything to help. The other thing is, Jenna keeps me calm. I'm going to need her more than ever if I have to live miles away and start a new school. It all feels rubbish.

I have more worries. One of my questions from the Family Meeting (that I never got to ask) was how will Mum and Dad get to the Council every day. Google Maps said that it takes 2 hours and 14 minutes to get from Stockford to Applemere Bridge. That's a nightmare. They'll be travelling for over four hours every day. And Grandma would still have to come and look after us and then travel back. They haven't thought it through.

Thursday 16th June

If I were typing, I'd use the face palm emoji now. I've been stupid! Actually, I haven't been stupid. I've not been given all the facts. Again.

Grandma filled me in. After school she was trying to find *Murder She Wrote* on the planner so I took the chance to ask her about the travelling she would be doing in September. 'What on earth are you on about, Leeza?' she said. She looked confused so I kept on. 'All the travelling to Applemere Bridge to look after us every day'. She was being very slow. Then she looked at me like I'd gone mad, then laughed, and explained it all.

Apparently Mum and Dad have decided to leave the Council! I am flabbergasted. (Word Wall!) They're setting up their own Human Resources consultancy and not travelling anywhere. The house they've found has room for an office. They'll use some of the spare money from the house sale to set it up. Also, because they've done something called 'taken voluntary redundancy', they get a lot of money for leaving their jobs. 'Does this mean we're rich?' I asked. Grandma looked at me for a second or two. I'm not sure what she was thinking. Maybe she thought I should mind my own business. Maybe she thought children shouldn't know what is happening in their own lives and should be kept in the dark. Eventually she said, 'No, not rich. But you'll be all right. Your mum and dad can try their best at this new life without scraping for pennies straight away.' And that was that.

When she was leaving later on, I was sitting on the stairs when Mum was showing her out. I didn't hear all they said, expect for Grandma hissing, 'For goodness sake, Molly, you've made a real hash of explaining this to them.'

Friday 17th June

I thought I was going to hate today. For months I've thought today would be awful. The reason? After lunch, most of Year Six left on a coach for the Year Six holiday. When Mum found out about it (a couple of months ago) I told her I hadn't wanted to go. I probably had really, but we had no money so there was no point. The funny thing is, Year Six are spending the weekend in - *can you believe it?* - The Lake District. I guess I don't feel like I'm missing out on anything anymore. Maybe next year will be like one long Year Six holiday.

Meg came to school with the biggest rucksack I've ever seen. I'm not being mean but the idea of her camping makes me laugh. I don't think she realises what she's let herself in for. I saw her at playtime linking arms with Ellie Rogers (who still looks scared stiff of her). I've stopped caring.

Jenna didn't go on the holiday either. Neither did Jamie Kingston, Olivia Tyler and Josh Willis. Except those three didn't come in to school today. All morning I thought they'd made the right decision, but when the afternoon came, me and Jenna were sent to Reception class to be helpers! It was brilliant. I read stories all afternoon. It was like reading to Kenny except they were a year older so listened better. While I was doing that, Jenna was in the role-play area. I could see her out of the corner of my eye trying to squeeze into an age four to five pirate costume. By the time the bell went, I was shattered. Being a teacher is exhausting and all I did was sit on a beanbag and read.

Something else happened today too. I told Jenna about the house move. She was very quiet at first but then she fake punched my arm and said, 'That's for leaving me with Moody Knickers.' (It's what she calls Meg now.) 'But don't worry. When my dad annoys me I've got somewhere to run away to now.' I laughed. I have no idea if that was the right response. It's done though, and I've told her. I feel rubbish inside.

Saturday 18th June

Dad came into my room this morning. He said, 'I'm guessing this is for you.' He passed me a print out of an email. He shook his head and said, 'Not that it matters for much longer, but please tell Jenna my work email isn't for her personal correspondence.' I sat up and looked at the paper. It was titled: PLEASE DON'T READ THIS PRIVATE EMAIL, LEEZA'S DAD. SORRY FOR HAVING TO GO THROUGH YOU. THIS IS FOR LEEZA MCAULIFFE.

Hey Leez,

I just wanted to say that I'll miss you millions when you go. I don't care you're leaving me with Meg because I can handle her. And I don't care you're having a brand new life, because that's exciting and I'm happy for you. But... don't lose touch! Once your dad leaves his job I won't even be able to use this address in an emergency. Please promise that we can have emails or phone calls or even visits? I can easily find my way to you if I save up the pound coins from my dad's loose change tray.

When you told me yesterday, you said you were worried about what I'd say. Don't be worried!! I'm not weird like Meg. I'm excited for you. And the thing is, you KNOW I'm excellent at making people laugh. So Year Seven in Stockford High will be full of people that I can make be my friend. We'll be long-distance best mates. Easy.

Happy Weekend, McAuliffe!
Jenna x

Something has become clear. It's now my mission to convince Mum and Dad that I NEED a phone.

Sunday 19th June

A lazy Sunday. Mum watched *Pretty in Pink* in bed. This always makes us laugh because of the character, Blane. He's the reason *our* Blane got his name. Mum says the actor who played him was the most beautiful man she'd ever seen when she was fifteen. At least 'Film Liesl' in *The Sound of Music* gets a couple of good songs to sing. 'Film Blane' doesn't do anything.

When it was over and Mum was happy, I showed her Jenna's email. She thought the title was hilarious. She said to Dad, 'Mac, have you seen this?' and Dad raised his eyebrows and said, 'Oh yes, I saw it.' I don't think he cares about work anymore so deep down he found it funny too. As she read through it she smiled a lot and said, 'Ahhhh'. When she was done she passed it back to me. 'I'm sure you'll keep in touch, Leeza'. And you'll make new friends as well.'

I hadn't thought about making new friends - I'm not ready to think about that yet. I just want to keep my old friends and not move house. But I need Mum and Dad to realise it's time to let me grow up. I didn't say anything about a phone, but I've mentally started to plan.

<u>Monday 20th June</u>

Happy 6th birthday Blane! *That's* why Mum watched her film yesterday. The family rule stands - he got to pick his favourite tea. I wasn't impressed with his choice. Jam sandwiches aren't really my thing but I ate them anyway.

School was interesting. While we were milling around on the playground waiting for the bell, Meg came bounding over. I don't mean she walked over. I mean she bounced and ran and skipped all at once. Her first words were, 'I'm so glad to be back. I had a great weekend but I missed you both loads. How were your weekends, guys?'

Jenna openly laughed in her face but I was confused. It was like Old Meg was back. I didn't know what to say, but Jenna, who's never stuck for words, said, 'What's up with you? Not wearing your moody knickers today?' before cackling at her own joke. I said, 'Why are you speaking to us?' Meg just said, 'Don't be silly, we're best friends.'

Then the bell went and we walked in. Meg's so weird.

Tuesday 21st June

Meg was all smiles again today. She's acting like the last couple of months haven't happened. I'm not ignoring her, but I don't feel comfortable pretending we're mates again.

In other news, I finished typing up my work early so I got to do more secret research. This time I ignored the map and searched online in general. When I typed 'Applemere Bridge', I got a few references but not many. I now know that it's a linear village, it has stone houses dating back to the 18th Century and there's a church. None of us go to church, I don't know what linear means, and the houses are ancient. I'm none the wiser.

Wednesday 22nd June

Before school, Mum suggested I invite Jenna and Meg to Friday Fooday this week. I am a bit wary to do this. I've no problem with Jenna, but I'm still annoyed by Meg's randomness.

When I got home, Mum had taken it out of my hands. She'd talked to Meg's mum and Jenna's dad and it was on. I think she's realised I'll be leaving my friends behind soon. Maybe she feels guilty?

I asked, 'Does Meg's mum think she's still having puberty or has that finished now?' Mum smiled and said, 'I don't think puberty is finished by eleven. But as far as I know, things have settled down at home recently. Why?' I wasn't sure what to say. It's like it was all in my mind, except it wasn't. I know what's gone on, even if she's pretending it hasn't

I'll chat to Jenna tomorrow and see what she thinks.

Thursday 23rd June

Jenna, it seems, is too excited about eating round mine to care about Meg. It made me laugh how she said it. After I'd poured my heart out about feeling uneasy about picking up where we left off, Jenna threw her arm around my shoulders as we walked and said, 'But McAuliffe, we'll be having halloumi! Meg can't beat that.' And just by being her usual silly self, I felt better. I'm really going to miss Jenna.

I also knew I needed to tell Meg about the house move before tomorrow night. It didn't feel like a big deal. At least it wasn't a big deal to break it to her. I'd felt much more nervous telling Jenna. I left it till after lunch, as we were lining up to go back into school. The dinner ladies were shushing everyone and making sure we were settled before Ms Archer came.

I lined up behind Meg and just came out with it. I said, 'By the way, I found out last week I'm moving house, so I won't be with you in Year Seven after all.' We stayed standing there as Ms Archer arrived and waited for quiet.

A few seconds later, I heard a noise. Ms Archer could hear it too. A sort of snorting and gasping. It sounded like crying. Really loud crying. As I realised that, Ms Archer came over to Meg and put her arm around her. I could hear her whispering, 'What's the matter Meg, what's happened?' At that point the dinner lady ushered us all inside as Miss dealt with Meg. I was a bit stunned. Nothing had happened. Maybe she'd been stung by a bee without me seeing.

Of course when we got inside, it all became clear. Meg was an emotional mess because I'd told her I was leaving. She kept trying to speak through the sobs. 'I... *sob*... just... *sob*... thought... *sob*... we'd... *sob*... be... *sob*... friends... *sob*... forever.' I was utterly bewildered. (Word Wall!) Thank God for Jenna, who shouted out, 'Meg don't be such a drama queen. You haven't spoken to Leeza since the baby news. Stop making this about you.' Ms Archer looked at the three of us and realised this wasn't going to get sorted in five minutes. She told us to take a minute to gather ourselves (it was only Meg that needed to do that) and we'd talk about it at afternoon playtime.

It turned out, (after the entire fifteen minutes of my break were taken up) that Meg had found the past weeks difficult. She was last to find out about the baby (not true - she was second) and then she realised that me and Jenna weren't going on the Year Six holiday. She said she felt like we were ganging up on her. RIDIC.

To be fair to Ms Archer, I think she found this a complete waste of time too. Once Meg had calmed down, Miss explained there were many reasons why people didn't go on the holiday, and it wasn't about being friends or not. Once again, Jenna cut through the rubbish by shouting, 'Yeah, my dad's skint. We're not all spoilt like you, you weirdo.'

The upshot was, we all had to shake hands, Ms Archer made it clear no one had done anything wrong except misunderstand feelings, and that now everyone knows I am leaving (clearly Miss had already known) we should make the most of our last weeks together.

I'm emotionally drained and I haven't had any emotions. Meg is exhausting.

Friday 24th June

After all the drama of yesterday, I was dreading Friday Fooday.

I'd told Mum that Jenna was banking on halloumi, so she got some in. Grilled halloumi pieces, home made dips, (pepper and feta - mmmm) chunks of bread with veggie sticks to dunk, and sweet potato chips. It was gorge.

It turned out that Meg was on her best behaviour. She politely asked for things to be passed to her, and it was obvious she was really trying. Jenna was also on good behaviour but I think she just likes eating new things. Her dad doesn't get to eat with her much so she uses the microwave to heat up ready meals. I always think this sounds very grown up. I would love the chance to get my hands on a ready meal. But when I see how happy she is just because of cheese, I think maybe it isn't as much fun.

When Dad was washing up, and we were clearing the table, I heard him say to Jenna, 'I got your latest email. Maybe now's the time to delete my address from your contacts?' Jenna said, 'No problem. Did you read what I said?' Dad said, 'Yes. Thanks for your efforts, but there's no need for all that research.' Then Jenna turned and winked at me.

I've literally no idea.

Saturday 25th June

Last night ended up being really late. Meg's mum came to pick her up at 8 o'clock but then stayed for a glass of wine. After she'd been there for an hour, she messaged Meg's dad to come round too. They were all very loud.

Me, Jenna and Meg stayed in my room, laughing at them. Meg was defo embarrassed about the way she'd been in school but we didn't tease her. Who knows, puberty might happen for me next. It'll be my turn to be 'an absolute cow'.

Sunday 26th June

I wish I hadn't left my homework for today. It took ages. I'm sick of doing transition booklets for a school I won't be attending.

I haven't thought much about my new school. I guess high schools are all very similar. It'll be like Stockford High but with more green around it on the map.

Monday 27th June

This morning Ms Archer showed us a film. It was a cartoon of *Romeo and Juliet*, which I've heard of. It was quite good even though everyone dies at the end. Well, Romeo and Juliet do anyway. (Auction Bidders - SPOILER ALERT. I should've warned you before I gave the ending away. Sorry.)

The exciting news is that we're going to be doing *Romeo and Juliet* as our end of year play! Some of the words were really hard in the cartoon but Miss said our script would be simpler. Auditions are Wednesday lunchtime. Everyone's excited.

Tuesday 28th June

Grandma has heard of *Romeo and Juliet*! 'Leeza, it's the greatest love story ever told,' she said. I replied, 'But they both die?' She was quiet for a moment and then said, 'I didn't say love was happy.' And that was that.

I wonder if things aren't going so well with Willard the Tree. I didn't ask.

Wednesday 29th June

It seems the whole of Year Six wants to be in *Romeo and Juliet*. We had to go to Mr Eskbrook's room at lunchtime if we wanted to audition. When I arrived, there were at least fifty of us. Ms Archer walked in and panicked. She decided they'd audition Mr Eskbrook's class today and us tomorrow. It's all anyone can talk about.

According to Joshua Willis, the audition was standing in front of Ms Archer and Mr Eskbrook and being told to act in different ways. Josh said he had to be sad, happy, confused, worried and excited. That was all. I'm not nervous about tomorrow now. It'll be easy. Especially the acting worried part. I do that most days. Except I'm not acting.

Thursday 30th June

The audition went well. I used all my best facial expressions to show how I was feeling. I think I did all right. I don't want to be Juliet by the way. Maybe one of the party guests? With all the turmoil at home, I don't think I can handle the pressure of a main part. Meg is desperate to be Juliet. She can't understand why I'd want to be in the background. She's not a background kind of person. And Jenna isn't bothered at all. She only auditioned so she wouldn't be bored on her own outside.

We find out next week.

* * *

7.

All Change

Friday 1st July

Grandma stayed for tea. While we were eating, Dad turned to her and said, 'How are things with the lovely Willard? Still bothered by his dress sense?' Grandma smiled, half shook her head, then said, 'Willard is proving to be quite the tricky customer.' She tried to leave it at that but Mum wasn't having it. 'What does that mean?' she said. 'You can't leave us hanging.' It was obvious Grandma didn't want to talk about it. Eventually she said, 'All I'll say is that he isn't the kind of man I'm used to.' Mum kept asking her questions but she didn't say any more.

I don't know what kind of man Grandma *is* used to. Mum's dad wasn't very nice according to Mum and I don't know about her other boyfriends apart from Brian the Lecherer.

Saturday 2nd July

I told Mum about *Romeo and Juliet* this morning. She'd been nagging Spike to wash his face in lots of different voices. She did a begging one, then a really strong Mancunian one, then a warbly singing one. It made me laugh and reminded me of the audition. When I told her about it, she was excited. (Unless she was acting!) After finally getting Spike to pick up the facecloth, she went into her bedroom and rooted in a box. When she came back she had a DVD in her hand. It was *Romeo and Juliet*! This was very unexpected. It had real actors, not cartoon characters. She said I could watch it tomorrow if I helped Dad take stuff to the tip.

I didn't mind helping. I like the tip. I like swinging each bin bag into the skip as high as I can. Mum said if I was exceptionally helpful we could have popcorn with the film. I swung sixteen bags into the skip. I brushed the backyard where all the rubbish had been stored for the past fortnight. I even offered to make

Dad a cup of tea. I'd say that was exceptionally helpful, thank you very much.

Sunday 3rd July

Romeo and Juliet is weird! In the film, Romeo's friends had guns instead of swords and they wore normal clothes. Mum said it was very different from how other *Romeo and Juliet* films look, but the words were the same. I think I enjoyed it. It wasn't boring and there were some parts where I laughed out loud. I also thought the end was very sad.

Even though I was confused quite a lot, it was a good afternoon. Mum watched it with me. At one point, Spike walked into the lounge just as Romeo and Juliet were having a big kiss, so he made sick noises for the rest of the day.

Monday 4th July

As soon as Ms Archer came out to get us, everyone began asking who had been given parts. She got flustered and said they were still deciding and it'd be tomorrow. It's all anyone is talking about.

Tuesday 5th July

The funniest thing has happened! Jenna is Juliet! HAHAHAHAHAHAHAHA.

Wednesday 6th July

I couldn't concentrate on anything last night because I was finding everything too funny. Meg was fuming when the parts were read out. She really thought she would be one of the main ones. Instead she is 'Capulet Family Member'. She wasn't happy.

When Miss said '...and the role of Juliet goes to...Jenna,' I looked at Jenna. She had a shocked look on her face for a couple of seconds before she threw back her head and laughed. She found it hysterical. It *is* funny, even though I feel a bit sorry for Meg.

The other shock news, which added to Meg's strop, is that Romeo is...Alfie Diggs! When Miss said that, Jenna pulled a face and shouted, 'Urghh Miss, I'm not snogging him!' Everyone laughed (except Meg, obvs).

I'm quite happy with my part. I'm the Nurse. I can't remember the Nurse from the film because I don't think there were any hospital scenes but it's nice to be in it somehow.

Thursday 7th July

Meg's doing her very best not to be grumpy with us. I don't think she wants the hassle of Ms Archer having to intervene and make us all give up a playtime to shake hands. She's defo not happy, though. She's used to getting her own way. Me and Jenna are being our normal selves. I think Jenna is secretly proud to have been picked as Juliet but she just laughs whenever I ask her about it.

Also, I got confused. The Nurse is Juliet's *nanny*. I remember her now. I have real lines to say and everything. Today we got our scripts. The people with speaking parts went to Mr Eskbrook's room for a read through, and the people without lines stayed with Ms Archer to learn the dance that they do at the party.

Swapping rooms for the last two lessons felt like high school. I've started to wonder what my new one will be like. I can't put off thinking about it much longer.

Friday 8th July

I asked Mum about my new school. She said she'd been planning to arrange a visit for me before we break up. I defo want to see it before September but the insects in my tummy are scurrying around like mad!

I don't know why I'm so worried. I know what to expect. I spent the day in Stockford High and it was fine. There'll be a load of Year Sevens in exactly the same situation as me, only they'll just know the area better. I need to stop worrying.

Friday Fooday was roasted vegetable and halloumi bake. Jenna would've loved it.

Saturday 9th July

I've spent all day learning lines! I'm shattered. Not achy in my body, but tired in my head. This is how Julie Andrews must have felt when she filmed *The Sound of Music*. She had loads of lines in that.

I'm lucky. I only have a few scenes where I speak. Jenna has almost all of it. We're going to practise together tomorrow. When I asked Mum if Jenna could come round, she said, 'Has she been doing anymore research lately?' When I asked what she meant, Mum changed the subject to what I wanted for tea. I can't be fooled. I let it go this time, but I won't forget.

Sunday 10th July

Phew, I've worked so hard for a Sunday! Me and Jenna have been at it for hours. We decided we would learn the scenes with Juliet and the Nurse together. That way it helps both of us. We're lucky that Ms Archer changed the language from the original play because it'd be a million times harder if she hadn't.

Our first scene is where the Nurse is helping Juliet get ready for the party. I have to pretend to brush her hair. Whenever I tried to act like I was doing it, we started giggling. When Jenna gets the giggles, she can't stop for ages. It took most of the day to get through it. I'm not sure how useful it was in the end. I had fun though.

Monday 11th July

We did our first run through. Most people still have the words in their hand, not just me. I was pleased with the hair-brushing scene though. Neither of us laughed once.

What's interesting is that now Alfie Diggs has a main part, he isn't messing around as much. He's trying his best with his behaviour. I don't think he's ever done that before.

Tuesday 12th July

Mum rang the school in Applemere Bridge. I'm going to visit on Friday.

I suppose they'll have had their taster days already so it'll just be me on the visit. I wonder if the canteen will be like Stockford High. I was looking forward to having hot meals for lunch once in a while.

My sensible head is telling me to chill out. I've already done one high school visit this year and enjoyed it. This'll be the same.

Wednesday 13th July

More rehearsals today. The weather's been warm the past few days so we took our chairs out to the playground and rehearsed there. We sat in a circle and when it was our turn to act a scene, we did it in the middle of everyone. By next week, Mrs Whitely (caretaker) will have put the stage up in the hall so we can practise there.

Only a week to go till *Romeo and Juliet* is performed. That doesn't sound long but we've stopped doing everything else. While all the other classes are doing real lessons, we're rehearsing, trying on costumes and making posters to put around school. This is defo the best part of being in Year Six.

Thursday 14th July

I told Jenna I was going to be off tomorrow because I was visiting my new school. All she said was, 'Just remember you're banned from making new friends, McAuliffe.' I promised her I wouldn't.

The thing is, even though I know she was joking, I don't want to make new friends. It'd have been OK if

I went to Stockford High because I could make new friends whilst keeping my old ones. But moving away feels like I'm betraying my old friends by trying to replace them. I honestly won't be able to replace Jenna. She's good for me. She stops me worrying.

Tomorrow's an early start. Mum's taking the day off and driving us to Applemere Bridge. I'm really *really* intrigued about it all. The Internet still won't tell me much. I haven't found many pictures of what the town's like. Hardly any. Tomorrow I'll get answers to my questions.

In other top secret news, I got my SATs results! Ms Archer gave them to Grandma in an envelope because the rest of the class gets theirs tomorrow. I'm *at* the expected standard for SPaG and Reading and *working towards* the expected standard for Arithmetic and Reasoning. Well duh! I could've told Miss exactly that but without the hassle of the tests. I'm good at English and not so good at Maths. The same as I've been since Reception. Mum looked at the results and said, 'Leeza, this was a colossal waste of your final year but we love and support you. Well done on getting through it and always remember that adult life is full of calculators.' Then she started to make tea.

Friday 15th July

Well that was a looong day. Mum summed it up best - shattered.com! I saw the outside of the new house, though. Not sure what I think yet. Well, I think a lot of things but they are all jumbled. I'll work out what I have to say as I sleep. My stomach is what I'd describe in a story as *churning*.

Saturday 16th July

I've had a good think about yesterday. Here's a list of what I learnt.

- Applemere Bridge takes longer to get to than online maps say.
- There's a lot of countryside between here and there.
- Traffic jams are rubbish.
- My new school isn't in Applemere Bridge at all.

- I have to get a bus from the village for twenty minutes - every day.
- I only saw a couple of classrooms.
- The uniform is a reddy-brown colour.
- I met my new form teacher - she seemed OK.
- I can't remember her name.
- I hadn't realised I'd be getting a bus on my own.
- I have forms to send off for a bus pass.
- We weren't in the school for long.
- I asked Mum if I could see the house.
- She said I could.
- The road I'll be living on is more like a track or lane.
- The house looks big, but is really, really, really, scruffy.
- Mum says it just needs a lick of paint and it'll be good as new.
- I didn't get to see inside because the estate agent had the keys.
- There were no other houses near us - we are at the end of the lane.
- You would never hear your neighbours row in Applemere Bridge.

- I made Mum drive through the village three times.
- I saw a butcher's shop, a mini supermarket, a village hall and a pub.
- I did not see a library.
- Did I mention the house is really scruffy?

This morning Dad asked me whether I'd enjoyed the visit. I just said, 'It didn't look terrible,' which is almost true. Dad laughed and said, 'It's going to be a great big adventure.' I smiled but it was forced. I didn't think it looked terrible but I didn't think it looked great either. I feel blank and numb.

<u>Sunday 17th July</u>

I suppose I'm lucky. I've been to visit. Spike and Blane won't know anything about it until we move.

I had another long think when I was in my room. 620 Tyson Road has been home all my life. I feel sad that I'm going to be leaving it, which I guess is normal, but there are bad things about it too. There's no room for us all and defo no privacy. Spike barged into my room looking for Blane as I was lying there, proving my point. Yet. Applemere Bridge seems so...drastic.

Monday 18th July

It's the start of my last week of primary school! I've no idea how I feel. It's all a blur right now.

Today the people that are buying our house are coming for another viewing. I'm glad I'm in school. I don't think I want to see them. It made me smile to imagine Grandma having to show them in though. She might make them change their minds.

The rest of the day was taken up with *Romeo and Juliet* rehearsals. I've finally learnt all my lines. I managed to put down the script this afternoon and only needed prompting once. To the surprise of everyone, Jenna had learnt most of hers too - and she has loads! Ms Archer kept smiling at her and saying she knew it was a good decision to give her the role. I got the impression she felt it was a risk. Jenna doesn't know if her dad's coming yet. He has to get across town after work.

When Grandma picked us up, I asked about the house buyers. It's a young couple with a baby. All Grandma said was, 'They seemed perfectly pleasant people. But then so did Hillary and Roger until they won the lottery and thought their new conservatory made them better than the rest of us.'

I don't know who Hillary and Roger are but I don't think it matters.

Tuesday 19th July

It's the last full day before the dress rehearsal tomorrow. I'm not nervous. I feel calm and ready. But Alfie Diggs still forgets his lines most of the time. I think he was a risk that didn't pay off.

Meg is being mega-clingy. It's like she's suddenly realised she's been acting stupid for ages and is running out of time to make it up. She walked around the playground linking my arm for most of lunchtime. Jenna's getting good at teasing her again. She did a really funny impression of how she was walking that made me laugh. It wasn't being cruel. Meg laughed a bit too.

When we leave school on Friday, Meg's going to Portugal for two weeks. By the time she comes back, I'll have left. It feels weird to think of it like that. Everything's happening so fast. When we break up on Friday, that'll be it for me and Meg.

I'm not as sad about that as I would've been at the start of the year.

Wednesday 20th July

Dress rehearsal day. We're doing two run-throughs for the school in full costume. I love days like this. It seems so long since we had real lessons.

I knew that the Nurse wasn't a 'sick people' nurse and more like a nanny. But the costume I have makes me look like a nun! It's a black dress, a white apron and a sort of veil on a hat. Jenna fell about laughing when I came back from Mr Eskbrook's classroom. Juliet's costume is much nicer. Like a princess dress I suppose. It looked funny with her scuffed trainers sticking out the bottom.

We started the first rehearsal once everyone was dressed. It was for Key Stage One. I could see Blane watching from the middle of his row. I think he enjoyed himself. It's always hard to tell what's going on behind his shyness.

Alfie Diggs still didn't know his lines! Ms Archer went mad at him after the first run through. She made him stay in at lunchtime and practise. I think her nerves are fraught. At one point, Jenna, who was supposed to be in love and happy on her balcony, hissed, 'Alfie, you're doing my head in'. Everyone laughed except Ms Archer. She knew Jenna had a point.

The second run-through was better. It was for Key Stage Two. I saw Spike get moved for talking in the middle of the Capulet party. He was spellbound when it came to the sword fight though.

Thursday 21st July

It's *Romeo and Juliet* day! I can't believe we've put together a whole play (OK, a shortened version of a whole play) in two weeks. It's flown by.

We had to be back at school for 5 o'clock to get into costume. We even had stage make-up on. Mrs Miles came to help. She put red circles on my cheeks to look like blusher, and blue on my eyelids to look like eye shadow. I would have been embarrassed except everyone looked as over the top as me. Jenna laughed and pointed at every single person she saw. I hadn't felt nervous all day. It wasn't until I saw the hall set up with rows of chairs that I felt the familiar butterflies.

Meg was in a good mood. She'd managed to convincc Mr Eskbrook to make her the lead dancer, so she's at the front when it comes to the party scene. She isn't shy at making sure she's noticed. Her parents were on the front row with a massive camera. They didn't seem shy either. I could see Mum and Dad in the middle of the hall. Grandma was next to them. It was hard to see between the heads. I was trying to see if Jenna's dad had made it or not, but I didn't see him.

I know it sounds big headed but I think we put on a brilliant performance. Alfie Diggs remembered *most* of his lines, Jenna did her dying scene without laughing, and everyone was really quiet because of how sad it made them feel. Then when we did our bows, the clapping was so loud! I could see people standing up, and Meg's dad's camera flashed over and over. I felt the happiest I've ever felt. I'll remember it forever.

The other perfect thing was that Jenna's dad managed to make it after all. At the end, when we'd left our costumes in the classroom, we walked out to the parents and he was there. Jenna had been her usual silly self the whole time, but when she saw her dad she screamed and ran over to him. He picked her up and whizzed her round for ages. It turns out she hadn't even told him she was the main part. He'd managed to get to the play ten minutes after it started, thinking she wasn't in it much. I've never seen Jenna so happy. Mum and Dad kept grinning and everyone was smiley. Even Grandma.

While we were at the play, Willard the Tree was looking after the boys on his own. It seems he's still 'on the scene'.

Friday 22nd July

Wooohooo! I'm no longer a primary school pupil!!!!

I say 'woohoo' but there are defo mixed emotions. It wasn't that long ago that I was looking forward to walking down Tyson Road holding files. I can't see myself having the same mature look avoiding the muddy puddles on the lane in Applemere Bridge.

Ms Archer did a speech for me before break. She said the whole class wished me well on my new adventure. I think every adult who hears about the house move describes it as an adventure. It's like they're trying to make it sound better than it is in reality. It was nice of her anyway.

Meg brought me a present. Ms Archer said we could open it at lunchtime after we were back from eating. It was a big, flat rectangle that I had to be careful with. I worked it out before I got all the wrapping off – a photo frame. When I saw the front of it though, I properly choked up. It was a big collage of photos of Meg, Jenna, and me from when we were four right up to now. One of the pictures was from last night!

Meg's dad had to print it off and stick it on after they got home. I hate crying but I had to wipe my eyes as I looked at it. It's mad how long I've known them both.

Home time was sort of happy and sort of sad. I can't explain it. When the bell went for the final time, everyone cheered really loudly. We'd signed each other's shirts so we all looked really cool. But then as we walked outside, it came time to say goodbye. Meg's flying off tonight so this was it for her. We gave each other a hug and I thanked her again for the photo frame. She was crying a lot (she might have been exaggerating a bit) and made me promise to keep in touch. I will try. I think. I did feel sad but managed to control it more than she did.

Jenna walked home with me and helped me carry the big frame. I don't move for another couple of weeks so I'll still see her. Also, she stayed for Friday Fooday. It was a day filled with feelings - some floaty, some achy.

Tea was...a chippy tea!!! They said it was a 'Leeza's (and Jenna's) Leaving School Celebration' but I think

Mum and Dad didn't have the energy to cook. The landing and hallway is full of boxes that have been packed. I didn't care. I love chippy chips and curry sauce.

Saturday 23rd July

I had the biggest lie in ever. After 1 o'clock!

Sunday 24th July

According to Mum, today was 'Operation Chuck It Out'. We were given a bin liner and told not to come back from our rooms until we'd filled it. When I tried to protest that I didn't have any rubbish I was told I was *speaking* rubbish! (Mum thought that was hilarious.) She said I had to go through everything in my room and decide if it really needs to move with us. Once again it has to be said, I don't have much. In the end I found a few old notebooks that were full of doodles and some dried out felt pens. They didn't fill a bin bag though.

Spike did better than me. He realised he didn't need any of his school uniform anymore so filled the bag with that. He's not as daft as he looks.

Monday 25th July

This should be the first proper non-school day of the Summer holidays. Instead the house is in chaos. There're boxes everywhere. Spike is going mad because he wants to build dens with them but Grandma keeps telling him off.

I packed all my belongings into two cardboard boxes. All the things I won't need for a few weeks anyway. Mum will be packing our clothes herself, so apart from that, there wasn't much. Mainly books and some old toys I keep because they remind me of being small. My room is really bare.

If a bookshelf has no books on it, is it a bookshelf, or just a shelf? I asked Grandma that question as she was cleaning, but all she said was, 'For pity's sake Leeza, I'm trying to make the back of this fridge fit for human use.' I guess I'll never know.

Tuesday 26th July

Grandma had us at her house today. But the interesting thing was that Willard the Tree was there.

As soon as we walked in, Spike ran over to him and pretend-punched his arm. Without saying anything, Willard clutched his hand to his shoulder and fell to the ground like he'd been really hit. Spike loved it. Then he sat on him as he threw more fake punches and Willard did more fake pain. I was shocked at first. This is what they must've been like when everyone was at the play. It carried on until Grandma walked in and said, 'Enough!' Spike stopped and Willard got to his feet, both of them grinning.

Then Willard high-fived Blane, who seemed to have left all his shyness behind, and high-fived him back - reaching up really tall and giving it as much power as he could. Willard pretended Blane had hurt his hand and shook it like it was sore. Blane's smile was massive.

That left Kenny. Willard picked him up, whizzed him up on his shoulders and twirled him round. Kenny giggled the whole time, in a way he's never done before. It's like Willard is magic and can make everyone laugh the second they meet him.

After he put Kenny down, he came over to me. He offered his hand to shake, which I did. Then he said, 'Leeza, congratulations on a fantastic interpretation of Shakespeare's Nurse. I've read the reviews and I believe you were the star of the show.' I couldn't help it - I started to laugh too. Then he walked past Grandma, who was standing in the doorway, and said, 'Come on Ursula, let's go and get ice cream'. Then we were all bundled out of the door to go to the café down the road.

I agree. He's nothing like Grandma's type, whatever that is. He's fun! The other thing I noticed today was that Grandma laughs more when she's with him.

Wednesday 27th July

Blane came into my room this morning. (Without knocking, obvs.) He said Grandma had sent him because he'd been asking what the new house was like. She said I was the one with the answers.

The past week's been so busy I've forgotten to think about the new house. I've seen it from the outside, at a distance from the end of a path. All I could tell him was that it looked bigger than ours and there was grass all around it. He wanted to know more, but I didn't tell him anything else.

The only other information I could've shared, was that the grass was overgrown with weeds, the paint was peeling from the outside walls, and it looked like it'd been empty for years. It wouldn't have been a good idea to pass that on.

<u>Thursday 28th July</u>

Every day there's something to organise for the move. Today I returned my library books for the last time. I asked Grandma if I could go on my own. I've done it twice so she can't really say no. She wasn't keen at first but in the end she texted Mum who said it was OK. I set off after lunch.

I've loved going to this library. It's always warm and it smells old but in a good way. As I handed back my books, I passed a card to the woman behind the desk. I'd made it myself. I know she doesn't really know me, and it's not always her on duty, but I wanted to say thank you to the whole building. (I'm pretty sure there's no library in Applemere Bridge.) I said, 'I'm moving away next week so I wanted to say goodbye'. As I said that I felt a lump in my throat even though it was only the library woman whose name I don't know. She was really nice to me and said, 'It's a pleasure to have been of service.' Then she reached into a drawer and gave me a badge and a pen. Both of them said *Stockford Library Service* on them. I didn't make a card to get free stuff but it made me feel glad that I had.

Friday 29th July

Mum and Dad had their last days at work today. Dad was, as Grandma would say, 'cock-a-hoop'. I've never known what that actually means but Dad was defo *it*.

When they got in at home time, they had lots of presents and cards. Most of the cards wished them good luck on their adventure. There's that word again. I can't help feeling that the people that call the house move an adventure have never had an adventure for real. If they had, they'd know that moving to the middle of nowhere is a *nightmare* or *disaster*, not an *adventure*.

The good bit was that Mum let us eat her chocolates. Mmmmm.

Saturday 30th July

I spent the day at Jenna's. I hadn't seen her since school and Mum told me to do something that wasn't under her feet. As she said that, I noticed her tummy is looking properly pregnant now, not just fat. It's an actual bump. She keeps resting her glass of water on it when she's talking to Dad. It makes sense that it's obvious now. The baby's due in six weeks. I felt sorry for her having to bend to clean the toilet with her massive tummy in the way. Not sorry enough to offer to do it though. I'll help some other way tomorrow.

Jenna was asking me about Dad. She wanted to know if he'd said anything about her. I didn't know what she was on about. His work email's cancelled now so she can't email me through him anymore.

Sunday 31st July

My heart sank when Mum woke me up. (I'd been awake for ages but I hadn't felt ready to get out of bed.) She said, 'Family Meeting at three, OK?' I felt an immediate panic. Family Meetings are so stressful. They shouldn't be called 'Family Meetings', but 'Parent Meetings Where Children Are Told Massive Events That They Have No Control Over.' I must've looked nervous because she said, 'Nothing to worry about, Leez. We just want to make sure we're all feeling good about the move.' I nodded and she went. Inside my head I said, 'Fat chance of that, Mum.'

When three came, we sat round the table. Mum said today was about asking any questions we have so we wouldn't worry about next week. It made me realise how soon everything is. Next week!

Spike asked if there'd be space to build a wooden den or a tree house. Mum and Dad looked panicked at the thought of Spike with a saw but they told him there was lots of room outside. Spike looked happy. Mum and Dad looked nervous.

They asked Blane if he had any questions. He shook his head and sucked his thumb. Dad told him that with all the space, he'd get rid of his stabilisers in no time. Blane sucked his thumb harder. I think Dad might need to give up on that and find something Blane actually *wants* to do.

Obvs I had questions but I needed to be careful. I have lots of concerns about the state of the house but I don't want to make the boys feel as worried as I am. Because in five more sleeps, we'll be living there for good with no turning back. In the end I said, 'Will we be doing any decorating when we get there?' I like to think that was a subtle way of showing that I know it *needs* decorating, without actually saying it out loud. Mum smiled and said, 'We'll be treating this like a massive adventure...' - *yes, she really did say the A word!* - '...and working on turning it from an old, empty building into our family home. It'll take a while but we'll do it together and it'll be worth it.' Then Spike said, 'Why's it empty? Where're the people that live there?' It was a good question and not one I'd thought about. Mum said, 'It belonged to an old man who died last year. It's been empty since then so has started to get a bit tatty.' Dad spoke up then. 'To be fair Molly, I think it's been a bit tatty for years.' They both laughed like it was a funny joke instead of it being a depressing thing to say about our new home. Spike was made up though. 'Cool, I hope the old man's ghost haunts us.' He's so random.

My final question was something Jenna had made me think about yesterday. It was something I hadn't thought about until she mentioned it and it was the most important thing. 'Is there Wi-Fi?' I asked. Dad laughed. There will be when we sort it, yeah. Don't worry, we need the Internet for work so it'll be a priority. Speaking of which...' - Dad got up and walked to his workbag. He got a flat box out of it and came back to the table - '...You can thank Jenna for this. If she hadn't mithered me for weeks, it mightn't have happened.' He opened the box to show us what was inside. Spike saw it first and gasped. 'An iPad? No way!' He tried to grab it from Dad who was having none of it. 'Hands off Spike! It's still new. Now before anyone gets carried away, this is a *family* iPad. You can use it for homework or games, or for keeping in touch with people. Jenna was adamant you had to have access to her.' Dad showed Spike how to turn it on whilst I sat there speechless. I now owned my own iPad. (Yeah, yeah, family iPad, whatever.) All because of Jenna? She is quite literally the best friend

I have ever had. I sat there speechless, teary and happy all at once.

I wish I wasn't moving away in five more sleeps.

* * *

8.

There's Nothing Cosy About Grey Walls

<u>Monday 1st August</u>

Another day at Grandma's. It's hard to move around at home with all the boxes. To get from the hall to the lounge you have to squeeze through a tiny gap.

Grandma's house was fine but Willard wasn't there. I don't want to be mean but she isn't as much fun on her own. When he's there, all her posh china and straight-backed chairs feel much more cosy. He softens everything around him. Especially Grandma.

<u>Tuesday 2nd August</u>

Dad has set up the iPad so today was all about contacting Jenna. I messaged on Mum's phone to check she was free, and then FaceTimed her. I know I've done it before, but it felt so much better knowing I was using my own (yeah, yeah, it's for the family) device. We pulled funny faces and laughed at each other. She told me she'd been emailing Dad with tablet prices for weeks. She said she never dreamed he'd get an iPad. She'd been looking at cheaper options and ones on eBay. I think Mum and Dad have realised that if we're moving to a scruffy house miles away, we might need some nice things to see us through.

Dad's sorted an email account for me. It isn't private and he set the password himself (HALLOUMI - Auction Bidders, do not hack me!) but I don't care. He promised that him and Mum wouldn't read my emails unless they were worried about me, and I'm only allowed to give the address to people I actually know. I'm so happy to have a proper way of staying in touch with Jenna (and Meg I guess) that I'll accept anything.

I felt relaxed for a bit today. It's funny how up and down I get.

Wednesday 3rd August

Grandma had us again but still no Willard. I asked how he was and Grandma replied, 'He's perfectly fine Leeza, why on earth do you care?' I wasn't sure why I cared really. It was more than being polite. I think he's fun for an old man and I was sad I wasn't going to see him before we left. I said, 'I just wondered if he was OK. Are you still going out with him?' She snorted and said, 'Leeza, at my age you do not *go out* with someone.' This confused me. I thought she met him on the *Never Too Old* dating site. But if they're just friends then he isn't her boyfriend. And that's a shame because he makes her smilier.

When I asked Mum later, she laughed her head off. 'Of course they're going out with each other. They've been inseparable for months.' This confused me. Again. Grandma is giving out mixed messages. I hope *Willard* isn't confused and stays around. He'd make her visits to Applemere Bridge a lot more fun.

Thursday 4th August

I was supposed to be at Grandma's again but Mum let me go to Jenna's instead. It's safe to say that Mum is *frazzled*. She looks constantly sweaty even when it's not hot. Dad checked the weather forecast. It said it'd be dry overnight so he moved some boxes into the backyard. It gave us more space in the house but only a bit. I never thought we had that much stuff before, but we defo do.

Being with Jenna was happy and sad at the same time. It's my last day in Stockford. My last day with my friend. I love that I can email her now but it won't be the same as being together. We spent most of the time on her iPad where she showed me which apps to install. Dad tried to show me the other day but Jenna is better at knowing the stuff I am interested in. Also she hasn't got Spike trying to snatch it off her.

When it was time to go, I had a little cry. I think Jenna felt like she wanted to as well but she managed to control it. She fake-punched me on the arm and said, 'If you don't keep in touch, McAuliffe, I will hunt you down!' Then we gave each other a hug. Her dad said he'll sort something so that Jenna can visit one day. I know he means it now, but I can't help thinking that once I've gone, everyone will move on.

I'm in bed now. My bedroom is empty and we've an early start when the removal van arrives. Goodnight 620 Tyson Road. I have loved living in you.

Friday 5th August

Saturday 6th August

Sunday 7th August

Monday 8th August

It's late, I'm shattered, and it's the fourth night in my new home. It's called The Farmhouse. This makes it sound sweet and countrysidey. I'm not sure if that's true. Tomorrow, when I've had a sleep, I'll write about the last few days. All I know is, Stockford feels a million miles away.

Tuesday 9th August

It's freezing. Not outside - outside it's a summer's day - but inside, especially at night, it gets really cold. Mum said the first job is to sort the windows. (They got quotes before we even moved here. It's all booked.) I think there are a lot of jobs to be honest.

We got here on Friday. It took ages. When I asked Mum how long we'd been in the car, she said casually, 'Just a couple of hours', like it was nothing. But it felt like days. It rained the entire journey and I was squashed between Blane and Spike on the back seat. On my knees was a bin bag of dirty washing that hadn't made it to the removal van. This was my view for the entire way there.

Because I couldn't see much, arriving at the farmhouse was a surprise. When I say farmhouse, I don't mean it's an actual farm. It was once, but now it's just a house. The driveway was full of massive puddles. I walked as carefully as I could around the one by the front door, just in time for Spike to jump two feet first into the middle of it. Mum went mad. He'd splattered mud all over the door. We had to take our shoes off outside before we could step into the new house. Not the best start to an *adventure*, really. Not one bit.

More tomorrow. I'm going to get under the extra blankets and try to sleep.

Wednesday 10th August

The inside of the farmhouse is interesting. It's big. That's the first thing to say. The kitchen and lounge are open-plan in the centre of the house where there's room for a massive table. The one from Tyson Road is tiny in the middle. There's a real fireplace (although no one's worked out how to light it) and the lounge area has space for at least three sofas. All our furniture is there and there's still loads of room.

I'm sitting in my bedroom now. I don't need to be here to get away from everyone quite so much, because there's space downstairs but I'm going to try and describe it.

First the good stuff...

- It's twice the size of my old room.
- It has space for more than one bed (if Jenna came to stay).
- The window looks out onto fields.

Now the not so good stuff...

- It's freezing.
- It's dingy - the walls are painted grey!

- Even with all my stuff out, it still feels empty.
- I don't like being in here as much as I used to like being in my old room.

I need to stop thinking about my old room. I miss it.

Thursday 11th August

A few days ago Dad took us on a walk. It hadn't rained since we arrived but there were still puddles along the lane. Spike was warned not to mess about.

When you walk down the drive and out the gates, you turn left. This is a narrow lane with fields on either side. If you walk for ten minutes it gets wider and more buildings appear. I recognised them from my visit with Mum. We walked past the butchers (which we'll never go in) and went into the mini-supermarket. Dad bought bread and beans for tea and then we left. It wasn't anywhere near as big as the supermarkets at home but it had the basics.

It doesn't matter how long I live here, Stockford will always be home.

Friday 12th August

Applemere Bridge is really quiet. I knew it wouldn't be full of traffic, but I didn't realise how few people I'd see every day. The only time I've seen another human being is when we walked to the village. The man behind the till chatted to Dad about us moving to the farmhouse. He was friendly and smiley and said, 'Welcome to Applemere'. Other than him, there was no one.

Saturday 13th August

Mum asked me how I was today. I said, 'Fine' and left it at that. I don't feel fine. It's like we've gone on holiday to a place that isn't that good, where we have to stay forever.

Sunday 14th August

The last boxes have been unpacked. Everything's in place but it still feels bare. I decided to take control of the situation. As Mum and Dad were sitting at the table making *To Do* lists, I grabbed my chance. 'Can I paint my room yellow?' I asked. I tried to sound casual but I think it came out in a desperate way. I can't sleep in that grey room for much longer. I wake up feeling sad.

The good news is that Mum and Dad didn't even hesitate. 'Of course you can,' Mum said without looking up. I wondered if she'd misheard me, but she didn't because she said, 'I'll add it to the list.' Then Dad said, 'I'm going to B and Q in a bit if you want to come and choose your colour.'

I must have filled the room with my smile. A drive to a normal shop! Being able to choose my own bedroom paint! Not having to ask for months and months only to be told we've no money! The house move has turned Mum and Dad into parents like everyone else's. This is exactly what Meg's mum and dad would be like.

Monday 15th August

By the time me and Dad got back from B and Q, it was too late to start painting. (Everything is miles away when you're in the middle of nowhere). We *did* go past a chippy on the outskirts of Applemere though, so that was tea sorted.

In my head I'd decided yellow was the best colour. I needed something to cheer me up and make me feel sunny inside. But when I got there, there was so much to choose from. I spent ages in the paint aisle while Dad got the boring screws and handles he needed from the rest of the shop. In the end it came down to a sea-blue turquoise or a golden yellow. I really did love the blue one but after lots of thinking I decided to stick with my original plan.

I don't think Mum and Dad had planned to sort my walls out so soon - their *To Do* list is massive! - but because I had the paint, they said I could start today! This meant getting up very early, which was the hard bit. I had to move all my furniture into the middle of the room so Dad could cover it with a plastic sheet. I could move it all myself except for the wardrobe. Dad helped with that. Then he put tape around the doorframes to keep them clean. Once we were ready to start, he poured paint into the tray, gave me a roller and we got going.

At first it was really relaxing. I liked how easily the paint spread over the wall and how much space I could cover with just a few strokes. I could only reach half way up so I did as much as I could, while Dad did the taller bits. He also did the edges with a brush. By the end my arms were aching but it didn't take very long to do the first coat. When I stood back and looked at the room as a whole, it defo seemed a little brighter. It's patchy right now but the second coat's going on tomorrow. This means I have to sleep at the end of Mum and Dad's bed! I'm far too old to do that normally, but at least it will be warmer.

Tuesday 16th August

When I woke up the muscles in my arms were killing! I don't think I could ever be a painter. It's so hard to do a second coat when you've pushed yourself too far on the first one.

We had another early start but by lunchtime it was done. I think my achy arms weren't as good at being neat today so I ended up getting covered in yellow paint. By the time I went downstairs, I was ready to flop. I have to say I'm very proud of my (and Dad's) efforts. The yellow looks like a deep sunshine and it's made everything look better. Tomorrow I'm looking forward to waking up in a room that doesn't look like a prison cell.

The rest of the day was spent resting my sore, aching arms. Mum suggested I have a bath, but I'm not ready to deal with that yet. The bath is a big old tin. It's got stains around the inside of it and looks disgusting. Plus, there's no lock on the door. This isn't as much of a problem in the shower as there's a curtain all around. And when I'm on the loo I can put my legs out and block the door being opened (it's always Spike trying to get in) but in the bath I'm helpless.

It's OK though. I saw Dad buy a lock from B and Q the other day. It's on his list.

Wednesday 17th August

Today I had the best FaceTime with Jenna. I'd been holding off until I wasn't in a grey room (she'd have been worried for me) but now it's bright and sunny I can show her. We chatted for ages. It was so good to see her, even if she's miles away. I walked the iPad around the whole house. She agreed that my bedroom is the best part. I think she was impressed I'd done it myself.

Today Dad is helping Spike put shelves in his room. Mum has spent the day dealing with bathroom people who are giving us quotes. Soon we'll have windows with no draughts and a bath that isn't disgusting.

Thursday 18th August

Everything feels different from Stockford. In the holidays, me and the boys are off school so I usually find things to do that get me away from them all. I go to the library, or I go to Meg's or Jenna's, or I read on my own. Since moving, I've realised I've spent every single day with Spike, Blane and Kenny. Every. Single. Day.

There's nothing wrong with Spike, Blane and Kenny (except when Spike is trying to burst into the bathroom when I'm having a wee) but I'm not used to being with them constantly. I need to find things to do in Applemere that don't involve them. I spent the afternoon with the iPad trying to find local activities. I put *Applemere* into the search box and kept adding words after it. Applemere *Park*, Applemere *Library*, Applemere *Café*, Applemere *Pool*, Applemere *Children's Things...*

I gave up after a while. Nothing came up. In the end I asked Mum if I could go for a walk down the lane. She wasn't up for it at first. Then she remembered that there's nobody here and nothing to do. Also, I'll be getting the school bus from the village in a few weeks. She had to let me.

I wore my wellies - even though it hasn't rained since we've been here - and walked down the lane. It didn't take long to get to the first shop - the butchers. I went slowly so I could take everything in. I'd no money (obvs) so I couldn't go into anywhere. I just wanted to get the feel of the place. Once I'd walked to the end of the mini-supermarket, I turned around to go back.

That's when I heard a voice. 'Hello again!' it said. I'd been in a world of my own so it made me jump. The voice said, 'Sorry to scare you, come and get a lollipop.' I looked across at a man carrying crates into the shop. He was the old man behind the till the other day. I think I froze a bit. He's defo a stranger and I know not to talk to strangers. But he's also the man that chatted to Dad and was friendly. I smiled and said, 'Thank you, it's OK. I've no money.' (Also, I'm far too old for a lollipop, thank you very much.) I started to walk on but he said, 'Nonsense, you don't need money. Here you are.' He put the crates down, picked up a lolly from the counter and came back outside. I smiled again and took it, all the while remembering the stranger danger films from school. 'Tell your parents that if they need anything at all, come and see Tom. I'll sort them out. Food, drink, and anything else. It's good to welcome new faces to the village.' I smiled again, kept remembering to be alert inside, and finally said, 'Thank you, I will.' Then he was gone.

I need to find out if it's OK to speak to Tom. He seems nice, he has thick white hair like a grandad in a film, and he gave me a lollipop. He could be a baddie, though. In Stockford, you don't get shopkeepers giving their lollies away for nothing.

Friday 19th August

In all the excitement of yellow bedrooms and working out the local shopkeeper, I'd forgotten Grandma was coming to visit. This'd been planned before we even left and it's why Mum and Dad have been working extra hard at ticking off things from their *To Do* list. (The bathroom lock is still in the packet.)

We waited by the window to see her arrive. She hardly ever drives in Stockford because there're buses, but now she has no choice. It would take days to get here on the bus. When she drove through the gates we all cheered. It shows how much we've missed seeing people if we cheer when Grandma turns up. I don't mean that in a nasty way. It's just that we never cheered when she looked after us Monday to Friday.

As soon as she walked through the door, she said, 'My goodness Molly, you're the size of a house. How on earth do you stay upright?' Mum said, 'Cheers', under her breath and I saw Dad squeeze her arm, as Grandma's back was turned.

I could tell she was trying to be positive. She kept saying how much *potential* everything had. As I looked around with her, I tried to see it through her eyes. I knew deep down she'd be thinking it was terrible. Her house is so *finished*. I wonder what she'd have thought if she'd been with us on day one. Mum and Dad have crossed off loads from their *To Do* list. It's still scruffy but not as bad as it was.

Apart from the odd sarky comment from Grandma, it was a nice day. She had baked us a cake, which we had with cups of tea (I had juice). She also bought Spike's birthday present for next week. It got quickly hidden before he could start nagging to open it. Dad teased her about Willard the Tree. He asked why he hadn't come and she said, 'Sebastian, we are not joined at the hip.' Then Mum said, 'But is he still on the scene?' and Grandma said, 'If by *on the scene* you mean the occasional dinner date and a walk around the garden centre of a weekend, then I suppose so.' Mum and Dad started laughing. They love winding Grandma up. At least Willard's still around. He's lasted longer than any of her other men friends.

Grandma left in the evening to go to her hotel. She said at sixty-eight she's too old for an airbed. I think Mum and Dad were relieved. She'd have had lots to say about the breeze at night. We're going to her hotel for breakfast before she goes home. I'm very excited about a drive out of Applemere.

Saturday 20th August

Baked beans, veggie sausage, tomatoes, mushrooms, hash browns, fried eggs and toast! I LOVE hotel breakfasts.

Sunday 21st August

The sun has been shining for a few weeks now. We spent the day in the back garden trying to make it look less wild.

Me and Spike were on weed duty. This was a never-ending task. We had to decide to stop, rather than get to the end of it. Every so often Spike would pull out a ginormous weed and put it on his head like a ponytail. I guess he had to make it fun somehow. While we were doing that, Mum sat outside on a reclining chair reading a book called *Keeping Chickens for Dummies.* Whilst she was doing that, Dad was planting things in a big patch of soil. Every so often she'd look up and say, 'There's just no way, Mac. Sorry, but no.' I don't think we'll ever have chickens. As an on-and-off vegan there's no way she can work it.

I'm not getting excited but according to Dad we will have tomatoes, potatoes and a load of herbs in no time. We'll see.

Monday 22nd August

Mum and Dad started work today. Sort of. They set up an office in the empty room upstairs. It'll be their freelance Human Resources consultancy. They want people to pay them money so they can give them advice about their businesses. I don't really get it.

Once the desk area and filing cabinet were in place, they put up a wall calendar and said it was done. Dad laughed and said he could handle workdays like that more often. Mum said that as long as people pay at some point, it would all be fine.

I really hope they've thought this through.

Tuesday 23rd August

Since there's no rain at the moment, we're taking it in turns to water Dad's new plants. I don't think any of them will grow for real but I quite like using a watering can. It makes me feel like there's something to do. I've started to wish school would start to make things less boring.

Normally I love the school holidays and never want them to end. This time I feel like I've spent far too much time with the same people. We've been here less than three weeks but it feels like forever. Even though I'm nervous I need to see new faces.

Mum said I could walk to the village again. I thought she realised I was feeling trapped but actually she had a shopping list. I didn't mind one bit but I pretended I was doing her a favour. I had to buy a loaf of crusty bread, tomatoes, mozzarella and rosemary. This means tea will be posh cheese on toast. (The herbs make it posh.)

When I got to the mini-supermarket I looked for Tom, but he wasn't there. He's still a stranger but (so far) not a bad stranger. I found the things I needed and then waited at the till. Eventually a boy came out from the back. He saw me and said, 'Oh', and then scanned my stuff. I reckon he was a teenager. Not an adult, but older than me. He said, '£4.98', and I said, 'Here's £5'. Then he gave me 2p change. As I walked to the door he said, 'You the new girl at the farmhouse?' I nodded and then walked out. He wasn't as friendly as Tom - grumpy really. And he didn't give me a lollipop. (Not that I wanted one at my age.) On the plus side, I've seen another human being in this place.

I don't like being known as 'The New Girl at the Farmhouse'. It doesn't feel like me.

Wednesday 24th August

I've read my books, I watered the plants, I tidied my room (it didn't need it) and now I'm writing this in the afternoon because there is nothing else to do. I'm so bored.

Thursday 25th August

Spike is eight today. I'm sure it won't make a bit of difference to how childish he can be, but still - Happy Birthday Spike! He got a construction kit, (*another* one) some garden tools, and his own packets of herbs to plant. I think Mum and Dad are trying to steer him in the direction of gardening. He seemed quite excited though. I hope he uses the fork and trowel sensibly. In the wrong hands they could be weapons.

The kitchen is still not up to full working order. The grill and hob are OK but not the oven. We've been eating a lot of beans on toast and sandwiches. When Mum asked Spike what he wanted for his birthday tea, all he said was, 'A proper hot meal'. I thought he had no chance but I was wrong. Mum said we could go to the pub. I know! That never happens. It really was an excellent idea. Firstly, it felt amazing to be leaving the house together. Secondly, the pub is further on from the mini-supermarket - a bit of the village that I haven't walked to yet. Thirdly, it did really gorge food. I had sweet potato, lentil and spinach dhansak. It was the loveliest thing I've ever eaten. I wanted to hug Spike for making us all come out, but I didn't. That would be weird. We don't hug but I was really happy with him today.

It feels ages since I've smiled for real.

Friday 26th August

I'm learning more about the village. Since yesterday I know that past the mini-supermarket is the pub. It's called the Applemere Arms and it's on the opposite side of the road. Next to that is the village hall. It gets used for meetings and Christmas fairs. On the other side of that is the school that Spike and Blane will go to. (It's tiny!) I think the day Mum and me visited, Applemere was one big blur. I couldn't remember how it all fitted together until I saw yesterday.

When we were in the pub I saw Tom the Stranger. He was standing at the bar when we walked in. He said hello to Dad and met Mum for the first time. After we sat down, Mum said, 'What a nice man.' I think this means he's OK. Also, he's no longer a stranger. I'll be friendlier next time I see him. The pub wasn't busy but had a few people in that I've never seen. I asked Mum where they all lived and she said, 'Probably the houses in the village.' I asked, 'What houses?' She said, 'The ones in the village.' She didn't see how this wasn't making it clearer. Plus, she was rubbing her stomach and looking uncomfortable in the pub chair so I didn't go on. I had to ask Dad later. It turns out that if you walk past the mini-supermarket, pub, village hall and school, you get to houses that carry on along the road. It had started to feel like it was just us, Tom and the boy at the till.

I also found out that the boy is Tom's grandson. He said, 'My Jake is about your age. You'll see him around, no doubt.'

I just smiled and said, 'Yes, probably.' I didn't say I'd already met him and he wasn't that nice.

Saturday 27th August

It rained. Pasta and sauce for tea.

Sunday 28th August

Mum called a Family Meeting. I'd forgotten about having them. They feel like they belong to a different person's life.

We sat round the kitchen table at three. Something about doing that made me feel a little bit happier. It was familiar. Like old times.

Mum said she wanted to keep us in the loop about what was happening. I had an awful feeling it was going to be another huge announcement about something terrible. *We've changed our minds and decided we're going to live on the moon.* It turned out she was telling us about the house renovations. Tomorrow the windows are starting. There was a cheer from Spike when she said that. (He's been sleeping in a woolly hat since we got here.) She also said that a new oven had been ordered and would be here soon. I cheered about that. Our meals have been basic. I can't wait for Friday Fooday to start again. It was the highlight of my week.

The other things that are happening will be a few weeks away, but they include a new bath, new curtains for the main windows, and the fireplace in the lounge being cleaned out. Then it will work. Right now it is blocked and filthy.

Dad asked if we'd any questions. I hadn't really. I had a lot of *comments* but there's no point making them. For now, I'm just happy that the house will soon be warmer.

Monday 29th August

All the windows have been taken out and it's freezing - even worse than at night! There're sheets on the floor where glass has landed, and a lot of banging. Dave and Billy are the window men. They're loud and they have a radio. It doesn't matter what the song is, Billy sings along to it. He isn't even a good singer. I think he'll drive me mad before the windows are finished.

Mum lay on the bed most of the day. I asked her if she wanted me to get anything from the shop and she said, 'Yes, can you get me a muzzle for Billy and a clock so they get a blasted move on.' She was quite angry but then smiled and said, 'No thanks. Enjoy the peaceful walk.'

Mum is due soon. I've no idea where the hospital is. I only hope they have looked it up. When Mum went into labour with Kenny, she was in the car on her way home from Grandma's. She ended up turning round and driving herself to hospital. I don't think it'll be that simple this time. She's going to have a long journey, wherever it is.

<u>Tuesday 30th August</u>

Billy is still winning the 'Loudest Man in the World' competition but the downstairs windows have been done. Once the curtains are up it'll start to feel like a real place to live. Hopefully.

When I walked into the village yesterday, I saw Tom's grandson, Jake. He was on his bike, wheelie-ing up and down. He didn't smile but nodded at me. I nodded back but I automatically smiled too. Then I felt stupid because he didn't do it back. So then I stopped. I know that isn't real news but not much happens here.

<u>Wednesday 31st August</u>

Mum and Dad have a client! It's Gina, Mum's mate from University. She isn't hiring them because she feels sorry for them (I asked them that) but she needs a new HR person because her other one has gone on maternity leave. I didn't bother pointing out that Mum is also about to go on maternity leave. They were too excited. Gina has something to do with ethical skincare.

Mum spent the day lying on the bed, reading things out to Dad who typed up what she said. They both seemed happy. I wonder if they're happy for real, or fake-happy like I am. I wonder if they're enjoying the 'adventure' they wanted for us all. I wonder when I'll stop missing Stockford.

* * *

9.

Harvest Time...In More Ways Than One

Thursday 1st September

Two more weekdays before I start my new school. I thought I'd be nervous but I'm *so* ready to have something to do. Dad drove me along the bus route so I'd know where I'm going. It isn't that far but it feels weird to know I can't walk home if I want to. Not that I would walk out of school, but I'd like to think I could if I had to. If there was a bad guy chasing everyone. Or a big fire.

My uniform's been hanging in my wardrobe since we got here. I tried it on today, in case I'd shrunk or grown. I have not. It looks fine. I call it reddy-brown but Mum calls it maroon. Stockford's is grey. I prefer grey. (But not on my walls.)

I've had loads of messages from Jenna since I've been here. She sent me a bunch of pictures the other day - photos of herself making silly faces. They were ace. It was brill to laugh properly.

Friday 2nd September

I spent this morning watching Blane ride his bike. He still has stabilisers. I dragged a kitchen chair to the front of the house and day dreamed while he pedalled.

I didn't spot Jake from the mini-supermarket. Not at first. He was on his bike, cycling up and down the lane. He'd gone past the drive a few times before I realised it was him. Then he shouted, 'What's your name, new girl?' I didn't like the way he spoke to me - sort of cocky and rude all at once. I pretended I hadn't heard. He shouted again so I ignored him again. When he did it a third time, Blane shouted back, 'It's Leeza but Spike calls her Loozer.' Jake laughed and rode away.

I sat there feeling annoyed at everyone.

Saturday 3rd September

It's the first full day of windows! It makes such a difference to have a draught-free bedroom. Spike said he'd still sleep in his bobble hat though.

The other good news is we now have a lock on the bathroom door. Mum did it today when she couldn't sit comfortably any more. I think she hates being pregnant. Every time I see her she looks fed up but then puts on a smile when she notices me watching. I can't be fooled.

Sunday 4th September

I left my uniform on the back of the door last night so it was ready as soon as I got up. I decided to wear my birthday crop top underneath (because I'm in high school now) as well as black socks. No one will see my socks so I just picked the first clean pair I found.

I wonder who'll be in my class. I wonder where all my lessons will be. At the Stockford High taster day, I got lost a few times finding my way around the building. I know the school is smaller but I've only seen a bit of it. I wonder if lots of children from the village will be there. Everything will become clear tomorrow.

Monday 5th September

How can five classrooms be an entire high school?

Tuesday 6th September

No really. I mean it. How can five classrooms be an entire high school? I thought it'd be the same as Stockford High just with more countryside. But it's smaller than Irwell Green! I'm confused.

I got the bus outside the mini-supermarket at 8.34am. It stops at Applemere before picking up at some other villages too. I was the only person at the bus stop right up till the bus arrived. Then, at the last minute, Tom's grandson, Jake ran out from nowhere and jumped on with me. I didn't pay him much attention. I was too busy trying to show my pass and find a safe seat.

When we arrived, I followed everyone into the building. The new Year Sevens were directed straight to the hall to meet our form tutor. That's when I started to realise things were different. It turns out I'd seen it all on the visit with Mum. I'd assumed it was only a tiny bit at the time. Also, there were ten Year Sevens. Just *ten*. I mean, whaaaat?

Miss Wilkinson took us to our form room. I met her on the visit. She's in charge of Year Seven and Eight. Both year groups are taught together. As she led us into the classroom, the Year Eights were already there - including Jake! I must've stared a bit because he looked at me and said, 'All right Loozer?' and then laughed. There were about twenty-five people in the room. I thought back to the taster day at Stockford High and how there were nearly two hundred of us.

Jenna would find this unbelievable.

Wednesday 7th September

I'm still getting my head around the smallness of everything. The bus has been OK so far. I sit on my own. That's fine, and there are loads of empty seats anyway. It takes twenty minutes to get to school. I see a lot of sheep on the journey.

I've found out some things about Jake.

1. He's called Jake Woolton.
2. He lives with Tom in the village.
3. He's already thirteen - his birthday was last week.
4. He's the most annoying boy I've ever met.

Even though we've different work, he still tries to copy what I'm writing. He'd be in a completely different classroom at Stockford but I'm stuck with him here. When he called me Loozer for the fiftieth time today, I snapped and called him Joke (instead of Jake) 'because you think you're so funny'. It wasn't the best comeback but it showed I won't put up with his teasing. Even Spike gets bored of it after a bit and he's a kid.

Thursday 8th September

Work wise, school isn't too hard. That was one of my worries about moving into Year Seven. When I think back to all the pressure of the SATs it's a complete change - much more relaxed. I don't know if all Year Seven is like that, or just this school. I'll ask Jenna. She'll have been back since Monday too.

So far, Miss Wilkinson has given us some assessments to see where we're up to. They weren't like proper exams so it was OK. Because we're doing different things most of the time, it takes longer to get organised. I think I'm getting into the swing of it. The rest of the class seem fine. I haven't spoken to anyone much because they all seem to have friends already. But it's fine. I'm still settling in, so I don't have the energy to be chatty too.

This afternoon all of Year Seven and Eight (or Class One as we're known) were together for the same activity. It was to research and write about Harvest festivals. I remember the Harvest festival from Stockford every year. We'd be asked to donate a tin from the cupboard for the old people. One year I was mortified because the fruit cocktail Dad handed me that morning had a use-by date from three years before. None of us like fruit cocktail so it'd been left.

It was interesting to hear how the middle of nowhere celebrates Harvest time. It seems a much bigger deal than finding an in-date tin of fruit. The whole of next week will be full of events. I told Mum and Dad about it while we had tea. Then Spike piped up that he'd been learning about it in his school too. (Blane and Spike's primary school only has two rooms! Can you even imagine?)

I feel stupid when I think of how little I understood about everything here.

Friday 9th September

The baby is due today! Mum didn't seem to care about that when she was standing on a stepladder, hanging the new curtains.

Saturday 10th September

It's Jenna's birthday on Monday so I walked down the lane to post her card. Jake was wheelie-ing up and down outside his shop. He said, 'All right Loozer,' and I said, 'All right Joke,' and then he rode away. When I was on my way back, he rode over to me and said, 'What're you doing?' and I said, 'I'm walking home.' Then he said, 'Are you coming to the Harvest night on Friday?' and I said, 'I don't know.' Then he said, 'You should, it's fun.' And that was it.

I wish he wouldn't call me Loozer.

I can't remember what the Harvest night is. I read loads of different things when I was researching the other day. I know we start the week with a special assembly. Not that it'll feel like an assembly when there's only about fifty of us in the whole school.

Sunday 11th September

Mum's still pregnant. All my brothers were born late. Spike was the latest, arriving eleven days after he was due. This sums up his entire attitude to life. Needless to say, I was two days early.

Monday 12th September

Jenna is twelve today! We sent each other messages before school. I miss her loads. I need someone to make me laugh like she used to.

We started our Harvest themed week in school. Class One got to spend the afternoon outside in the school allotment and pick what we could.

The allotment was on the back-field. When we got there, Jake pulled my arm and said, ‘Look Loozer, this is where I planted my stuff.’ His section had all kinds of stalks and leaves coming out of it. He grabbed a trowel and started to dig. Almost straight away, he had a handful of potatoes. I think I must have looked surprised because he glared at me and snapped, ‘Don’t just stand there, give me a hand.’

After about twenty minutes we had a plastic tub full of them. I don’t think I’ve ever seen real grown vegetables before. I mean, I know they’ve all grown at some point, but by the time they’re near me they’re in a plastic bag. It was quite an eye opener.

Maybe this means Dad’s plants will work too. Possibly.

<u>Tuesday 13th September</u>

The school hall is full of vegetables. At least that’s how it looks when you walk in. There were about twenty adults sorting them out into wooden crates. Miss Wilkinson said they were volunteers from the local villages. I got a bit of a surprise halfway though the morning. I heard loud talking coming from outside and when I looked up it was Billy the window man! Apparently his daughter is in Class Three. I heard him shout, 'Seven hampers to Sunset Court, yeah?' before carrying a load of stuff to his van. Everyone was busy and we were put to work carrying and fetching things for the adults. I stood next to a lady called Doris, who looked kind. She made me hold my finger in the middle of the bows she was tying, to keep them tight as she did them. She said I was very helpful.

Over tea, Dad said he'd seen a poster in the village about Friday night. He said we should all go and experience a real Harvest festival for our first Applemere soirée. I don't know what a soirée is, and I'm not entirely sure Dad does either. But it's something to do. Friday Fooday hasn't happened for ages. I think it's because we have no proper kitchen facilities. Also Mum is too fat.

Wednesday 14th September

It was another day of harvest helping. The whole school are involved - all fifty-odd of us. Jake said that once this week is over, we don't mix again till Christmas. I don't mind either way. The older ones don't talk to the younger ones even when we're in the same room. They're probably worrying about their GCSEs and their periods all the time.

We had registration and then got sent to the hall. I've realised that during community events, the school children are used as slave labour. There's no end of jobs to do. Doris nabbed me again. She said I was a hard worker. Jake ended up with his grandad, who'd come to help. Tom joked saying, 'I'm the only one that'll put up with you,' as he ruffled his hair. Jake said, 'Geddoff', but laughed as he did. I haven't seen Jake laugh at anything, apart from calling me 'Loozer'.

By home time I had helped to sort the final vegetables into crates, label them with the right addresses, tick off the addresses on Doris' list and then carry twenty bottles of homemade wine to the back of Billy's van. Tom made a funny joke while I was doing that. He said, 'Those'll do me, but what about the wine for everyone else.' Doris laughed and Jake rolled his eyes. I also laughed. It wasn't that funny, but it felt like we all shared a little moment. Then Miss Wilkinson came over with a boy called James. For a moment, James and Miss Wilkinson didn't know what we were laughing at and it felt like we had a private joke.

I didn't mean for James to feel left out. I wasn't trying to be mean. But seeing someone else as an outsider, even for a minute, felt nice. I was in on the joke. I've been the outsider since I arrived here. I'd forgotten how good it felt to be part of something.

James didn't care one bit. He dragged Jake off to help him carry boxes and I was left with Doris and Tom, wiping down folding chairs with a sponge. For a whole hour! Grandma would've been proud of me.

Thursday 15th September

Today is the official start of Applemere Bridge's Harvest festival celebrations. I've been so busy thinking about food parcels and sticky address labels in school, that I forgot that my own village is where it's all happening.

When I got off the bus, the village had been transformed. There were stalls and tables selling different types of food. There was a marquee on the field behind the village hall, and the pub had opened a bar outside the front door. Tom had said it started today but I didn't realise how big it would be until I saw it for real.

I told Mum and Dad when I got home, but they said they'd wait for tomorrow night. Mum was lying down and Dad was filling a hot water bottle for her back. They had their hands full. As I was leaving the room, Dad said, 'But you can have a wander down, Leez. Can't she Moll?' Mum groaned but in a positive way, which we all took to be a yes.

After tea, I walked down the lane. As soon as I'd left the front door I could hear the music and the buzz of voices. By the time I'd got to the mini-supermarket, there were loads of people standing around. Lots of them had drinks and the air smelt of toffee apples and cooking. I didn't have any money (as usual) but being there was exciting enough. There were so many things to see - fresh bread, cider, cheese, punch, sausage rolls, pies, jars of pickled vegetables - it was like the Farmers' Market in Stockford except everyone knew each other.

Tom was standing outside the pub with a plastic glass of beer. He was chatting to some other men. He waved when he saw me and raised his glass in the air. It felt like when we'd had the private joke in school. Like someone here saw me as being part of it all. It made me tingle, and feel happy and sad all at once.

I'd been there for ten minutes when I saw Jake. He was standing by the traditional sweet stall. 'All right, Loozer,' he shouted. I pulled a face. I will never forgive Blane for telling him that was my name. 'All right Joke,' I replied. (I know 'Joke' isn't that funny but I have to do something to feel in control when he starts.) Then he said, 'I've been trying to get Mum to give me free samples. She will if you ask her.'

Jake has a Mum! All I knew was that he lived with his grandad. I looked at the woman behind the stall. Jake's mum was quite young. Younger than Mum anyway. She had short black hair, a pierced nose, and a big tattoo on her arm that looked like a bird with massive wings flying out of a fire. She gave me a big smile and said, 'Leeza, it's great to meet you. My dad says you've moved into the old farmhouse?' I smiled back. It was weird because she was talking at me like she knew me and I'd only just found out she existed. I said, 'Yes, we've been there six weeks now.' She smiled and said, 'I bet it feels strange after coming all the way from a city. A bit of a difference isn't it?' And all at once I felt like I was going to cry. I wanted to say, '*Yes it's a massive difference. I don't know whether I'm coming or going. I feel lonely. I feel miles away from the people I know and the things I recognise. People are friendly but it's like I'm watching them through a screen and their friendliness can't get through to me properly. I miss home so much. Everything is rubbish. Everything feels wrong. I miss my old life. I miss feeling like me. I wish I was back in Stockford. Nothing feels right anymore.*' Instead I swallowed down the lump in my throat, forced a smile, and said, 'Yeah, it's a bit different'.

As I headed home, Tom shouted after me, 'Don't forget to bring the family tomorrow night. It all kicks off on the Friday night, Leeza.'

Friday 16th September

As Dad said later, 'Tom really knew what he was talking about.'

I'd told Dad what Tom had said when I got in last night. I said we should go down to see the village because it'd been a really good atmosphere (before I got emotional on Jake's mum). So after another memorable (sarcasm!) meal of tinned tomatoes, chickpeas and wilted spinach on toast, we walked down the lane with Kenny in the pushchair. Mum joked that she should swap places with him. We *did* have to walk very slowly to stay at her speed. Luckily it's not a long road and eventually we got there. It was just the same as last night except it was busier. I asked Dad where all the people lived - there aren't *that* many houses on the other side of the village - but he said it was advertised in other villages nearby. People travelled to it every year. I don't think I believed him. Why would anyone travel to

Applemere? (But then the next obvious question is, '*Why would anyone move to Applemere?*' Exactly.)

Everything was going well at first. Spike had spotted a kid from his class so he'd gone off to play. Someone had given Blane a balloon, so he was holding that with one hand and the handle of the pushchair with the other. Kenny was asleep and oblivious to everything. Mum and Dad were walking slowly. Then it happened.

I didn't realise at first. I was watching Blane's balloon bob in the air. Then I heard Dad say to me, 'Watch the pushchair will you. We're just going over here.' I nodded and kept walking. I was even slower now I had Kenny and Blane in convoy. We pottered along, past the pie stall and towards the traditional sweets. At that point I stopped and looked back. That's when I realised that something was happening.

Tom was running. Not fast but quicker than a walk. I saw him make signs at another man to help him. That other man ran to Tom, listened to what he said, then turned and legged it past me, and up to Jake's mum on the sweet stall. I saw him say something to her, her eyes went wide, and then she hurried off too. They both headed towards the village hall. Everyone else was carrying on chatting so I kept walking. I didn't think anything more about it. I looked at the balloon, checked Kenny was still asleep, and wondered if Mum and Dad had bought any spending money for us. Then Jake ran over. He didn't say 'Hi' or make a stupid joke. In fact he looked deadly serious. He just came out with it. 'Loozer, your Mum is having a baby.'

I wanted to say, 'Duh, of *course* she's having a baby,' but then I realised what he meant. She was having it now! I just said, 'Oh. Right then.' I mean, what else could I say? Jake continued. 'They've rung an ambulance but it's going to take ages. Billy's on standby with his van and my mum's with her because she's a nurse. I'll take you now.' And with that, he pushed through the crowd, letting me, Blane, and Kenny follow behind in the gap he made.

Mum and Dad were sitting on a hay bale in the village hall. Mum was doing deep breathing and Dad was rubbing her back. I was relieved to see she was fully clothed. I'd worried she might be at the pushing and screaming stage and I wasn't sure me and Jake needed to see that. They both smiled as we walked in. Dad immediately jumped up and gave me a hug then said, 'Leeza, everything is under control. You're not to worry about a thing.' Obvs this made me worry a million times more. Mum looked up, and said, 'It's fine Leeza. Cait's a nurse and I've done this loads of times. We'll be grand.' It turns out Cait is Jake's mum. She said, 'Josie the doctor's here somewhere. She'll be able to provide some pain relief when my dad finds her.' (I could see Mum give a grateful smile at that. For all her talk about peppermint tea being better than Rennies, she's always happy to take the drugs for childbirth.) Eventually I found my voice. 'What shall I do?' I said. Dad thought I meant '*How can I help?*' when I actually meant, '*What about me in all this madness?*' He said, 'Keep an eye on your brothers and enjoy the evening. We'll be in here until the ambulance arrives.' Mum nodded in agreement. 'I am NOT giving birth in Billy's van.' And with that she carried on breathing and Dad carried on rubbing her back. Jake led me outside and we all sat on the village hall steps. Jake gave Blane a sweet out of his pocket, and a bit later Doris bought us over some juice and cake. I think I was in a bit of a daze.

Josie the doctor arrived at some point. She had a bag with her, so I'm guessing it was full of drugs. Cait came out a couple of times to see if we were OK, which I suppose we were. Jake was still there. He kept Blane entertained. He showed him how to pretend his finger had been cut off, by bending it over. Blane loved it although it seemed pretty silly to me. Spike ran over at one point and said, 'Is it true that there's loads of blood?' I told him it wasn't true in the slightest, so he ran back to his school mate feeling disappointed.

Time dragged. It was dark and most of the crowds had gone. Jake said the Friday night of the Harvest festival ends when the last person leaves. He said it usually means that his grandad and his mates are still sitting on hay bales when the sun comes up. It was at this point I asked him what time it was. Midnight.

I remember asking about the ambulance. There'd been an emergency in Carlisle and it had gone there first. With Josie, Cait and Mum an expert in labour, they'd been given support down the phone and left until further notice. My mum still refused to get into Billy's van.

Blane fell asleep against my shoulder. There wasn't much else to do. Jake stayed with us, looking tired. I felt sorry for him. He said that there was no point going home on his own. His mum and grandad wouldn't be leaving until the ambulance arrived. Or the baby.

And so it happened. At 3.55am the baby was born. Dad came out of the hall. He looked shattered but he was smiling. In his arms was a little bundle, wrapped in an Applemere Bridge Harvest Festival bag for life. 'It's a girl', he shouted. Everyone cheered. Tom clapped and whooped. Doris gasped and cried. Billy and his mates started singing. I smiled I think. I felt relieved. I mouthed, *'Is Mum OK?'* at Dad, who nodded back. More relief. Childbirth is like a horror film. I was doing my best to ignore the mess on Dad's top as I smiled at the news that everyone was all right.

I looked at the little crowd. Everyone was smiling, everyone had hung around to make sure we were looked after. Even Jake had kept Blane amused. The lanterns and fairy lights flickered on people's faces and made it look magical. I suppose it was magical when you think about it. I had a sister. A tiny baby sister.

And the best part was, now we'd moved, I wouldn't have to share my room.

Saturday 17th September

Everyone is exhausted. Mum and The New Baby finally made it to hospital, but came home a few hours later. Dad has slept most of the day and Doris came round with leftovers from the cake stall. No one bothered with tea. We went straight for the cake.

Sunday 18th September

Every time I walk into the hallway, there's another bunch of envelopes on the mat. It seems everyone at the festival has posted a congratulations card. People are very nice. I FaceTimed Jenna and held the screen over The New Baby's cot. She was sleeping. (The New Baby, not Jenna.) Jenna thought the birth story was the funniest thing she'd ever heard. She wouldn't think that if she'd been sitting outside till all hours. She wouldn't think that for one second.

Grandma arrived this afternoon. We heard the gravel crunch as the tyres rolled over it. The first thing she said was, 'To think my fifth grandchild had to enter this world on the floor of a village hall! What will I tell them at Zumba?'

Grandma does Zumba now.

Monday 19th September

News travels fast. The fact that Mum gave birth at the Harvest festival was the talk of Class One. Miss Wilkinson said, 'Your mum deserves a medal.' James asked me what the baby was like. Owen, who I've never spoken to before, asked me if anyone had fainted. It was like being a celebrity.

The one thing they all want to know is something Grandma keeps asking. 'Molly, will you stop shilly-shallying and give my granddaughter a name!' That's not what they say at school, obvs, but they do keep asking what she's called. I don't even know what was on the shortlist. I'm not sure Mum and Dad got round to discussing it. By the time you get to child number five, it isn't a pressing issue.

I'm Liesl from *The Sound of Music*. Spike is Spike from *Press Gang*. (Some TV show Mum loved.) Blane is Blane from *Pretty in Pink* and Kenny is Kenny from Kendal - where Mum and Dad went on holiday for a long weekend the year before he was born. (We stayed with Grandma. It *was* a long weekend as I remember. There were chores.)

Tuesday 20th September

Grandma went home today. She said to Mum, 'I'd been hoping to be told in person what the name would be, but if you're playing silly beggars with my granddaughter's identity, then so be it.'

I don't think Mum and Dad are playing silly beggars, whatever that means. I think they're just shattered. So far, they're sleeping as much as The New Baby.

Wednesday 21st September

Jake sat on the bench with me at break. He joked, 'It's just like the other night except no one's having a baby inside.' I smiled. The other night feels like it happened to someone else. Now that the cycle of dirty nappies, crying, sick and sleep has begun, everything in the house has fallen in line with the routine. Not a routine that suits anyone except The New Baby, but still a routine. We all recognise it from when Kenny was born.

In some ways, having The New Baby has made everything feel familiar again. It's like old times. Just old times in a big farmhouse that still hasn't got a proper bath.

Thursday 22nd September

It was announced at breakfast time.

'We've got it,' Mum said. 'Do you want to know?' She didn't need to explain any more. We were all waiting. Calling her The New Baby didn't seem fair now she was coming up to a week old.

Dad kept making toast, as Mum stood up from her seat. She picked up The New Baby, held her out in front of her and said, 'Ladies and Gentleman, let me introduce you to the newest member of our family, Harvest Sky McAuliffe.'

There was a silence. Then Spike said, 'You what?' I think he spoke for us all, to be honest. Mum carried on. 'This is Harvest Sky. We'll call her Harvest. Or Harvey if you like.' Spike piped up again. 'Harvey's a boy's name.' Mum replied, 'Well if we call our little girl Harvey, then it's a girl's name isn't it.'

I hadn't said anything but I obvs looked less enthusiastic than I was supposed to. Mum spoke firmly. 'Kids, she was born at a Harvest festival. It was either going to be Harvest, Festival or Cheese Stand. I personally think Harvest is the best choice.' She had a point. And it's quite a nice idea really.

Except most people are born in hospitals and you'd never think to call them *Ward Nine* would you? I ate my toast and didn't worry too much about it.

One thing did make me smile. Grandma was going to hate it.

Friday 23rd September

Something we can say about Harvest...she's not shy at making her feelings known. There's been a lot of crying so far. I did my homework straight after tea because she was asleep. If I leave it till tomorrow it's a massive gamble that there'll be quiet.

Saturday 24th September

Grandma came back. The best bit was, she bought Willard! When we saw them pull onto the drive, Spike shouted, 'Yesssssss', and got Blane in an excited headlock. We all perked up. This was quite impressive seeing as we were awake with Harvest's crying most of the night.

I tried to spot Grandma's reaction to the name *Harvest*, but she managed to cover any irritations she had. She held her for ages but was smiling the whole time. No comments or anything. (I bet she had loads in her head though.) Willard was funny. He gave Mum a big hug and said, 'You're a trooper Molly,' but then Mum had to disentangle herself because milk was leaking on her top. Willard laughed, said, 'Oops, my fault', and then backed away quickly. It made us all laugh. Mum's been leaking milk for days now. We're used to it.

Because we had visitors, Dad said we should go out for tea. We all cheered at that. When we walked into the pub, loads of people spotted us and came to say hello. I didn't know most of them but they all knew us. One man clapped Dad on the back and bought him a pint of beer. The lady behind the bar told Mum her drinks were on the house all night. Even Billy came over. All he said was, 'I'm just relieved we didn't have to use my van', and then he went back to his table. Grandma's face was a classic. Proper surprised. 'It's like you're famous,' she kept saying. Mum half smiled. 'You try keeping your anonymity when you've given birth on a pile of hay', she replied.

Sunday 25th September

Grandma and Willard stayed at their hotel last night but came round this morning for breakfast. Willard was so much fun. Spike took him outside to show him the area of the garden he keeps digging up. It's meant to be his allotment, but he just hacks into the soil and moves it around. Willard was soon stuck in and covered in mud, while Spike grinned a lot. Usually it's because someone has made a smell or fallen over. This was good smiling - smiling at something positive. If you can call digging into a piece of garden for no reason positive, I suppose.

By the time they went home, Willard had taught Blane a magic trick (how to pull a coin from a person's ear), he'd lifted Kenny up to the ceiling over and over (because Kenny kept saying, 'Again, again!') and he bounced Harvest on his knee until she stopped crying and went to sleep. He's like a superhero - he knows exactly what to do for everyone. As for me? He lent me a book! He said, 'Leeza, I've no idea what you'll think of this, but you might like it. It's about a boy who is fed up with all the adults in his life.' It was called *Catcher in the Rye* and was written the year he was born. 'You might hate it so let me know, I'm really interested in what you think.'

Blimey, Willard the Tree is gooooood.

<u>Monday 26th September</u>

Jake sat behind me on the bus. He leaned forward onto my seat and said, 'So, how's Harvey?' He's the only person that's called her that so far, even though Mum said it was one of our options. I said, 'She's fine. She came out for tea with us on Saturday.' Jake said 'I know. Grandad said. She was the talk of the pub. Mum said, tell your mum she should come over for a cup of tea soon.' And then he leaned back on his own seat and we carried on to school.

<u>Tuesday 27th September</u>

I told Mum about going for a cup of tea with Cait. Mum replied, 'You know what, I think that'd be lots of fun.' Next thing I know she's writing her phone number down for me to pass on to Jake to give to Cait. I think technology was created to stop having to use paper and pens to pass on numbers, but I didn't say anything.

Tea was aubergine curry and cauliflower rice. Not as nice as the pub curry but not bad.

Wednesday 28th September

When I got back from school, Dad was coming down the stairs cheering. He grabbed my hand from the front door and pulled me into the lounge where Mum was feeding Harvest. 'Ladies, I have great news!' Mum looked doubtful and I think I probably did too. He carried on. 'We've just had an email from Gina. We have received our first payment!' I think my face still remained blank but Mum's changed into a big smile. 'Nooooo. We've been paid? You mean, Hart and McAuliffe Business Consultancy has made some money? Woohoooo!!!!' Mum stood up and carefully put Harvest in her chair before throwing herself on Dad. Yuck. I think it was just hugging but I still didn't need to see that.

I'm pleased for them. But honestly, I think they might need to calm down a bit. They were never like this on payday in Stockford.

Thursday 29th September

Mum was still in a good mood today. I said, 'You're happy,' as I ate my breakfast. She said, 'Leeza, it's a beautiful autumnal morning, I'm full of good hormones, and Hart and McAuliffe are going places.'

I nodded and let her get on with it.

Friday 30th September

Great news! An oven's been ordered. It's fair to say, whilst we haven't starved, our meals have been *dull.* I said, 'Does this mean we can have Friday Fooday again. Dad said, 'That is most definitely the plan, Leeza.' Then Spike said, 'Does this mean we can have roast beef and Yorkshire puddings?' Dad said, 'That is most definitely *not* the plan, Spike.' And then laughed. 'Nice try,' he said.

Dad used to eat meat before he married Mum. I wonder if he misses it. As I thought that, I had a sudden flashback to the ham sandwich Jenna's dad gave me that time. I'm a little bit nearer eighteen now, so the time I can choose is getting closer.

In other news, *Catcher in the Rye* is weird but good. I've no idea what's going on, but I like how the author writes the words like someone is talking. Not formal and boring, but sort of... relaxed. It's hard to describe. I love how Willard thought I might like it because it's really hard. He must think I'm like a teenager, which I nearly am.

10.

More Drama

Saturday 1st October

Mum got dressed up tonight. She still wore leggings and a top, but added earrings, lipstick and perfume. Dad told her she looked beautiful and she smiled and said, 'Mac, I look like the back end of a bus.' But she defo looked better than she's done for a while. As Grandma would say, '*Pyjamas do favours for nobody*.'

Mum was going out with Cait. They were going to go to the pub and then back to Cait's if Mum found the pub chairs too hard. (She's still getting over having Harvest. I can't handle all the grisly details.) Mum isn't breastfeeding Harvest anymore. She did for a bit but it wasn't really working. I heard her telling Grandma that when she was here.

I'm writing this at nearly midnight and she's still not back. Grandma would say, 'Molly, you're a dirty stop-out!' I *do* enjoy imagining what Grandma would say. It always cheers me up.

Sunday 2nd October

I came down to find Mum on the sofa, drinking a glass of Berocca. She has that when she's got a hangover. I smiled and said, 'Good night?' in a sarky but funny way. Mum smiled through her headache. 'Leeza McAuliffe, it won't be long before I'll be saying the same to you, now give over.' The rest of the day was a duvet and film day.

Tea was veggie sausages, mashed potato and gravy. Mum needed the stodge.

Monday 3rd October

Jake spent the bus ride leaning forward onto the back of my seat and reporting back. Apparently Mum and Cait came back to his house after their meal and then drank lots of wine. Mum kept saying, 'I'm owed nine months of alcohol,' every time her glass was filled.

I wasn't sure whether I should feel embarrassed or not. My parents are always a bit embarrassing no matter what they do. In the end I said, 'Sorry if she made a show of herself'. I wanted him to know she wasn't always like that. He shrugged and said, 'It was better than the telly.' Then added, 'It was nice to see Mum with a friend'. Then he sat back on his seat and didn't say anything else.

I'm never sure whether he's normal, or whether he puts on a normal act and deep down he's Spike.

Tuesday 4th October

Mum got a text from Grandma. She read it to Dad as I was getting ready. It said, 'I could see you were struggling last week so I've booked a few days at the hotel. I'll help around the house - it'll give you time to run a comb through your hair. Don't thank me, it's my pleasure. See you tomorrow.'

Neither of them said anything for a second. Then Mum said, 'Cheeky cow.' I'm not sure I was supposed to hear that.

Wednesday 5th October

Grandma was here when I got back from school. I'd say the atmosphere was tense. She had a bowl of water and was scrubbing the window frames. The *new* window frames. I'm not the tidiest person in the world but even I could see that was a complete waste of time. Mum was holding Harvest, looking annoyed.

I went to my room and had another bash at *Catcher in the Rye*. If only Willard were here. He'd be impressed with how I'm keeping going with a hard book. He'd also be chilling out Grandma.

Thursday 6th October

When I got in, Grandma was ironing a pile of tea towels and sheets. Who cares if tea towels have creases? Who actually cares?

I heard Mum say, 'You really don't need to do that,' but Grandma said, 'I won't have my family live like ruffians.' I don't know what a ruffian is, but I guess it's not a good thing. Mum took a deep breath and went to check on Harvest. I think she's keeping a lot of her thoughts to herself at the moment. Maybe she needs her own diary?

Friday 7th October

It all kicked off today. Grandma turned up from her hotel before I'd even left for school. She marched in and said, 'Today is the day we polish!' Mum was standing at the sink. I watched her turn round and say, 'What exactly do you think we have that needs polishing, Ma?' Grandma was already rolling up her sleeves, as if there were a mountain of things to polish right there in front of her. She didn't even stop or look up. She said, 'Oh Molly. Everything! Shoes, silver, wooden surfaces, all kinds of things.'

Mum did a little laugh to herself. Except it wasn't the kind of laugh when something's funny. It was an *angry* laugh. She took a breath and then went for it.

It was mostly shouting. Mum kept saying, 'Who do you think you are?' over and over again. Grandma kept saying, 'I only want to help,' and also, 'You need some help, look at the state of the place', which didn't help matters. Dad came in after a few minutes and guided me out of the room. I could still hear them though. I sat on the stairs with Dad as we listened. At one point he said, 'Best let them get it out of their system.' And that was it.

By the time Mum had got it out of *her* system, she'd told Grandma to go back to the hotel, pack her things and go home. And by the time Grandma had got it out of *her* system, she'd told Mum she was making a fool of herself by thinking that running away from all she knew was going to make her happy. I don't think either of them meant it, but they said it. Out loud too.

Grandma stormed out of the house and Dad went into the kitchen to hug Mum. I got my coat and my bag and took myself off to the bus stop. It wasn't even 8.15am.

Saturday 8th October

After the drama of yesterday, today was very dull. Mum was quiet, but now and then would smile if any of us were nearby. Dad was his usual self. I remember how worried I was after Nappy Gate and whether we'd ever see Grandma again. Now I get it. She has a big personality and so does Mum. Every so often they explode.

When I thought more about it, I realised I've grown up a lot since Nappy Gate. Even though it happened this year, it feels ages ago. Like it happened to a different person.

In other news, a man came to unblock and clean the downstairs fireplaces. There was lots of black dust everywhere. Grandma's tidying would've been much more welcome today.

Sunday 9th October

I was thinking about home today. Old home. Stockford. I even read through the early part of my diary to remind myself of how things used to be. Everything was simpler.

I wanted to FaceTime Jenna but I haven't spoken to her in a while. I didn't know if she'd be free. I found myself emailing instead. Like an old person. I just typed a quick, 'Hi, how are you?' style message and left it at that. I'll get in touch properly another time.

Monday 10th October

After Mum's forced cheerfulness over the past few days, she seemed smiley for real today. She took Harvest for a walk into the village this afternoon so ended up meeting me from the bus.

It's OK. It wasn't like she was waiting for me at the bus stop - that would've been a disaster. She was coming out of the mini-supermarket as the bus pulled up opposite. The weirdest thing happened though. When she saw Jake she gave him a big grin and crossed the road to high-five him. An actual high-five! Jake did a big smile back and said, 'Nice to see you Molly. Not singing today?' Mum laughed and said, 'No not today.'

When he'd gone I asked her what he was on about. I wish I hadn't now. Apparently the other night at Cait's, the pair of them had been singing Madonna songs on a karaoke machine. Jake had to come out from his bedroom to tell them to pack it in so he could sleep. I felt my face go red. How embarrassing! Mum found the whole thing hilarious. At one point she even said, 'Lighten up Leeza. At times you take after your grandma.'

Low blow, Mum. Low blow.

Tuesday 11th October

The weather's changed. The past few days have gone from the end of Summer to full on Winter. Autumn's been missed completely. I came down this morning to frost on the window ledges and a really cold kitchen. Dad was doing his best to light the fire. Since they've been cleaned he's managed it a couple of times but it takes ages. He keeps saying, 'I just need to find the knack and I'll be fine.' He was still looking for the knack this morning.

Wednesday 12th October

I think I'm getting a cold. My throat feels scratchy and my nose is sniffly. I've no doubt this is due to the Arctic conditions I'm living in. Every time I walk past Harvest I tuck the blanket around her a bit tighter.

Dad spent all of breakfast messing with the fireplace in the kitchen. I thought he was making my toast.

When I realised he wasn't, it was time to leave for school. I was starving all morning.

I can make my own breakfast. I don't need Dad to do it. It's just that he's usually done it before I come downstairs. I found myself having a moan to Jake. I think it's the first time I've started the conversation. To be honest, it wasn't really a conversation. I said, 'My dad spent all morning trying to light the fire so I ended up with no breakfast. I'm so hungry.' To which Jake replied, 'Nightmare.'

And that was that.

Thursday 13th October

Mum's bought a heater. It's to keep us going while they 'get a handle on things'. It's plugged into the kitchen wall and is the nicest thing to walk past ever. Harvest's carrycot is parked next to it. We dragged our kitchen chairs over to it this morning which made Dad say, 'Don't you think you're being a little over the top, kids?'

For what it's worth, I don't. He's not the one going to school with half a loo roll shoved up his sleeve. (My nose is running like a tap.)

Friday 14th October

I'm so glad it's Friday. I've been hanging on for the weekend so I can stay in bed with my pyjamas. I hate having colds.

When I got in from school, something was different. I opened the door and felt warmth! It was unbelievable. Then I heard voices. In the kitchen, Mum and Dad were sitting at the table with Cait and Tom. Tom was giving Harvest her bottle. I couldn't work out why it was so warm but then I saw the fire! A proper roaring fire. Cait said, 'Leeza, come and look what your dad did!' Then Dad said, 'I made a fire, Leeza!' Mum laughed and said, 'Look at his little face! We're all proud of you, Mac.' And Cait and Tom laughed too. Everyone seemed to be having a jolly old time.

It turned out, after I'd had my moan to Jake, he'd told Cait and Tom. They came round and gave Mum and

Dad lessons in how to light a fire. They'd practised all afternoon. When I got in, they were eating cake and drinking tea in the warm. What a *lovely* time that must have been. I'm being sarky, obvs. I was battling with snot and having to get a bus home while they were having cosy cake fun.

Really, it's me who should be proud. If I hadn't said anything to Jake, we'd still be freezing. I saved the day. (With Jake's help, I guess.)

Saturday 15th October

I'm not so grumpy today. It's amazing what a warm house will do for your mood. I got up quite early for a Saturday. I wanted to sit by the fire as I ate my toast. My nose has calmed down too. I only need to wipe it every few hours now instead of constantly.

Sunday 16th October

Grandma is still being silent. I asked Mum if she'd heard from her but she said no. Actually what she said was, 'Grandma needs to take a long hard look at herself.' I get the gist, obvs. It means Mum isn't happy with her. But still, what a strange thing to say.

Sometimes I think adults talk utter rubbish. They're so *phoney*. (I got that word from Willard's book. The main character uses it a lot. I like it.)

Monday 17th October

One of the hardest things to do is leave the warm kitchen and get the bus in the morning. Dad is getting quick at lighting the fire now. He does the one in the kitchen before we all get up. Even though there's an office upstairs, I think Mum and him work at the kitchen table most of the day. That's so Mum can lie on the sofa and still be part of the discussions while Dad is at the laptop. If she still worked for the Council she'd be on maternity leave for the next eight months. She keeps reminding us of this at regular intervals. Usually when one of us has left our underwear on the bathroom floor (Spike) or got ketchup on the walls (Spike) or made Blane cry (Spike).

Tuesday 18th October

The big news of the day: the coriander seeds have worked! We've enough coriander to make curry on Friday night. I don't think I was as enthusiastic as Dad wanted me to be. He kept going up to everyone with the plant pot to show us. It's true that there's a lot of coriander. I'm just being realistic. We'll eat it on Friday and then it'll be gone. It seems growing our own food is a long process that won't actually feed us for real. Dad was very pleased, though. With that and the fire, he's full of achievements this week.

Wednesday 19th October

So yesterday I was fake-excited about the coriander. I mean, I'm happy for Dad and everything, but it was sort of a joke that we were all proud of him. But today, something exciting happened for real - and not before time. THE OVEN ARRIVED.

I can't explain how happy I am that our food options have expanded. (I heard Mum say that to Cait on the phone - 'You'll be pleased to know our food options have expanded.') There've been so many changes recently that not having Friday Fooday has been unbearable. When I got in from school, Mum and Dad were reading the manual. I said, 'Does this mean we can...' and Dad said, 'Yes it does. Friday Fooday here we come. With coriander!' Then we all laughed.

I don't even know if I like coriander.

Thursday 20th October

Jake leant forward on his bus seat this morning and whispered, 'Congratulations Loozer.' I said, 'What for?' He said, 'The coriander of course.' Then he laughed a lot. I suppose he was quite funny. No one really thinks growing herbs is a big deal. Especially not people who live in the countryside for real. When he'd finished laughing he said, 'Your mum sent a photo of your dad holding the plant pot. Grandad said he needs a certificate.' Then he laughed again.

Oh good. I *do* like it when my family are the topic of village fun. (That was sarcasm. I do *not* like it.)

When I got home from school, things were quieter. Dad was typing away and Mum was doing something on a calculator. Mum asked me if I had much homework but I told her I'd do it at the weekend. That's when she told me. Grandma had been in touch. She's visiting on Saturday. Mum said, 'You never know Leez, she might storm off after ten minutes and you'll have loads of time to work. But just in case, best be organised, yeah?' I said I would.

I predict tension with a capital T.

Friday 21st October

I refuse to think about tomorrow. Tomorrow will come and I'll worry about it then. (Except it's me I'm talking about, so obvs my stomach's been playing up.) But enough of that. Today was great. Today was the first Friday Fooday since we moved house. Woooohoooo!

I wasn't bothered what we ate as long as we made it special again. All day I was thinking about it - in registration, in Maths, in History and on the bus home. It was all I could concentrate on.

When I got in I could smell the best food ever! The music was on, Mum was stirring something in a pan and Dad was rolling out dough. Now they work together from home, they can both take Friday afternoons off. It was like a new version of old times. It felt good. Even Spike was in a good mood. He ate seconds and didn't try to leave the table as soon as he was done. Friday Fooday changes people. Mum had lit candles and everything felt glowy. I don't think that's a word but it should be. *Glowy*. It's my favourite feeling.

Tea was butternut squash and coconut curry (and coriander!) with naan bread and rice. It was delish.

Saturday 22nd October

Grandma turned up around ten. I was still in bed but I heard her voice downstairs. After the loveliness of last night, I felt like staying there and keeping the happy feeling for as long as possible. I lasted half an hour before Dad came up and told me I had to get ready and come down.

When I made it to the lounge, Mum and Grandma were sitting on the sofa. Grandma looked very subdued. Not like her usual self. And Mum? She looked sort of upset. I said, 'Morning Grandma,' like I would normally do, but just as I was about to walk off to get a drink, she grabbed me and hugged me. She hugged me! Grandma is not a hugger. I was totally surprised. Mum raised her eyebrows and sort of smiled, in an expression that said, *just go with it, Leeza*. When she let me go, I went to the kitchen where Dad was. I didn't even need to ask. He could see he needed to explain. He whispered, 'Grandma's upset. She's split up with Willard.'

I have to say, I was *not* expecting that. Everything froze. I nodded and got my drink but inside I was really cold. What'd gone wrong? Willard was the nicest person in the world. I was still in the middle of his book. What was the problem? Surely they could work it out?

I got my drink and took it back upstairs. I wanted to be on my own. I wanted to cry but no tears would come. I know we only knew Willard for a little bit, but he was a lot of fun.

Sunday 23rd October

Grandma didn't stay long yesterday. Mum said she was upset and had wanted to apologise for last week. They'd decided to split up a few days before she arrived. She was trying to distract herself by cleaning our house. I can't imagine ever being so upset I would want to clean.

I asked Mum *why* they had split up. I didn't want to at first. I didn't want to hear that Willard had turned out to be horrible. Some people can put on a good act, can't they? They're nice in front of everyone but behind closed doors they're bullies. Mum was quick to reassure me. She said, 'We were right to like Willard. Grandma still likes him a lot too. They just want different things from the future.' I can't imagine what that would be. They're both so old. Their future is limited. When I told Mum that, she smiled and then stopped herself. She said in a serious voice, 'For old people, they still have lots going for them.'

I feel sorry for Grandma now. If I'm feeling sad about Willard, I guess she's feeling worse.

<u>Monday 24th October</u>

Everything is normal but feels flatter. School was fine. Miss Wilkinson was all right. Jake was his usual self. He noticed I was down. His actual words were, 'Hey Loozer, what's up with your face?' I fake smiled and told him to mind his own business. Then he stopped joking and said, 'But seriously, is everything all right?' I didn't really know what to say. Sometimes he's a pain and then other times it's like he's being kind. I just said, 'My grandma's split up with her boyfriend and it's all a bit of a drama.' He was quiet for a second. Then she said, 'Soz about that Loozer.' And that was that.

Tuesday 25th October

Four days till half-term and four days till Friday Fooday. It can't come soon enough. We all need cheering up.

Wednesday 26th October

School was all right. Miss Wilkinson said I'm getting better at equivalent fractions so that's good. As well as being my form teacher, Miss Wilkinson also teaches me Maths. There's a lot of doubling up here.

Thursday 27th October

Tea was pasta bake. Being able to put it in the oven to brown the top is so much better than stirring the sauce through a pan of bow ties or shells. It's just my opinion. (But I am right.)

Friday 28th October

Finally it's half-term. It's strange that I've been here long enough to have done half a term. It only seems five minutes since I was in my room in Tyson Road. I really need to FaceTime Jenna. It's been ages. I'll do it tomorrow.

Friday Fooday was a nice distraction from feeling sad about Willard. (I wonder *why* Grandma didn't want a future with him.) We had home made flat breads, hummus and veggie sticks with caramelised Mediterranean vegetables. It was a taste sensation, according to Dad. We all smiled at him but deep down it felt like everyone was putting on a brave face.

Saturday 29th October

At breakfast, Mum said, 'Right you lot, I've had enough. It's time to shake off our blues and get some fresh air.' I looked around. She was talking to all of us, not just me. Spike was looking angrily at his toast,

Blane was drinking his water with a sad face and Kenny was crying quietly to himself. (I'm not convinced Kenny was feeling down about Willard. I think he was just having a whinge.)

Nobody said anything but I don't think any of us felt like moving. Mum threw hats and scarves at us whilst she got Harvest into her pram. She grabbed our coats from the hooks in the hall and told us to put them on. Then she opened the front door and said we had to go.

I love fresh air on holiday but not when it's forced on me in real life. Spike moaned a lot - mainly that it was his first day off and he didn't want to be going anywhere. I can't say I disagreed with him. It felt a bit much to be marched out of the house and dragged down the lane, just because things felt sad all the time. Going for a walk wasn't going to bring Willard back.

We ended up walking to the shop, getting some groceries and walking back. On our way home I asked Mum what I'd been worrying about. 'Why doesn't

Grandma want a future with Willard?' There was silence for a moment. Then Mum sighed. 'Because she's a stubborn old biddy? Because she's a control freak? Because she doesn't know what's good for her? Take your pick.' I must have looked confused because Mum ruffled my hair (get off!) and said, 'Grandma has lived on her own for so long she wasn't sure she could share her life with someone else. So she's chosen to stay single so she can have things her own way.' When Mum said that, it made sense to me. Of course you'd want things your own way, if you could. I hate that I have to share my life with six other people every day. It's too crowded.

When I got back, I still felt sad. Although I did feel like I had a bit more energy. And my face was all rosy from the wind. I read a few more chapters of Willard's book in the armchair near the fire. Willard wasn't phoney. He was really cool.

<u>Sunday 30th October</u>

I think Mum realised she'd been unfair dragging us out yesterday because today was a pyjama, duvet and film day. I had a shower, put on my clean pyjamas and watched *Mary Poppins*. Bert makes me laugh. He makes us all laugh actually.

OMG. I've just realised. Bert is exactly like Willard and Mary Poppins is exactly like Grandma! She has no hesitation whatsoever in giving us tidying jobs. I wonder if Mary Poppins would want to share her life with another person? Maybe just until the wind changes?

Monday 31st October

Happy Halloween!

It's weird being on holiday whilst Mum and Dad work from home. They told us that some of the time they'll be working upstairs so we need to be calm and quiet. I'm not sure how much they managed to achieve today. Spike cut his finger on his trowel, Kenny weed on the sofa (accidentally) and Blane broke a glass. At one point, Dad said, 'If I have to come down these stairs one more time, I'm cancelling Duck Apple.'

For Halloween we always play Duck Apple. Mum won't let us do Trick Or Treat because she says it's wrong to threaten someone just because you have a silly mask on. In Stockford, we used to keep a bag of sweets by the door. It was only ever the high school kids that knocked. I'm sure they were disappointed with a handful of Haribo.

Duck Apple was a laugh. We all had a go. I insisted on going first. I said it was because I'm the eldest, but really I didn't want anyone else's spit in the water. I managed to get an apple quite quickly. The trick is to push it to the bottom of the washing up bowl straight away, and take a big bite. It means your whole face gets wet but only for a second. As I ate my apple with a towel round my shoulders, I watched Spike getting soaked with every dip. The apple bobbed away from him every time he tried to bite it. He didn't seem to mind though. We all had a good laugh. In the end Mum let him use his hands. We gave him a clap anyway.

It was nice to laugh at something silly. Thanks Spike!

11.

New Friends, New Family

Tuesday 1st November

Day two of the holidays. Harvest bounced in her chair, Spike dug soil, Blane and Kenny watched *Peppa Pig* and I read my book. When I finally finish it, I'll have to give it back to Willard but I've no idea how I do that now. Will Grandma see him? I don't know. I let the words wash over me. It's still too hard but I'm sticking at it. It's made me feel clever for trying.

Wednesday 2nd November

It's Grandma's birthday on Friday so Mum asked her if she wanted to come for Friday Fooday. She got a *No Thanks* reply as she had plans with her Zumba friends. I think Mum felt she needed to make an effort because of Willard. Then she said we all had to make her a card.

Mum covered the kitchen table with pencils, felt tips, scissors, glue and the collage box. (It has feathers, glitter, ribbon and pieces of coloured paper in it. I have no idea how it survived being binned before the house move, but it did.)

I made an excellent card, even if I say so myself. It was a portrait of Grandma. I used brown pieces of fur to make her hair feel real. I added highlights with bits of yellow wool. I also gave her red glittery lipstick and green eye shadow. I'm not sure she would actually wear green eye shadow and glittery lipstick but I wanted her to look as colourful as possible.

By teatime, Grandma had four handmade and very different cards. Spike had drawn a picture of a plant, because as he put it, 'Grandma likes plants'. Blane had drawn a picture of a clown, although he didn't tell us why. Kenny did some cutting and sticking with bits of coloured cellophane. Mum said she would love them all.

I'm not being funny but mine is defo the best.

Thursday 3rd November

The cards are on their way! Dad took us to the village so we could post them. I saw Jake on his bike outside the shop. He shouted, 'All right, Loozer'. I said, 'That's an old joke now, Joke.' Then he smiled and rode off.

I feel less annoyed about *Loozer* on the inside so I'm not as bothered on the outside. It still bugs me a bit. Just not as much as it did.

Friday 4th November

Grandma's sixty-nine today! Mum rang her and made us sing *Happy Birthday* on loudspeaker. It was embarrassing but we wanted to cheer her up. It sounded like we had so it was worth it.

Afterwards, Mum said something weird. As I was eating my toast, she said, 'How about one week we invite Jake to Family Fooday?' I didn't say anything. I think I shrugged. It was a random idea. I know I see him a lot at school, but there's no reason to make him part of a family event. (And yes, Auction Bidders, I know he was part of Harvest's birth, but that was defo unplanned.) Yesterday I was thinking that he only bugs me a bit and not a lot, but that's still no reason to treat him like a long lost family member.

Later on I asked Mum why she'd suggested it. She said she'd been thinking of asking Cait and Tom to thank them for their help in settling in. I suppose when she put it like that it made more sense. If he came because his Mum was coming, it wouldn't be as weird.

I decided not to think about it. It might not happen.

Saturday 5th November

It's Bonfire Night! I've come to realise that Applemere enjoys celebrations. We wandered down to the village after tea. On the field behind the pub was a huge bonfire. You could see the glow as soon as we were on the lane. And the smell? The smell was amazing. Like a cosy, happy, winter smell. It smelt *warm*. I don't even think that's possible but that's how it was.

Mum spotted Cait. She'd bagsied two picnic tables outside the pub and was beckoning us over. I was glad. Last time we attended a village event, Mum's waters broke and everything was a nightmare. This time we all stayed together. I controlled my worries by keeping an eye on everyone.

While we were sitting there, Mum got a text. She read it, sighed loudly and said, 'Oh *great*. My ridiculous mother has invited herself for lunch tomorrow. *Goody*. That'll be a calm day of no rows, family togetherness and happy times.' She put her phone in her pocket and shook her head.

If I had to put money on it, I'd say she was being sarcastic.

<u>Sunday 6th November</u>

Grandma was supposed to be getting here for 11am. Mum had already said she'd no intention of cooking so that wasn't happening. Also, Dad never cooks for Grandma because she's 'too high maintenance'. (I think that means she's too fussy.) So that meant one thing - Sunday lunch in the pub. Whoop.

We heard the tyres on the gravel. Auction Bidders - remember how excited we'd been the first time she visited us? We'd all been at the window, waiting to spot her car. Today was different. We still felt down about Willard. Plus, we were tired from last night, so we stayed on the sofa. When the bell rang, Mum walked to the door, turned to Dad and said, 'Game face, Mac!' We all understood. Our faces had to look pleased to see her - not nervous of any rows that might happen and not sad that she was single again. We had to play a game.

But then...then it happened. Grandma's voice was talking and so was Mum's and so was someone else's. Then the lounge door opened and there was Grandma, Mum and...Willard!!!!!!

Yes! Willard the Tree walked in!

Everyone leapt up and started cheering. Blane high-fived him, Spike jumped up at him till Willard picked him up under his arm, and I just smiled really widely. Even Dad was excited. He shook Willard's hand up and down lots of times. It was brilliant to see him again.

Lunch was lovely. It would've been anyway because we were in the pub. But it felt even better because the tension was lifted. No one needed their game face because they had a happy face for real. When we'd given our orders to the waitress, Grandma picked up her glass and tapped it with a fork. We all stopped talking. Once she had our attention she said, 'I have a small announcement to make,' then she corrected herself and said, 'Sorry, WE have a small announcement to make.' Mum and Dad looked at each other and made the same face. All wide-eyed and eyebrows-raised. I turned back to Grandma. She said, 'As you know, myself and Willard have been friends for a while now...' At this, Mum fake coughed and Dad laughed and said, 'Yeah, friends, right.' Grandma ignored them and carried on. '...And so, after our little blip of the past few weeks, I have some happy news to share. On Friday, on my birthday, Willard asked me to marry him. And I said...' - we all held our breath and waited - '...Yes!'

We cheered and clapped and whooped! Mum jumped up and gave Grandma a big hug. Dad clapped Willard on the back, kissed Grandma on the cheek and said, 'Nice one, Ursula'. Spike jumped up and down on the spot in excitement. It was all too much. Next thing, Willard went to the bar for champagne and our food came. I can barely remember my cauliflower cheese in all the excitement. (Actually, I can. It was gorge.)

Monday 7th November

News of Grandma's engagement made it to the bus. Jake leaned forward and said, 'My mum's well excited. She loves weddings. She's going to help your mum buy an outfit.

How does Jake know my family news before I do?

Tuesday 8th November

Every conversation I have seems to be about Grandma and Willard. Even Miss Wilkinson asked me about it today. I don't know any details but people keep asking questions. Where? When? What's the dress like? What was the proposal like? I've no idea about any of it. I don't even know if Grandma knows the answers yet. Except, she must know what the proposal was like, as she was the one proposed to. Willard said it was in the garden, under Grandma's favourite tree.

I don't have a favourite tree. I don't understand why anyone would.

Wednesday 9th November

As Mum gave me my toast this morning, she said, 'Fajitas for Friday Fooday?' I said, 'Yes please!' in a silly voice. I haven't had them for ages so I was excited. Then she said, 'Tell Jake that's what we're having. Just in case he doesn't like them.'

Mum has done what she said, and asked Cait and Tom for tea. This means that Jake will be coming too. When I got to the bus stop, he was already there. He gave me a big grin and said, 'All right Loozer. I believe I'm guest of honour at yours on Friday.' I gave him a sarky look and made it clear he's *not* the guest of honour. He isn't even a real guest. He's only there because his mum and grandad are coming.

Thursday 10th November

At teatime, Mum opened an email on her phone. She said, 'Oh blimey, Ma's sent an essay.' Dad said, 'What's she on about?' and Mum said, 'The email's title is *Wedding Thoughts*?' Dad laughed and said, 'That'll keep you busy for a while.'

Mum said she'd work through it when she'd got Harvest to sleep. She sounded like me when I have homework I don't like.

Friday 11th November

As I got off the bus this afternoon, Jake waved and said, 'See you later, Loozer. Friday night is about to get Wooltonised.' It took me a second to remember his last name is Woolton. Even so, he's just ridic.

Saturday 12th November

Last night was late! I went to bed at midnight and could still hear the grown-ups talking. When I left, four entire bottles of wine had been finished. Tom had moved onto whiskey and Cait was teaching Mum yoga. I left them in the downward dog position, although neither of them looked like any dogs I've seen.

Jake had been all right. He was fast asleep on the sofa when I went up. All evening, he'd been friendly and polite. He'd had second helpings of the fajitas and even picked up the peppers that Kenny had spilt under his seat. This morning when I came down, the first thing Mum said was, 'I do like Jake you know. My only hope is that Spike behaves that way in other people's houses.' Then she laughed. I think we both knew there was absolutely fat chance of that.

Sunday 13th November

Nothing happened.

Monday 14th November

Mum got round to reading Grandma's essay. She said she'd opened it last night after gearing up to it since Thursday. (She said Grandma wouldn't mind as she often replies to emails, several weeks after receiving them.)

There were loads of ideas and plans on the email, but the most important one is this. I AM GOING TO BE A BRIDESMAID.

Woohooooooo.

Tuesday 15th November

We know a lot more about the wedding plans, now. It's all happening really quickly. On Wednesday 28th December this year to be exact. NEXT MONTH. Mum rang to find out if this was an official date or a pencilled-in date, but apparently it's all booked. Grandma said, 'I acted really old so the registrar would make sure the paperwork was in place ASAP.'

First of all, I didn't know there was paperwork for a wedding. It's because Grandma's been married before so they have to check she's actually divorced. (Not only is she divorced but Mum's dad is very dead. He won't be causing them problems.)

Secondly, Grandma doesn't need to *act* old. Just saying.

Wednesday 16th November

I FaceTimed Jenna. It took a while to get the iPad from Spike who was insisting he needed it for homework. I know for a fact, he didn't. He was playing games on it. I know *sometimes* homework is to complete a particular Maths game, but there's no way his teacher told him to play Fortnite for hours.

Eventually I got it. I took it to my room and rang Jenna. She answered straight away and it was exactly like old times. She shouted, 'It's McAuuuuuliffffe!' as I said hi. I couldn't stop laughing. Then when we'd calmed down she said, 'Look who I've got with me.' She moved her phone and Meg came into view. I was a bit surprised but I don't know why. I suppose I thought once Meg started Stockford High, she'd make new friends and ditch Jenna straight away.

I told them my big news. Well, Grandma's big news. It was exciting to tell people I'm going to be a bridesmaid. (People who know me properly.) But then things went a bit weird. As soon as I'd said it, Meg burst out laughing. She said, 'You? A bridesmaid? That's the funniest thing I've heard all year. I can't imagine you in a dress for one second.' Jenna looked at her like she was being strange, but she kept on laughing.

I know I'm not like Meg - all lip gloss and bra tops. But I've been excited about wearing a posh dress for a day. I thought I'd look nice. Now I'm not sure I will. Jenna pushed Meg away from the phone. She said, 'Ignore Meanie Meg. You'll look fab.' I know Jenna was being kind. But I also know that Jenna doesn't care much about dresses and clothes. Maybe Meg is right and I'll look stupid.

Thursday 17th November

I felt fed up all day. Mum asked me what was wrong, but I told her it was nothing. I don't think I want to be a bridesmaid anymore.

Friday 18th November

My insides have been aching again. I hate it when the thoughts in my mind make my stomach feel bad. I was glad when it was time for Friday Fooday so I could be distracted.

After last week's Wooltonised version, tonight's was very calm in comparison. Dad had found a kofta recipe he wanted to try - spicy veggie balls served with flatbreads and yoghurt. Very messy to eat but they tasted lovely. It's fun watching Mum and Dad cook together. Sometimes I think I should write down their recipes for when I'm older. But then I remember I'll be too busy making ham sandwiches and eating Big Macs, just because I can.

I was watching Dad roll the koftas after school. He seems very relaxed since we moved. He was always relaxed at weekends but now he's like that all the time. I think it's because he doesn't need to wear a tie to work anymore.

Yesterday he was in tracky pants all day.

Saturday 19th November

I said to Mum, 'Don't you think Dad is more relaxed these days?' She said, 'Hmmm?' because I don't think she was actually listening to me at first. I repeated myself. I said, 'Don't you think Dad's more relaxed now? Is it because he likes his job better?' Mum thought about it for a second or two before replying, 'I imagine it's a direct result of not having to deal with your grandma every day.'

I think the wedding emails are coming thick and fast now. Mum's phone pings, she reads something, rolls her eyes and then throws the phone on the sofa or the table. Wherever she is, she tosses it away.

I wonder if I'll be like that with Mum when I'm older.

Sunday 20th November

Dad invited Jake in for hot chocolate this morning. We NEVER have hot chocolate for no reason. Apparently, when he was clearing leaves from the path, Jake was riding his bike up and down and Dad felt sorry for him. (???) I carried on with my homework, but Jake kept chatting to me. In the end I gave up and chatted back. He was bored because his mum was doing college work and his grandad was in the shop. When Dad asked him if he wanted to stay for dinner, I wasn't at all surprised when he said yes.

I can't work Jake out. He's nothing like Meg and Jenna (obvs). But even though he started off like Spike (by that I mean annoying) he's better than that now. I still don't think he's a friend. Not while he calls me Loozer, anyway.

Monday 21st November

On the bus, Jake was full of how good yesterday was. I didn't get it myself. He kept saying how lively my home was. Lively is one word for it. I'd say noisy, shouty, and screamy. Grandma once described 620 Tyson Road, as 'walking into pure chaos'. I can see why she'd say that. Walking into her house is like being in a church. It's silent and smells of polish. Anyway, Jake kept going on about what a fun time he'd had yesterday. I suppose when his Mum and Tom are busy, he's on his own a lot.

I would love that more than anything.

Tuesday 22nd November

I finally finished *Catcher in the Rye*! I feel so proud of myself. I'm like a real grown-up, especially as Mum said it was one of the classics and a bit old for me.

I've no idea what was going on even now it's finished. It doesn't stop me feeling proud though.

I told Jake I'd finished it. I wanted to drop it into conversation so I'd sound clever and cool. He said, 'Nice one. What's it about?' That threw me. I didn't have a clue. It just kept plodding along in an easy-to-read writing style that sounded like talking. In the end I said, 'It's hard to summarise, but the writing is really easy to read.' I hope that made me sound intelligent. Jake nodded and said, 'Cool. Can I borrow it?'

I've never had a friend to share books with. That's something I've always wanted. I mean real books, not schoolbooks. I said, 'Yeah, sure. I'll check with Willard but I don't think he'd mind.' Jake said, 'Nice one, Loozer.' I must have looked annoyed because a second later he said, 'Soz Loozer. I meant Leeza.' Then he smiled.

Hmmmm. He called me Leeza. Do I have my first proper Applemere friend?

Wednesday 23rd November

There's now an *Ursula and Willard's Wedding Countdown* chart on the fridge. It arrived in the post yesterday. Mum stuck it up with magnets. Dad looked at it and said, 'And we have that on our fridge, why?' Mum shook her head and said, 'Don't start. Ma thinks we need a handy calendar to stay on track.' Dad said, 'On track of what?' Mum said, 'Dress fittings, page boy fittings, when to book a hotel, when to breathe, when to do anything my ridiculous mother wants me to do.'

Dad rubbed Mum's shoulder, then made her a herbal tea. It's going to be a long month.

Thursday 24th November

This weekend I'm going back to Manchester! It's a flying visit so I'm not stopping in Stockford. But I am going into town with Mum and Grandma. We're going to find me a dress.

On the one hand...wow! Manchester! I can't wait to see things I recognise. On the other hand, Meg's teasing is still in my head. '*You? A bridesmaid? That's the funniest thing I've heard all year'*.

I need to forget it. I need to pretend I'm happy about everything. I need to use my fake smile.

Friday 25th November

I took ages to fall asleep last night. When I did, I dreamt I was wearing a lime green frilly dress and a pink hat with a massive bow. Everyone was laughing and pointing at me. It was such a relief to wake up. I will find out tomorrow what horror I'm forced to wear.

Saturday 26th November

I had to get up at 7 o'clock. On a Saturday! There should be laws against that. When we got to Manchester, the city centre was full of shoppers even though it was still morning. Christmas lights were strung along Market Street but at 10am they weren't switched on. We met Grandma in Costa. She bought us breakfast and filled Mum in on the Wedding Countdown.

The toast in Costa (normal bread!) had been so lovely I'd forgotten why we were actually there. As my stomach started to churn again I decided I'd had enough. It was time to take control of the situation. As we were leaving I said to Grandma, 'What exactly have you got in mind for me?' Grandma smiled and said, 'Something as beautiful as you are.' I laughed out loud because I thought she was joking. She's not a horrible person but she never says things like that. Mum patted me on the back and said, 'Love does strange things to people. Let's just go with it.' To which Grandma replied, 'What are you blithering on about, Molly?' Mum said, 'Nothing Ma, just chatting.' We walked out of Costa laughing about the randomness of Grandma, with my butterflies a little calmer.

The rest of the day was long, and I mean loooooooooooong. There was lots of walking and lots of trying on dresses. The best place was Debenhams because there was so much choice. That meant I could stay in the changing room while Mum pushed the next dress through the curtains. In the end none of them looked right. That wasn't just my opinion.

That's what Mum and Grandma said too. If they'd asked me, I'd have said nothing looked right because they were dresses and I wear leggings or jeggings.

The last shop was Monsoon. My legs were really achy by then. It felt like we'd been wandering around for days. We walked towards the wedding section and looked for their bridesmaid stuff. One caught my eye immediately - a dark blue sleeveless dress. It had a fitted top half and a long net skirt. On the bottom of the skirt were little clumps of gold sequins. It reminded me of the stars in Applemere. I've never felt happy about a dress before, but I felt it about this one. It also came with a little jacket so it was good for the winter. Mum saw me looking and came over. She said, 'What do you think, Leez?' I can't remember what I said. I probably just mumbled. I really liked it. I have NEVER felt like that about clothes before. Mum found my size and I went to try it on. It was - even if I say so myself - utterly beautiful. I think it was the colour that I loved. Nothing too pink or pale or boring. It was bold and strong and looked like the sky on Christmas Eve. I felt amazing.

From outside the curtain I heard Mum say to Grandma, 'So do you think your colour scheme can incorporate cobalt blue with gold bits?' I'm not sure what Grandma said, but next thing I knew, we were paying for it at the till.

Sunday 27th November

Shattered today. I heard Mum asking Dad how yesterday went. He joked that they'd all enjoyed their boys' day. Mum said, 'Surely every day is a boys' day if you're a boy?' Dad laughed. He asked her how her girly shopping trip had been. She told him to stop being ridiculous.

Mum doesn't like gender stereotyping. She doesn't like the idea that you're predisposed to prefer certain activities because you're a boy or a girl. I hear her say 'predisposed' a lot. It's one of the big words she uses that I kind of understand when she says it, but not enough to use myself.

I know I'm supposed to love shopping and dresses, because I'm a girl. But I don't. So it's confusing that I love my bridesmaids dress and think it's the best dress in the world. I like leggings or jeggings every day but the dress made me feel beautiful. I liked the feeling of that. I still don't want to be a princess though. And I still don't like being told I should like pink.

Having opinions can be complicated at times.

Monday 28th November

I FaceTimed Jenna again. She was on her own so that was good. I didn't feel like talking to Meg. I told her about the dress. She said, 'Nice one, McAuliffe.' Apart from that, we didn't say much. We both had homework to do.

Tuesday 29th November

I passed *Catcher in the Rye* to Jake. Grandma told me that Willard had said I could lend it to my friend. I'm still not sure if Jake is my friend but he's not my enemy either. He's something in between. (But more a friend than an enemy.)

Jake said, 'Nice one, Leeza' when I gave it to him. It feels like 'Nice One' is all people say to me these days. Also he went straight for *Leeza* this time. I'll have to remember not to call him *Joke* from now on. Not if we're being respectful with each other.

Wednesday 30th November

According to *Ursula and Willard's Wedding Countdown* chart, today's the day they buy their wedding rings. I keep checking to see what's happening every time I walk past the fridge. Mum still rolls her eyes whenever she gets a new email, but now I'm not worrying about my dress, I'm getting excited.

The wedding is in a posh hotel in Manchester and we'll be staying in the hotel! I think that's the best bit. I've never stayed anywhere posh. With that and the dress, I'll feel like a completely different person.

This weekend, Mum is taking Spike, Blane and Kenny to do the same thing we did last weekend. Except they'll be finding suits not dresses.

With a new grandad as well as a new dress, I'm becoming unrecognisable from the person I used to be. And it doesn't feel bad at all.

12.

Feel the Glow

Thursday 1st December

It's Christmas month! The best month of the year. I hope I enjoy it all as much as I normally do, even though so much is different.

Friday 2nd December

Applemere's Christmas lights have been switched on. That means there are fairy lights strung between the trees, and a Christmas tree outside the pub. Compared to Manchester's tree, it's really small. Even so, when I got off the bus and saw it, I felt really happy. I liked the feeling it gave me. It's the *glowy* feeling that makes everything good.

Even better - Friday Fooday was slow-cooked vegetarian chilli with crusty bread. Mmm mmm mmm.

Saturday 3rd December

By the time I got up, Mum and the boys had left for their shopping trip. Dad made me breakfast and said he had great plans for us. I wasn't really in the mood for lots of activities. Last Saturday took it out of me and I'd been looking forward to a chilled day.

I needn't have worried. The 'great plans' were a roaring fire, hot chocolate and Christmas films! I watched *Polar Express* (my favourite), *Home Alone* (Dad's favourite), and *Miracle on 34th Street* (Mum's favourite). Even Harvest watched from her bouncy chair. I had a blanket over my legs and instead of meals at the kitchen table, we ate nachos on the sofa.

I have never felt so cosy.

Sunday 4th December

Something strange has been happening the past few days. It's an odd feeling but I've started to feel happier about living here. When I think back to Stockford, I'm not wishing I still lived there.

Also, my stomach hasn't felt bad since Dress Day. Normally it aches for some reason every day or so. This is completely unusual for me. It's weird. (Weird but good.)

Monday 5th December

Getting off the bus after school has become the best part of my day. Twinkly Applemere looks gorgeous as it goes dark.

Tuesday 6th December

Grandma and Willard are booking their honeymoon. That's what the countdown chart says for today. Last week I heard Mum ask Grandma where she wanted to go. She said, 'We've not decided yet, Molly. But somewhere romantic and secluded, we think.' Mum made a pretend sick face that made me laugh.

Grandma and Willard are nice people and work well together but none of us want to see them be romantic for real. Yuck. Also, Mum and Dad have started calling Willard, *Will*. Apparently most people do.

Wednesday 7th December

School is both hard work and fun these days. The hard work is because there are tests. The fun bit is that there are lots of Christmas activities too. At lunchtime I have choir practice. I'm in a choir!

I said I'd do it because I like Christmas. Practising carols gives me the glowy feeling I like. Jake said *he* would do it because the week before we break up, we get out of lessons and sing in Old Folks' Homes. His reason for taking part was a bit more selfish. Today we sang through all the verses of *Once in Royal David's City*. I didn't know there were so many.

Thursday 8th December

Today we did a carol I'd never sung before. *O Holy Night*. One of Class Three did a harmony on the high bits. It sounded amazing.

Apart from that, we had tests.

Friday 9th December

It was *O Come All Ye Faithful* today. Not bad but I already knew it. And the last test was Science. It was annoying, but nowhere near as bad as the SATs were. Funny - I'd forgotten all about them as soon as they were done. At the time they felt huge.

When I got in from school, Grandma and Will were there! (I'm trying to remember to call him Will, but I forget sometimes.) They only told Mum they were coming this morning so it was a surprise for the rest of us. Grandma said, 'We wanted to do a proper face-to-face about the wedding plans. Sometimes I don't think my emails make it.' I saw Dad hide a laugh when she said that. Her emails make it. They just get ignored.

This was Willard's first Family Fooday and he fitted right in. He'd brought a couple of bottles of red wine with him and he offered to help. Mum took the wine and said, 'That's exactly how you get invited back, Will. Well done.' Then everyone laughed. There was a lot of laughter all through the evening. It was a lovely atmosphere. Spike stayed sitting at the table till well after he'd finished eating. That's always a good sign.

Grandma and Willard stayed at our house this time. They didn't book a hotel. Mum and Dad kept making jokey comments about it. Things like, 'Oh, so the house isn't too dirty for you now, is it?' Or, 'I hope the rats and cockroaches don't get you in the night.' They found it hilarious. Grandma smiled along but deep down was getting annoyed, I think.

Saturday 10th December

When I woke up this morning I could smell breakfast. Cereal doesn't smell, so I knew someone was cooking. This never happens!

When I got downstairs, Willard - I mean *Will* - was in the kitchen, scrambling eggs and grilling veggie sausages. Grandma was making tea and coffee for everyone. Mum and Dad were sitting on the sofa looking amused. I don't think Grandma has ever acted like this. Willard the Tree has changed the dynamic for us all. Will said he wasn't much of a cook except when it came to breakfasts. He said his daughters loved having sleepovers when they were teenagers because he'd cook their friends a fry up the next morning. Yeah! Will has daughters! Mum's going to get two step-sisters. Even though that's big news, it's OK. It's just more to be excited about, is what it is.

In other news, scrambled eggs on toast is my new favourite meal. Also, things still feel nice in my tummy. I like it.

Sunday 11th December

I tried to FaceTime Jenna again but she wasn't there. Now I feel more settled, it's easier to think about Stockford without getting upset. I never cried when we left, but my tummy felt constantly *swirly*. Not like an upset tummy when I need the toilet all the time. It just felt *not* happy. Things feel so much calmer now. I think I might be happier?

Mum and Dad put the decorations up this evening. It was strange seeing things that used to be in Tyson Road being used here. Like the wooden sign that says *Noel*. Or the net of fairy lights that goes over the front window. It looked lovely when it was done. The tree is in the kitchen. Because it's open plan, we can sit on the sofa with the telly and see the tree behind us. Everything feels good. Better than good - it feels *glowy!*

Monday 12th December

When I left this morning, Cait was downstairs. She's going to help Mum look for a dress for the wedding. Cait had handed in her college work and Mum was taking a day off. (Although - as she regularly tells us - she *should* be on maternity leave. In the last week, she's said it when I asked her to check my homework, wash my school skirt, and pass me the scissors. It's her default setting.)

Mum and Cait went to Carlisle. Mum said she hoped to box off her dress in the first hour and then find a pub for lunch. I wanted to say, 'You can't go to the pub if you are on maternity leave', but I didn't. Mum and Cait dress very differently. Mum always wears leggings, a colourful tunic top and tall boots. Cait wears a lot of black. Today it was black jeans, a black T-shirt with some rips in (that were meant to be there) and chunky boots with laces. I like how Cait dresses but it's nothing like Mum.

When Jake saw me on the bus, he said, 'It's not fair that the mums are having a day out and we have school.' I said, 'Well they have to buy a dress so that might take ages.' Jake said, 'Nah. Your mum knows the one she wants. It's from Monsoon. She saw it when she was there the other week.'

Jake *always* knows more than I do.

Tuesday 13th December

The McAuliffe family are ready for the wedding of the year. That's what Mum said at breakfast. She got her dress yesterday. Jake was right. It was from Monsoon and she'd seen it last week. It's bright red, and sort of lacy. It looks like it might be see through but there is a secret layer under the lace that stops anything being on show. Mum said it was the best thing for a post-pregnant belly as there's ruching around the middle. I didn't know what ruching was before, but I do now. It's a posh word for wrinkles.

All new outfits are hanging on the back of Mum and Dad's bedroom door. (Dad's suit isn't new but he's hardly worn it.) Every time I go to the loo, I lift up the plastic to see my dress. It's perfect.

Harvest has a new Babygro for the wedding. It's white, but has a princess dress sewn onto it. It's sort of cute and sort of funny. Harvest might grow up to be like Cait, and only wear black. She might hate the princess Babygro but can't tell us yet. I hope she doesn't hold it against us.

Wednesday 14th December

I wonder when I'm going to start my periods. When I was with Meg I used to think about it all the time. That's because she used to *talk* about it all the time. Now I've sort of forgotten about it. The reason it was on my mind today was because a packet of sanitary towels has appeared in the bathroom cabinet. This means Mum's periods are back. Because of Harvest being on the way, it's been ages since Mum has moaned about stomach ache and hugged the hot water bottle. I once asked her if periods hurt, and she said, 'Hardly at all, Leeza', before swallowing paracetamol and curling in a ball on the sofa. She's such a fibber.

Thursday 15th December

Today in choir we learnt *Carol of the Bells*. It's very fast and we were split into three parts that sing different notes and words. It sounds fantastic when we get it right. Jake keeps getting it wrong. He says he'll mime that one.

The concerts start on Monday. We'll use the school mini-bus and go to a different Old Folks' Home every day. Even though I've teased Jake about only joining the choir to miss lessons, I'm *well* excited to get out of school. That's the real reason any of us are doing it, deep down.

Even though it's just a week till Christmas, it feels ages away. We've been focused on the wedding so much, we've forgotten to think about what's happening a few days before it. Mum's told us not to expect lots of presents. She said we'll have a couple of things to open but we'll have a lovely time regardless. To be honest, we don't get lots of presents anyway. I don't mind that. I just like the Christmas feeling that comes in December. I don't need things to unwrap as well. I'm almost exactly the opposite of Meg that way.

I wonder how Meg is. It's been ages.

Friday 16th December

Tonight is another 'Wooltonised' Family Fooday. Jake told me they were coming, at the bus stop this morning. If Jake's there it means I have someone to laugh with when the adults have too much wine.

School was fine. No more tests. Just fun stuff until we break up on Wednesday. I'm writing this in my room as we wait for Cait, Tom and Jake. Downstairs Mum and Dad are cooking chilli and I can smell bread baking in the oven. I'm a bit excited about it all. I think I like hanging out with Jake. He makes me smile and he makes my tummy forget to have butterflies. In films and stories, when people are friends and then they *have* butterflies in their tummies, it means they're falling in love. I don't like that. Why would anyone *want* to feel nervous when they fall in love.

Surely, you'd want to feel happy and relaxed? It makes no sense. I like that my tummy feels calm when he's around.

I've just read that back and it sounds like I think I might be falling in love with Jake. I AM NOT! We're just friends. That's all. It's hard to work out because it's different from Meg and Jenna. Not in a love way. He's just a different type of person from them.

Saturday 17th December

So tired after last night. There was no drunk yoga this time. Instead there was singing. After we finished eating, Dad put on his Christmas CD, and everyone sang along to the songs. Me and Jake didn't know most of them. They were from before I was born. Cait kept screaming every time a new one came on. She knew all the words. Mum got up to dance. At one point she tried to drag Spike to his feet to dance with her, but he shouted, 'No way, José', and crossed his wrists like Wonder Woman. She had to leave him be.

Me and Jake left them to it around 10 o'clock. We got away from the noise in my room. It was fun being there. We could still hear the goings on downstairs but with the volume turned down.

Jake spent ages looking at my things. He asked me about the photo collage that Meg's dad had done when I left Stockford. I found myself explaining my old life to him. It was nice to tell him things about myself, but it felt like a stranger's life. I'm a different person now. When I explained what Meg's like, I described how she'd laughed at me for being a bridesmaid. I tried to make it sound funny. Like she was just having banter with me, but Jake didn't smile. When I stopped talking, he said, 'Do you have your dress here?' I nodded. He said, 'Well show me. I'll give you my honest opinion so you don't worry about it.'

I wasn't sure this was a good idea. I really loved my dress but suddenly doubts popped into my head. Maybe the dress was fine but it still looked stupid on me? I wasn't sure what I'd do if Jake told me it didn't suit me. I would still have to wear it on the wedding day, but I'd feel rubbish. In that split second, I made the decision that whatever Jake said, I was going to keep telling myself that I liked the dress. That was what I felt when I saw it, so no one else's opinion should change that. I thought all this as I walked to Mum's room, got it out of its bag and got changed. I kept my leggings on because I didn't want cold legs, and then walked back to my room.

I was actually nervous. As I walked in, Jake looked straight at me for a moment and then said, 'I can honestly say that you look...' - I held my breath and my stomach flipped - '...really amazing.'

I gasped and then laughed. 'Really? You're not just being polite?' I felt I had to make sure. Jake was adamant. 'No', he said. 'Not being polite at all. That deep blue brings out the lighter blue in your eyes, and the gold stars make the whole thing seem twinkly and wintery. It's the perfect dress for a Christmas wedding. What shoes are you wearing?' I went back to Mum's room to get the gold ballet pumps and brought them back. He looked at them and said, 'Definitely. These work.'

Who knew Jake had a good eye for fashion? It seems funny how I thought he was like Spike when I met him.

Sunday 18th December

A boring day. Mum took the car to Carlisle to get some presents. The rest of us watched films. The best bit was having no homework.

Monday 19th December

It's day one of the carol concerts. After registration, everyone involved had to meet at the front entrance. We got in the mini-bus and drove to a nursing home about ten miles away. Me and Jake sat next to each other. I've realised since living here, I don't know anywhere else apart from Applemere. The journey to school goes down country lanes that look the same. Sometimes Jake will say the name of a place and I won't know if he means down the road or a hundred miles away. I think I need to look at a map to get my bearings.

The concert was fun. When we arrived, the old people were sitting in the lounge. We walked in and stood in position. Then we sang our songs. Some of the old people sang along and clapped. A lady called Alice kept saying ‘encore’ at the end of every carol. That was nice to hear. One or two of the residents fell asleep, but maybe they’d had a late night.

I always think Grandma is old. But compared to these people, she’s not. She is young-old instead of old-old.

<u>Tuesday 20th December</u>

Day two of the concerts. It wasn’t as exciting today as we knew what to expect. But getting out of lessons and driving around the countryside was way better than Maths.

Today there was no Alice. But no one fell asleep either. It went as well as it could.

<u>Wednesday 21st December</u>

We’ve broken up for Christmas! I’ve survived the first term at high school. To be honest, it’s all been fine. Sometimes I think it’s easier than Year Six. There feels less pressure, that’s for sure. And now I have two whole weeks off. That feels brilliant.

To celebrate, Mum cooked roast potatoes for tea. I think there's nothing you could do to a potato that I wouldn't want to eat.

Thursday 22nd December

Mum and Dad had their last workday till after the wedding. It meant they were in the study most of the day while we had to amuse ourselves downstairs. Spike spent the day outside even though it was freezing. He was trying to dig with his tools even though the ground's really hard. I didn't care though. It meant that me, Kenny, Blane and Harvest could watch films in the warm. Today was *Elf*. When Spike came in and realised he'd missed it, he made us watch it all over again. I pretended I minded, but I didn't really. I could watch Christmas films every day of the year.

Friday 23rd December

Grandma was on the phone for a long time this evening, going through last minute plans. I could tell it was Grandma because of the facial expressions Mum was making to Dad.

Saturday 24th December

Christmas Eve! Dad said he wanted to take us on a Winter walk after breakfast. This sounded exciting. In reality, I knew it was because Mum needed the house to herself so she could wrap presents and get things organised for tomorrow.

We put on our hats and scarves, and went outside. There was frost on the ground but the sun was still shining. It felt like my exact favourite weather. It could only be better if it were snowing.

The 'Winter Walk' ended up being a walk to the village to post cards. Some of them went straight into the post box (Dad said, 'I know they'll be late but it's the thought that counts.') Others went through letterboxes. I only really know Tom, Cait and Jake. It seems Mum and Dad have sent cards to loads more local people than that.

Blane fell into a puddle outside the pub. I felt sorry for him but he wailed so long that my sympathy ran out. After a bit, Tom came out from the shop to see what the fuss was about. He took one look at Blane and went back inside for a towel. In the end, we went in to get warm while he found some old clothes of Jake's. 'We can't have you getting a cold at Christmas, can we?' he said. Blane didn't manage a smile but he stopped crying so that was good.

Dad and Tom chatted for a bit before we had to go. Cait and Jake had gone to the theatre in Carlisle for the afternoon. They do it every year apparently. I was surprised. I couldn't imagine Jake at the theatre. No idea why, it just made me puzzled. There's so much more to him than I first thought.

As we were leaving, Tom told us to pop in tomorrow night for a Christmas drink. Dad said we would.

Sunday 25th December

Merry Christmas Everyone! I've just eaten the biggest Christmas dinner ever and I'm having a lie down because I feel so full.

Blane woke everyone up at 6am. I know it's silly but I was just as excited as he was. We went downstairs where we'd left our pillowcases. (We have pillowcases instead of stockings!) Mine was on the left of the fireplace. Mum came down and lit the fire so we could get warm as we opened our presents.

Considering Mum and Dad had told us not to get our hopes up, it was pretty good actually. I got marzipan fruits (my fave) like I get every year. I got a new diary (Auction Bidders - remember when Grandma thought I was depressed?!) and best of all, I got the pair of shoes that I'd *really* wanted to get, when I'd been made to get the bridesmaid ones instead. They're exactly the same style but instead of gold, they're red. I thought they'd look nice with jeggings. I couldn't believe it when I opened them. Mum said, 'I remembered when I went back to Monsoon for my dress'. That made me happy. Not because of getting new shoes, but because I hadn't gone on about it much but Mum had remembered I liked them.

Harvest got a plastic rattle. Dad kept putting it in her hand but she just giggled. Spike got seeds and bulbs to plant in the spring. (They're desperate to make a gardener out of him.) Blane got art stuff like pencils and sketchpads. (I think Dad's given up on teaching him to ride a bike.) And Kenny got some building blocks with phonics on them. He'll start school next year so I suppose he's getting a head start.

All morning the house smelt gorgeous because dinner was cooking. Back in Stockford, Grandma used to come for Christmas dinner. This year she's eating with Will. Mum got off the phone with her this morning and said to Dad, 'Apparently Ma's having a low key Christmas this year. But I just interrupted her smoked salmon and champagne breakfast in bed. Ridiculous.' Dad laughed and said, 'Nah, it'll be soggy toast and luke warm tea. She's having you on.' And then they both laughed.

Tonight we are going to the Wooltons' for drinks. It sounds so grown up!

Monday 26th December

I'm really tired. Or maybe I'm hung over!

Last night I tried Tom's homemade damson gin. I had a sip of Mum's to see if it tasted as nice as it smelt. It was very strong. I only had a tiny bit but I felt giddy afterwards. That must be what it's like to be drunk. So now I know. It was late when we left. But the nicest bit was walking through the village at night. The Christmas lights and the stars in the sky made everything feel nice and comfortable. Like...home.

Tomorrow we leave for Manchester. It'll be the first time I've ever stayed in a hotel. I won't sleep tonight. This week's been so much fun already. I don't see how anything can top it.

Tuesday 27th December

After the glow of Christmas, today was back to normal. Mum was running around trying to pack the car with our outfits, shoes, spare clothes and Harvest's twenty-three nappy bags that go everywhere with us. (I'm exaggerating about twenty-three bags, but for a tiny baby, she really does have a lot of luggage.) Spike was annoying Blane who kept bursting into tears. Dad said he was overtired from an exciting week, but I think that was letting Spike off the hook. I took charge of Kenny and kept him entertained whilst everyone was stressed. I read him *The Big Big Sea* because it'd been my favourite book when I was his age. He listened but I don't think he loved it as much as I did.

Eventually, we got into the car. Mum started the engine and reversed a bit before Dad realised he hadn't got his phone charger. Everything was a bit fraught. As Dad ran back into the house Mum said through clenched teeth, 'Who gets married at Christmas anyway?'

Once we'd set off, things were calmer. The roads were clear and Dad played his *Stone Roses* CD for most of the journey. In the end Mum said, 'Give it a rest, Mac. Let's have some quiet before we have to deal with my mother.'

The wedding hotel is massive. We got here around 3 o'clock. Me, Mum and Harvest are in one room. Dad, Spike, Blane and Kenny are in the other. I feel like I've drawn the short straw being with the baby that cries at night. Even though I'll be kept awake, the bed is massive and comfy. Mum won't be anywhere near me even though she'll be sleeping on the other side. I can't wait to get into it later.

Tonight we're having a quiet meal in the restaurant with Grandma, Will and Will's daughters. Grandma described it as a 'quiet meal', but I don't really know what that means. If we have to sit in silence Spike will really struggle.

Wednesday 28th December

Ahhhhhhh. Grandma and Willard got married today and it was lovely.

After a really early start (thanks Harvest!) all the women met in Grandma's suite. I'm counting myself as a woman because I totally felt it. Grandma had a hairdresser AND a make up person there. It's like she's on the telly. When we arrived (in our PJs!) Grandma said to the hairdresser, 'This is my daughter, Molly. Is there *anything* you can do?' Mum snorted and said, 'Charming', then poured herself a glass of champagne from a bottle in a silver bucket and got into bed. Like she was the Queen!

Grandma's hair was in rollers. I thought it'd look weird, but when it was all done, it was soft and wavy, not tight and curly. It looked lovely. She had a cream dress with lace sleeves. It was tight all the way down. When she saw it, Mum said, 'Fair play, Ma. Not many sixty-nine year olds could pull that off.' It was a compliment I think, although Grandma tutted when she heard the sixty-nine bit.

When we were about to leave to go to the wedding room, Mum and Grandma had a *moment*. In the doorway, Grandma turned to Mum and said, 'You do like Will, don't you? I *am* doing the right thing, aren't I? I know we've had our differences over the years, but I can trust you to tell me if I'm making a fool of myself. It's the right thing to do, isn't it Molly?'

It was a bit mad. For the first time ever, Grandma wasn't completely sure of herself. Mum had the power to make or break the whole day, by telling her not to go through with it. There was a small pause but then Mum turned to her, and with a really serious voice, said, 'Ma, Will is the best thing about you. He makes you a nicer person. I like you more when he's there. You need to cling on to him like there's no tomorrow because you're so much more *loveable* since he came into your life.' I guess this was a sort of compliment although it sounded really harsh. She carried on, 'You were hell to live with when I was younger, and I was *so* happy to leave when I was eighteen. Your money, your snobbery, your 'high standards' that mask your fear of what others' think about you. But now, Will has come along. He sees you for what you are, and he accepts it. Even better, he loves you. He's taking on *a lot* by marrying you, but he's happy to do it. Of course it's the right thing to do. It's the *only* thing to do.'

I mean, whoah! I was a bit shocked to be honest. Mum hadn't held back. I thought Grandma would go mad but she didn't. She listened and nodded, then said, 'You're right of course. He's an absolute wonder, isn't he. Thank you, Molly, for your candour. Now let's get this show on the road.' And with that, we went to the wedding.

It was such a good day. Mum walked Grandma down the aisle. Dad took lots of photos on his phone. Will's daughters had fun too. Last night they'd told us loads of funny stories about Will, at the 'quiet meal'. (It hadn't been so quiet after all.) Will had the biggest smile on his face all day. At one point, after the ceremony, he lifted Kenny on to his shoulders and walked around with him as he chatted to other people, like it was the most natural thing in the world. It's like he's always been our grandad. He doesn't feel like a stranger. When Mum did her speech, she said, 'I knew Will fitted in straight away because my kids adored him from day one. And if you can win over the fruit of my cynical loins then you're all right by me.' Everyone laughed. Mum used lots of big words and clever phrases when she spoke. Sometimes I forget she isn't just Mum but she has adult conversation too. She was really funny. At least the bits I understood were.

After the meal there was a disco. Grandma and Will did their first dance to *My First, My Last, My Everything* which I'd never heard before but was a fast song that made everyone get up and dance. I loved being able to wear my dress, swish about and feel like a grown up adult with all the other grown up adults.

I think today was my favourite day of my life.

Thursday 29th December

Harvest was kind to us last night. She only cried a bit. Mum got her out of the cot this morning and said, 'Thank you for knowing Mummy has a hangover. Good girl.' Then she carried her into bed with us and went back to sleep.

I didn't fall back to sleep because I was thinking about something that's happening today. I think it'll be good. I hope so, anyway. On the way back to Applemere, we're calling into Meg's house. I felt a bit nervous about it at first - when Mum first told me - but I think it's a good idea now. Mum planned it with Meg's mum a few weeks ago, once the wedding was booked. It's been so many months since I saw Meg. FaceTime doesn't work very well because it makes things awkward. Face to face in real life will be loads better. It'll be strange to drive down Tyson Road but I want to do it. I want to visit everything I used to know.

But before all that I'm going to have a long soak in the biggest bath I have ever seen. Hotels are brilliant.

Friday 30th December

I didn't write when I got back last night because it was late and I was shattered from the wedding. Going back to Stockford was interesting.

First of all, seeing my old house was weird. It looked exactly the same on the outside although there was a silver car where ours used to park. We went past Irwell Green, the library, the park and Stockford High. When we got to Meg's and the door opened, Mum and Meg's mum started shrieking like they were best mates. They acted like it was a big reunion. Then, as the door opened wider, Meg was there and she did exactly the same. Lots of screaming and hugging. I'd forgotten what she was like.

What was lovely for real was that Meg had invited Jenna over. When I walked into the lounge she was there and it was a big surprise. She stood up and said, 'It's McAuliffe back from the wilderness', and then fake punched my arm to show me she was happy. It was so good to see her again.

Mum and the boys sat downstairs and talked about the wedding. Me, Meg and Jenna went upstairs to fill each other in on everything. The first thing Meg said was, 'Oh my God Leeza, tell us about your dress. Was it terrible?' I found myself going red. But then I remembered how good I'd felt wearing it. I said, 'No, it was lovely in the end. I really liked it. It was blue.' I know saying it was blue wasn't really explaining it but I didn't know what else to say. Then Jenna said, 'So what's it like in Applemere Bridge? Is it boring?' I think these were genuine questions. I was about to answer and say that it wasn't boring at all but then Meg jumped in with, 'Of course it's boring, it's in the middle of nowhere. No wonder you're happy to see us. You must be lonely.' Again, I felt my cheeks burn and my stomach started to ache. I said, 'I've got friends. At least I've got one friend from school.' Meg made a fake sad face and said, 'Ah bless, just the one friend,' and then she laughed a lot. It was then that I realised that I didn't like her. She was never going to be happy for me. She was never going to listen to anything I had to say. It was always going to be about her. 'Yeah,' I said, 'His name's Jake. He's thirteen and he makes me laugh loads. Also, he's really kind. When he saw my dress he told me it looked amazing.'

I ended up saying the last bit quite loud - the bit about the dress. I wanted to show Meg that she didn't have a clue about me anymore. Jenna understood. She said, 'I bet you looked ace, McAuliffe. And Jake sounds cool. Is he your boyfriend?' The way she said it was so casual. Like he *could* have been my boyfriend. But I knew he wasn't. 'No, he's just a friend. But he's nice. Properly nice, you know?' And Jenna nodded.

I'm glad I got to see Jenna again. (We're going to sort her coming to stay in the New Year.) But I'm glad I don't need to see Meg again. Like ever. Most of all, though, I'm glad that I drove away from Stockford knowing I was going back home to where my mate Jake lives. And I'd be seeing him soon.

<u>Saturday 31st December</u>

I'm not planning on writing much today. We're all getting ready to go out to the pub for a New Year's Eve party - I'm doing all the grown up things this week! Everyone from the village will be there and the pub will be open late. Like 'tomorrow morning' late! Dad's excited about that.

Jake's just been round. Cait sent him here to find out what time we'll be turning up later. Then Mum sent him up to my room to see me, so I could show him some of the wedding photos. Jake said, 'Show me those in a minute. I've got to give you your Christmas present. Immediately I felt bad. I didn't know we'd be buying presents for each other. He noticed my face. 'Don't panic. It's from my mum really, but she told me to give it to you seeing as we're sort of friends.' I laughed as he said that. Sort of friends is good enough, even though I'd been bigging him up in Stockford yesterday. 'What is it?' I said. 'Duh, open it and find out, Leez,' he replied. He passed across a flat rectangular shape in gold paper. It was the size of a book but didn't feel like one. I ripped off the paper.

Inside a wooden frame was a photo. It was of me and Jake, standing in the kitchen next to each other, bent double laughing. I have tears coming from my eyes and Jake is pointing at something off to the side. It's the happiest photo I've ever seen. Jake said, 'Do you remember? It was the drunk yoga! I think my mum had just collapsed on the floor. And I think that might be when your mum said she'd weed a bit.' I burst out laughing at the memory. And I looked at Jake who was laughing about it all over again.

It's been such a busy week. I sat on my bed after Jake had gone and thought about everything that's happened. It's not just having Will join the family, or seeing Grandma looking happy at her wedding. And it's not just laughing with Jake and talking about how embarrassing Mum and Cait are when they have too much wine. It's more than that. Since I started this diary, so much has changed. I'm living in a new town, going to a new school, I have a new sister, I've got a new friend, and I'm one step closer to being a grown-up for real. This has been a year of change.

If someone had told me in January that all those changes were coming, I'd have panicked for sure. I'd have said, 'No way, José, I'm not interested in everything being different.' But I had no choice. The changes came whether I wanted them or not. It's like puberty. I can't stop that either. It's coming. I can't sit in the bath forever, waiting for my periods to start. (We STILL don't have a new bath, by the way. Mum and Dad's *To Do* list petered out a while back.) I have to stop worrying, get out of the bath, and get on with each day. I need to enjoy what's happening at the time, rather than worry about what might go wrong in my head.

For now, I'm signing off. It's nearly time to go the pub. Happy New Year Everyone! And a Happy New Year to the Auction Bidders. Thank you for buying this diary at an auction of my belongings, far off in the future. I hope your robots are cool.

OMG! It's 2.05am tomorrow morning. My periods have finally started!!! It happened AT THE PUB. Luckily Mum had a pad in her handbag. I used a pad! It's a new year and a new me! It's all kicking off. My tummy feels very grown up. Blimey. Right then. Night-night, everyone. This year has been MASSIVE.

ACKNOWLEDGEMENTS

Many people gave their time to make this book the best it could be. Thanks to everyone who read rough draft after rough draft, and gave feedback along the way. Mary Bond, Frank Bond, Dom Bond, Monica Bartley Bond, Beth McMahon, Ste Rew, Lucy Keavy, Ashley Preston, and Millie Crowther. I know you all have *far* better things to do with your time. Cheers.

Claire Dyer at *Fresh Eyes* was enormously helpful; encouraging, critical and supportive all at once. *Portal – Design and Communication* were fab, coming up with a perfect front cover, and managing to interpret my rambling ideas into something a million times better. And thank you to *The Poised Pen* writers' group. Listening to me (nervously!) read bits aloud, was hugely confidence-building.

Finally, special thanks to all past members of 1NB and 4NB, as well as the children I had the pleasure to mentor, back in the day. Whilst this is a work of fiction, I hope my school experiences helped add a bit of authenticity to the pages.

ABOUT THE AUTHOR

Nicky Bond was a Teacher and Learning Mentor before publishing her first book in 2017.

She is a Liverpool FC Women supporter, loves cooking (and eating) as often as she can, and her favourite time of year is Eurovision Song Contest day.

Nicky lives in the North-West of England.